Praise for Cordelia Kelly

"I was hooked from the start. Absolute banger read in two sittings."

"One of the most thrilling paranormal books I have read in a while."

"The story has this perfect balance of mystery, tension, and heart. I found myself flipping through pages faster and faster as I got closer to the end. It's one of those books where you think, "Just one more chapter..."

— BOOK REVIEWS FOR *THE CARNIVAL OF FOOLS*

An imaginative take on the teen-vampire trope with plenty of action and romance and a compelling antihero

— *KIRKUS REVIEWS* ON *THE WELL OF SOULS*

Atmospheric descriptions, vividly portraying tempestuous weather and the eerie ambiance of Duchesne Island, heighten the suspenseful mood. A gripping read that seamlessly blends adventure and emotion.

— *BOOKVIEW REVIEW* ON *THE WELL OF SOULS*

Stellar fantasy of a young woman facing a curse and daring to rebel.

— BookLife by Publisher's Weekly on *The Sibyl and the Thief*

Dynamic characters galvanize this entertaining, well-paced magical tale.

— *Kirkus Reviews* on *The Sibyl and the Thief*

THE SEABOURNE LEGACY

A PORT OF LOST SOULS NOVEL

CORDELIA KELLY

BCP

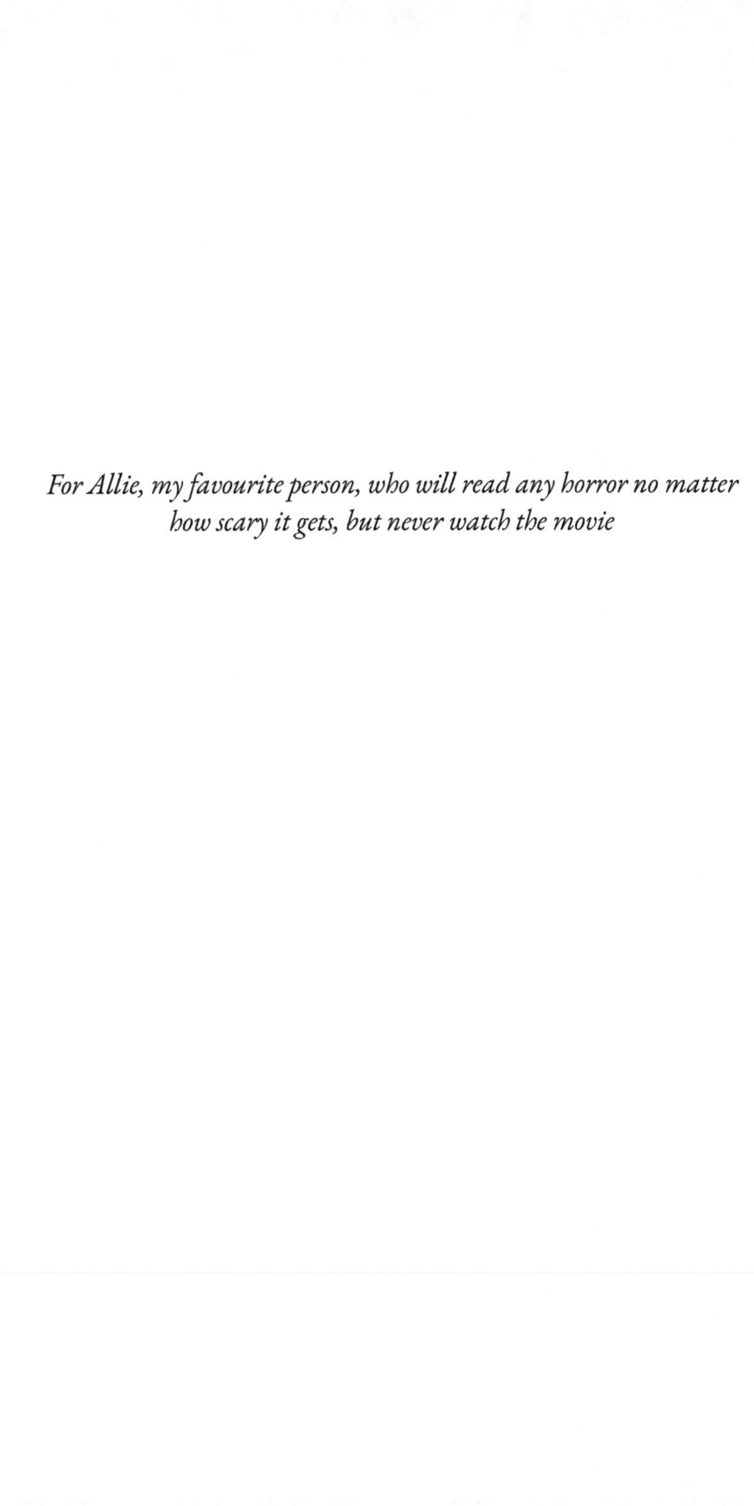

For Allie, my favourite person, who will read any horror no matter how scary it gets, but never watch the movie

Duchesne Island

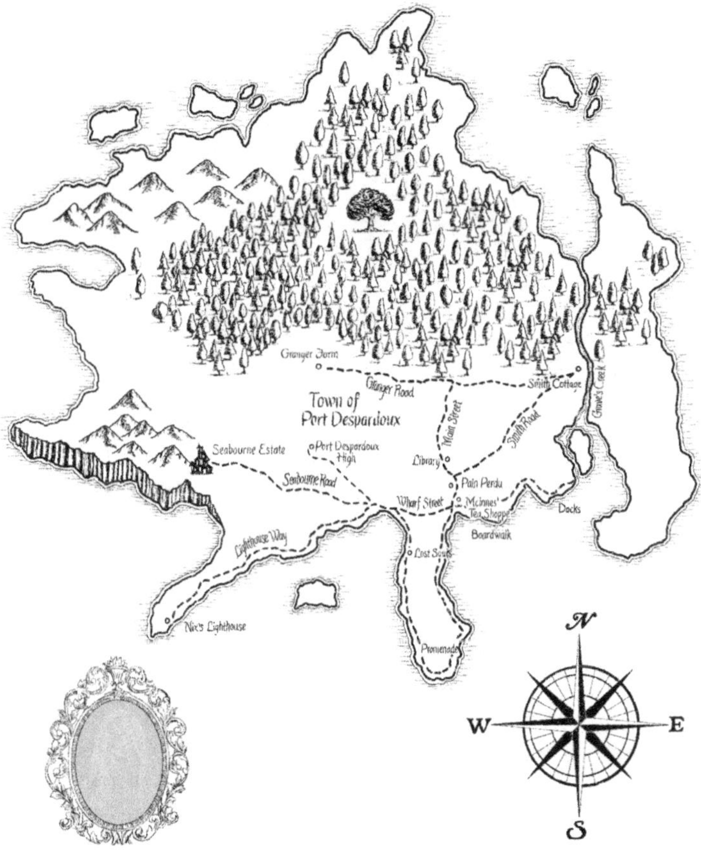

ONE

The firelight danced across the polished wood, casting restless shadows over walls lined with leather-bound tomes and ancient maps. The Seabourne Estate study might have at some point impressed Lola, but tonight it was stifling. She was too weighed down by the unease smouldering inside her since stepping off the ferry this afternoon.

She'd called her friends immediately, and they agreed to meet here.

With her back to the crackling fire, a stack of papers in her hands, she stood in front of them like a professor giving a lecture. Six weeks since she'd left Duchesne island to go digging—both literally and metaphorically. She'd scoured archives, traded favours with old contacts and taken risks she shouldn't have.

But as she faced the three people sitting in front of her, their expressions cast in amber light, she worried her findings weren't enough. At times like these, the chasm between herself and her friends seemed unfathomable, formed by her years of supernatural experiences and choices they could never fully understand.

She barely understood herself these days, caught between what she used to be and what she was trying to become.

"The Order of Hanta Cythraul."

Lola's voice cut through the quiet like the snap of a book closing. "A secret society of demon hunters, centuries old, ruthless and relentless. And now, we know they're here on Duchesne."

The faces in front of her reflected varying degrees of tension. Walt leaned back in his chair, a picture of practiced indifference. His expression was unreadable as ever. He could have been planning an escape or simply wondering what was for dinner.

Nix, by contrast, bristled with urgency. Her brows furrowed as though her thoughts were already sprinting ahead, assembling a thousand theories.

And then there was Gael, arms crossed, eyes dark and defiant, daring her to explain herself. His silence was the loudest.

Lola resisted the urge to flinch under his gaze, a reminder that some wounds couldn't be smoothed over with apologies or time. She swallowed hard and pressed on.

"From what I've discovered, the Order of Hanta Cythraul isn't some harmless group of folklorists. These people are trained with weapons from childhood, with centuries of blood on their hands."

She took a breath, drawing on the resolve that had carried her through the past weeks of nonstop travel and sleepless nights. Her fingers tightened on the edge of the desk as she spoke, the edges of the papers crumpling under her grip.

"What I don't understand," she continued, her voice low and taut, "is why I've never heard of them before. After all my searching, I still have no idea what kind of threat they pose."

"Six weeks away, and this is what you came up with?" Gael waved a dismissive hand. "Seems like a lot of nothing after what you put Faye through worrying about you. All of us—" Gael caught himself and looked away.

Despite herself, her stomach twisted. She'd hurt him, and he wasn't ready to let her forget it—not that she deserved to. Still, she wished he could see that leaving wasn't running away. It had been necessary.

"I'm sorry I worried you," Lola said, a healthy wave of guilt crashing over her. Since breaking up, they hadn't been in contact; she'd hopped on a boat a few days after and disappeared for more than a month. She'd messaged him, but he never responded. "I kept Faye up to date with everything I was doing. Well, the parts I could tell her."

"So, you travelled around digging up treasure you set aside for a rainy day?" Nix's sea-blue eyes sparkled at the thought.

"Something like that. I also liquidated some assets, moved some funds around."

"It was dangerous, though, right?" Gael said. "You could have alerted your old crew that you're still alive." His eyes glittered dangerously in the firelight as he watched her.

Lola sighed. It had been a risk she'd had to take. "I only went through bank accounts I'm sure Jacquotte knew nothing about. I've been storing assets for decades, away from the crew's prying eyes. But Nix wasn't far off; I had several caches of treasure actually buried in the ground. I exchanged them and made it seem like it was the inheritance coming from my recently deceased father in Paris. Which is the reason I've been gone for so long, in case anyone asks."

"All of this so you can get a new wardrobe?" Gael gestured at Lola's outfit. True, the clothes she wore were very different from what they were used to seeing her in: hand-me-downs or stolen sweaters. Now, she wore grey wool trousers with a white silk T-shirt and leather loafers. She shivered in delight at the luxe fabrics that brushed gently over her skin.

"Yes, I went shopping. Did you want me to live off Faye forever? Thanks to dearly departed papa, I'm a wealthy girl. And this is money I will use to set myself up as a human, Gael. This is me starting my life. I won't apologize for that."

"Don't apologize for any of it!" Nix clasped her hands together, practically bouncing on her toes. "Do you know how jealous I am, that you got off this island? That you went to New

York City?" She gave her a mock-serious look. "Next time you have to smuggle me in your suitcase. I won't even need snacks or air holes. Just pack me between your sweaters and I'm good to go."

"I'm sure we could give you a few air holes," Lola said.

Nix grinned and she tucked a strand of copper hair behind her ear. "Someday, though," she said, almost to herself. "I'll see all of it. The world's too big to stay in one place forever, right?"

Lola couldn't help smiling at her friend's enthusiasm. "I kept this for you. For when you visit." She handed Nix a folded paper from her bag: New York City's subway map.

Hands trembling, Nix opened the map, her finger following the criss-crossed coloured lines. "I've always wanted to go," she said, her voice scratchy. "It's just that..."

"You'll go, someday," Lola said. "We'll go together. I can show you everything."

"That sounds like pure freedom, to just go anywhere you want, nothing holding you back." The longing was tangible in Nix's gaze. "I've never left this island, you know."

"Really? Not even to go to the mainland?"

Nix shook her head, scarlet flushing over her cheeks. "It sounds ridiculous, I know, but between helping out at the shop and taking care of the kids, not to mention my dad running the lighthouse, there's just no time for us to get off the island. And it's expensive..."

"It'll happen, I promise you. Oh, I'll show you Paris!"

Nix looked as though she wanted to bottle that promise. "You don't know what it's like, being stuck here. Even Gael has gone places."

"I've been to Halifax. Twice." Gael's gaze softened as he took in his friend. "I'm not exactly your expert world traveller."

"And I only ever go to posh resorts so my parents can brag about them," Walt added. "Trust me when I say they're not pleasant experiences."

"But Lola, you've seen everything." Nix let her fingers trail over the lines on the map, tracing out her hunger to explore.

"But never during the day." Lola smiled at the thought of seeing mountains and valleys and city streets drawn out in shades of gold and amber sunshine.

Gael's gaze never left her. She could implode from the heat behind them; there was more than anger simmering there. "So, you'll see the world and leave everyone else behind, right?"

"It's not like that." Lola found she couldn't meet his eyes. Surely wanting to explore the world as a human wasn't a crime? Freedom was supposed to feel lighter than this. It wasn't supposed to feel like she had to cut ties with the people who grounded her. But the thought of staying, of letting the world shrink around her was unbearable.

"How did you get back into the country?" Walt asked, oblivious to the tension. "I'm assuming you're carrying more cash than would be considered legal?"

Lola cleared her throat, relieved to be released from Gael's gaze. "You're not wrong. I still have contacts along the coast. I sailed with an old friend from Maine across the Bay of Fundy, missing unfriendly ports that might ask questions. Like who I am, and why I'm carrying tens of thousands of dollars on my person."

Nix let out a choking gasp at the sum, and Gael scowled. "You smuggled money into the country?"

Lola let out an impatient huff. "I can't actually operate under the confines of your government here. My very existence is a lie. Yes, I'll have to bend some rules to survive. That's how I've made it this far."

Gael's eyes glinted darkly. "Lola Monteux, morally grey since 1942. You don't think the rules apply to you at all, do you?"

A loaded silence descended between them as they faced off. Lola raised her chin defiantly, wondering what other accusations he was going to throw at her.

Nix cleared her throat. "Back to the order of Hanta Cis-whatever," Nix said, tripping over the word. She brushed her curls out of her face with a brusque hand. "The Order of HC. Reiko is one of them, a demon hunter? Like, they are a part of the Otherworld?"

Nix had fallen for Reiko over the summer, but the girl hadn't been honest about who she was or why she was here. She'd used Nix's crush to get closer to Lola and her ties to the Otherworld.

"She's a part of the Order, but I'm not sure of their actual place within the Otherworld. It seems to be influenced by the mythology of many cultures, from Japanese to Scandinavian—a real international mix. They take secrecy seriously, though. I was a vampire for eighty years and I've never heard of them before."

"Where did you get this information?" Walt stood and began to pace, tracing his finger along the book spines. "If they're so secret."

"I tapped all my old contacts in the Otherworld," Lola said. "At least the ones that were still safe to approach."

With her fragile human body, she found travelling through the Otherworld took a toll on her. She returned to the island exhausted, dark shadows spreading under her eyes, barely able to put one foot in front of the other.

While off the island, she felt stretched thin, as though her essence was drifting away from her. She would wake up with her head foggy, full of unsettling dreams of the oak forest of Duchesne, the memory of a voice calling out to her already forgotten. The dreams had followed her every night until she resisted falling asleep.

Dreams weren't her biggest fear, though. Far scarier were her demon contacts now that she was no longer a vampire. Some would have known immediately that she was human, and she stayed away from them. Others were a decent bet they wouldn't kill her on sight, and she tried her luck with those. Very little had any good information. The Order of Hanta Cythraul was more legend than reality.

"I wish I could have gotten information on what they want and if they're a threat to us."

"If it helps, Reiko has started at Duchesne High and is now right in there with the hyenas," Nix said, referring to the pack of popular kids who had bullied her most of her life. "Besties with Sam Lynch, if you can believe it."

"That *is* shocking," Lola said. "Sam is a nightmare. Maybe Reiko thinks *she's* a demon."

"Why are we assuming the Order is bad?" Gael asked. "I mean, isn't killing demons good?"

"But what is their agenda? *Why* are they killing demons?"

"To make the world a better place?" Gael raised his eyebrows as though this was obvious. "Demons are evil; they kill demons. I'm pretty sure I'm on their side."

"Not all demons are evil, Gael." When he snorted, she rolled her eyes. "Not all creatures from the Otherworld deserve to die. Some are neutral, just trying to live their lives."

He wouldn't let up with his hard stare. "But do they deserve to live in *our* world?"

Lola placed her hand over her mouth, hiding the quiver. Gael had changed so much from the innocent boy he was before she'd introduced him to the wicked side of the Otherworld. Before he met her, Gael recited poetry and believed in kindness before all; she wouldn't have to convince him that not everyone from the Otherworld deserved to die.

She had done this to him, taken someone wholly good and brought darkness into his life.

Glancing away, she concentrated on the room where her friends huddled around the carved mahogany desk. The Seabourne's study reflected their wealth and status on Duchesne Island: Walt's father a wealthy trader and his mother, the mayor. The study was scented with the faint vanilla aroma of pipe tobacco.

Her gaze caught on a particularly dark and foreboding

painting that graced the wall behind the desk. A grim man in a stiff pose glowered down at them.

"Walt, this guy looks just like you."

Nix let out a snicker and Walt coughed. "Thanks, Lola."

"I mean, not his expression. But look at the eyes, and the jaw. If you turn out to be a miserable old man who kicks puppies, this would be you."

"I will hug puppies every day from here on out, then." Walt approached the portrait with wary steps. "My illustrious ancestor, the very first Walter Seabourne. He made the family fortune."

"Let me guess, through hard work and good deeds?" Gael asked.

Walt's smile lacked humour. "He was a rum-runner during Prohibition. Duchesne Island was a great place to smuggle contraband booze; the massive network of caves on the island was a perfect hiding place. I've even heard legends that this house was built with tunnels that access the caves underneath. Apparently, the original Walt Seabourne became paranoid as his smuggling business got serious, and the whole place is full of secret passageways, hiding places and escape routes."

"Have you ever found any?" Nix's eyes were round.

"A few." Walt's gaze sought out the darkened shadows of the study. "That's my dark secret. My family fortune came from criminal activity."

He sounded glum so Lola nudged him. "Don't worry, most of them do."

Gael snorted, but Lola couldn't tell if it was scornful or if he was trying to hold in a laugh.

When she looked at him, he schooled his face into passive indifference. "You start school tomorrow, then," he said. "Two weeks late."

Lola waved her hand. "I'm sure the tragic passing of my father in France will help smooth things over. I'll admit I'm a bit nervous.

My education has been...thorough...in many ways, but I've never been to a formal school. That I can remember, anyways."

"How did Faye explain that one?" Walt asked.

"She only repeated what I told her," Lola said of her guardian. "I attended a boarding school in Europe that focused on life experience."

"Like treasure hunting and jewelry heists?" Nix asked. "But nothing about calculus?"

Lola let out a pent-up breath. "After everything that's happened, I just want things to go smoothly. Keep my head down and get through these next two years."

"I don't really get why you're doing this." Gael's words began to heat up again. "Going to high school. It seems so trivial compared to what you've done. I mean, you have all your money. You have all your *life experiences.* Why bother?"

"Staying on the island for another two years and completing high school gives me an effective backstory. I can go to university and develop a normal human life. I want to be free to do whatever I want."

"You'll stay for two years, and then what? See you later? *Sayonara* Faye, I'm done using you too!" His words spat out in a jumble, then he reared back as though he hadn't meant to say that.

"I'm not using Faye; I never meant to use anyone." Her shoulders slumped. Starting over was supposed to be simple: hide in plain sight, finish school, build a life. But the shadows of her past were never far behind. "She's aware that I'm not planning on spending my whole life on Duchesne, and she *wants* that for me. It's a normal thing to want."

"I still don't understand why being normal matters to you," Gael said.

"You don't have to." Lola swallowed the snap in her voice. "I've never had the chance; my life was taken from me. It's fine if you don't get that."

"I just think you're being unfair to Faye. It's obvious she cares about you, and you're already preparing to check out of her life."

"That's not what I'm doing at all!" Lola stormed towards him, getting close enough that she had to crane her neck up to take in the near-foot difference in their height. She was tired of dancing around his hurt feelings.

A spark of heat erupted in her chest; the way his eyes lit up, she was certain he felt it as well, whether it came from anger or desire. She pointed a finger in his face. "How dare you—"

The door to the study flung open. Standing on the dark threshold, lit up by the light of the fire, stood Walt's mother, pale as a ghost.

"Your father is coming," she said in a strained whisper.

Two

Walt shot to his feet, his fists clenched tight as his gaze darted around the room. "I thought he was gone until tomorrow."

"His trip was cut short. I didn't know until now. I get the sense things...didn't go well." She hesitated. "It would be best if he had the house to himself."

Walt's mother, the mayor of Port Despardoux, looked wan, her stick-thin figure propped against the door frame as though she'd faint without the support. Her blonde hair was pulled back in an elegant chignon, and though she was at home for the evening, she wore tailored slacks and a cashmere sweater.

But her dark lipstick was smeared around her mouth, and the sour scent of old gin drifted from her.

All the colour drained from Walt's face. His hands trembled as he ran them through his hair, his fingers tangling. "Sorry, guys, we'll have to cut this short."

"There's no time." Mayor Seabourne's voice was barely audible. "He's at the front gate. There's no way of leaving without being seen." She met her son's gaze, squinting to keep him in focus. "You have to hide." She gave a meaningful nod, then slowly shut the door soundlessly behind her.

Lola's stomach churned, clutching her bag as her skin crawled. Lola had only seen her the mayor as a laced-up politician, cold and severe. To see her undone like this, dishevelled with fear, brought back memories from Lola's past.

Back when her ex, Beau, thought she belonged to him. His moods would change with the wind, and he would make her hurt for stepping across an invisible line she didn't know existed. The sour taste of bile rose in her throat, and she forced herself to take a deep breath.

Lola may have been a monster in the past, but she also knew what it meant to have to hide from those who should have cared for her.

Nix looked to Walt, half-laughing, expecting him to tell them it was a joke. When he didn't, her face crumpled. "Wait, what? We're talking about your dad, right?"

Walt flinched at her words, not meeting her eye. "If he finds us here, it won't end well."

Lola grabbed his arm, her voice calm but firm. "Where can we go?" she said, keeping her tone steady. People needed someone to rely on in moments like this—someone who wasn't panicking.

"Go?" Walt looked to Lola blankly, as though he could see right through her.

"You said there were hiding places in the house, right?" When Walt didn't answer, she squeezed gently. "Walt, focus. We need you right now."

"Hide, hide…" His lost gaze darted around the room, then fell on something that made him brighten. "Of course, there's a place we can go. I'm not really supposed to, but Mom showed me when I was little, told me to use it in an emergency."

Had Walt's mother shown a young boy places to conceal himself for his protection? How much of Walt's life had he spent hiding? His reticence at letting people close to him, his awkward way with others, began to fall into place.

"Everybody pack up." Lola was already grabbing her cross-body bag, carefully stacking the pages about the Order of Hanta Cythraul before placing them inside. She shrugged into her leather jacket and wrapped a scarf around her neck.

Nix clutched her schoolbag to her chest. "I don't understand," she said, sounding very young.

"We just need to go, Nix." It wasn't Lola's issue to explain, but she didn't think Walt was up for spelling it out right then. "Grab your stuff."

Gael had already packed his bag, watching Lola with burning eyes. "Where to?"

Walt strode to the back of the study, past his gloomy ancestor's portrait. He ran his fingers over the embossed book covers on the bookshelf next to the fireplace. "Which one, again?" He let out a long breath as he tried to calm himself.

As he hesitated over the books, a low groaning resonated from the very walls of the house.

"What the eff was that?" Nix asked, her blue eyes nearly popping out of her head. Her freckles stood out in high definition on her pale face as she huddled closer to Lola.

"This one." Walt's hand settled on a book near the end of the shelf; its green leather bound with gilt. He took a shuddering breath and yanked the book. It tilted sharply with a faint click that echoed in the unnaturally still room.

With a puff of stale air, the bookcase swung inwards on silent hinges, revealing a dark opening to a narrow passageway. The air within was musty, smelling of ages-old dust and rotting wood.

The light filtering in from the study behind them showed wooden wainscotting along the bottom half of the walls and heavy damask wallpaper above. A rickety wooden staircase led to the lower level.

"Cool," Gael whispered.

A bang sounded outside the study, coming from down the hall. Walt's head whipped towards the door as though expecting it to blow open.

"We need to go." The skin around his eyes was tightly strained as he pleaded with them, betraying how much effort he was putting into appearing calm. He stepped into the darkness first. Nix and Gael followed while Lola took up the rear.

The door shut with an echoing thud behind her, leaving them in total darkness. Something feathery soft brushed her cheek, and Lola batted at it, hissing in disgust.

"What's wrong?" Gael's voice floated towards her.

"Just cobwebs," she said, trying to control her shudder. "Is there any light down here?"

"The electricity isn't hooked up down here," came Walt's whispered reply.

A harsh beam of light shone directly into her eyes, and Lola jerked back, raising her hands as a shield against it.

"Sorry," Gael said, redirecting his phone downwards.

"We need to get downstairs," she said, blinking the bright flashes from her vision. "Away from the study, in case we're heard." Pulling out her own phone, she turned on her light as well.

The sweeping beams illuminated the suffocatingly narrow stairwell that headed down into the gloom.

"This is the creepiest thing ever." Nix's eyes gleamed in the reflected light.

Lola inspected the passageway; she'd seen many in her life. This one was warm and dry, if somewhat musty. It didn't even crack the top twenty creepiest places she'd ever seen.

"What is this place?" Gael asked.

"The bottom level of the house; they used to call it the Below-stairs," Walt said as he took a tentative step onto the stairwell. "It's where the servants lived and worked for the most part. The original Walter Seabourne wanted them to be able to access the rooms without being seen by the family. But it was also a way to hide, in case the cops came."

"Charming," Nix muttered.

"It's been years since I've been back here," Walt said. His hand trailed along the wall and came away grimy. He grimaced and wiped it on his pants.

Lola listened to the sound of each stair creaking softly underfoot, like a ghostly echo of the servants who used to scurry through the darkness. In single file they descended without a word, hearing only their stifled breaths and uncertain footsteps.

When Lola reached the bottom, the others huddled at the base of the stairwell as though reluctant to explore any further. A corridor stretched long ahead of them, their flashlights barely touching the darkness.

"That's weird," Lola said as she beamed her light over the wooden plank floors.

"Everything down here is weird." Nix wrapped her arms around herself.

"No, look. The floor is bare. The walls and these old lamps, they're covered in dust and cobwebs, but the floor has been recently swept."

They all peered at the clean floors. "That's not possible," Walt said, cracking his knuckles and glancing over his shoulder as though expecting someone to jump out at him. "Nobody knows about this place. Our staff isn't forced to hide in dark, dusty hallways. Anymore."

"How nice of you," Nix said, an edge of bitterness sharpening her voice.

"I just meant this part of the house is blocked off," Walt said, still not moving. "My dad would kill me if he found us here."

"Where exactly is this leading us—besides into the creepy void of death?" Nix asked.

"Is there an exit down here?" Lola asked.

"There are a bunch of ways out of the Belowstairs, but all to other parts of the house," Walt said, then his eyes brightened. "Wait, there is a way out through the kitchens. Though that door hasn't been opened in decades."

"Let's try to find it, then," Lola said, trying to nudge him forward. "We're already down here, so we should keep moving."

"I'd rather not end up a horror movie cliché," Nix said, resentment creeping into her voice. "Why don't we vote on who gets to die first?"

"Can we just...not do this right now? Please?" Walt's voice sounded strangled.

"Let's just get to the kitchens, okay?" Gael said.

"Fine. I don't want to get trapped here." Nix brushed past Walt. Shoulders hunched around his ears, he followed.

A sound, very faint, reached Lola's ears. Like sandpaper being dragged along the wall. The sound was stuttering and irregular and grated at Lola's nerves.

Something about it was very, very wrong.

"Do you hear that?"

"What?" Gael hovered at her shoulder, eyes wide.

She took a few steps down the hallway. "Like a scratching kind of thing."

"Lola, it's probably rats."

She ran her flashlight beam over the floor, crouching down to peer in the corners. Again, she was struck by the lack of dust along the wooden boards. "I don't think so. I don't see any droppings."

"Know much about rats?" Gael asked.

Lola raised an eyebrow at him.

"Of course you do. More of that glamorous life experience, right?" His tone was acrid. "You've just done so many things."

"And I can guarantee you'd never want to do any of the stuff that involves rats." Lola huffed out her breath.

The rough sound nettled her as the scratching became louder, more frantic, as though whatever was making the noise was reacting to them. It amplified and echoed down the corridor.

"You can't hear that?" Lola was doing everything she could not to press her hands over her ears. Gael shook his head, mystified. Every hair on her arms stood straight up as the hallway seemed to stretch away from her, getting longer as she stared at it.

The heavy thumping of her heart sped up to match the frantic scraping. She took a few stumbling steps forward, trying to get away. The sound was right there, right next to her.

The air was colder here, like the touch of icy fingers against her cheek. She played the light from her phone over the wall, searching in the shadows for the source of the sound. There was nothing but dusty wallpaper, the pattern barely visible under the layers of dust.

The light on her phone flickered and went out, leaving her in darkness. The scratching stopped, so all she heard was her shaky breath as she turned, dread filling her insides.

Her light flickered on again, lighting up over a white face right next to her. The figure had hollowed-out eyes and a mouth stretched wide in an empty gaping void.

THREE

L ola startled back, her garbled scream choked off in her throat as she dropped her phone.

Gael was at her side, frantically flashing his beam of light as though it was a weapon. "Lola! What happened?"

The concern in his voice was so tender, so different from how he'd been treating her up until now, that Lola had to fight a momentary instinct to melt into him. She couldn't do that anymore. "I saw something. A girl. She was screaming; something horrible happened here." She pointed a shaky finger to the wall.

Gael aimed his flashlight at where she gestured and started to laugh.

The light bounced off a very dark, very dirty mirror. "Well, I wouldn't call you horrible, but you were definitely a screaming girl."

As the tremors from the shock worked through her, Lola approached the reflection.

Though the mirror was cloudy and speckled with age, it reflected only her face, nothing like the enchanted funhouse mirrors at the Carnival of Fools.

But she hadn't seen her own face, had she? "No, it wasn't me, it was..." She paused, trying to remember exactly what she had seen. A girl's face in the mirror.

Had her reflection frightened her to the point of screaming?

She pressed her hands over her burning cheeks. "*Merde*, I can't believe I scared myself like that."

"I think your time on the mainland made you soft," he said, a hint of a smile still held in his eyes. It was the most warmth she'd received from him since the summer, and she leaned towards it like a moth to the flame, as though he could warm her with his bonfire presence.

"I looked like a ghost; you would have been scared too." Without meaning to, her voice lowered, full of all the things she wished she could say to him: she missed him.

"I was never afraid of you. Not even when you were a monster."

Lola reached out and brushed her fingers over his arm, letting them linger on his forearm.

He looked down at her hand and his smile faded. "You're all good now." He didn't meet her eyes as he pulled away, leaving Lola to scramble on the floor to find her fallen phone.

"What's taking you guys so long?" Nix hissed from the shadows at the end of the hallway, her voice echoing strangely.

"Lola scared herself," Gael called, moving towards them. Nix's chuckle drifted back, and Lola's blood began to cool, but she cast one last look at the mirror, still expecting something different from her own haunted face to peer back at her.

She hadn't imagined the shock of horror and dread that emanated from this spot. If the Otherworld had taught her nothing else, it was to never ignore her instincts. Something terrible *had* happened here; she was sure of it.

With the trembly feeling that something lurking in the dark was going to lunge for her, she turned her back on the mirror. When she caught up with the others, they stood in front of a heavy wooden door reinforced with iron bands. Walt grabbed the rusted iron handle, which turned with a satisfying clunk.

The door creaked open to a large, simple room beyond. Walt and Gael both ducked their heads to enter, the low ceilings giving it a cramped, utilitarian feel. Plain wooden furniture filled the room, a long pine table surrounded by sturdy, undecorated chairs. Thin windows set horizontally near the ceiling showed they were partially underground, and a dribble of twilit light came in to cast blue shadows over them.

The air was thick with the scent of aged wood and mildew, and the faded floral wallpaper was from another era. Neglect and disuse permeated the room, with cobwebs draped like fine lace over dishes still strewn on the counters as though all residents left in a hurry. A stained teacup sat in a cracked saucer as though put down by someone who would be back in a moment.

"You used to make people live down here?" Nix eyed the area, her lip curling as she ran a finger through the heavy layer of dust.

"It obviously didn't look like this before," Walt said, some heat coming into his voice. "We haven't used this part of the house for decades. A modern kitchen was put in on the ground floor back in the fifties, I think. But generations ago, the staff would cook and eat here, like a common room."

Set into the back wall was a massive stone hearth. The fireplace was large enough to walk into, with insets in the wall on either side where a rod might once have borne a pot over a snapping fire. On the mantle overhead were cracked ceramic vases and, between them, an old-fashioned candle holder, a candle standing straight inside of it.

Lola lit the wick with a match from an old pack sitting next to it, letting the guttering flame catch before she picked up the holder. She crouched down to peer at the floor. "It's been cleaned here, as well," she said, holding the flame over the recently swept floor. There was a faint stain on the stones that could have been old blood. "Walt, are you sure no one uses the Belowstairs?"

His face was stretched out and gaunt in the flames from the candle. "There's no way," he said, eyes opened wide. "Nobody would even know about it."

"You do. And your mother."

"Have you met my mother? Could you see her crawling around down here in the filth?"

Nix let out a scoffing laugh under her breath, and Lola had to admit it was hard to imagine Mayor Seabourne in this place.

Still, she knew better than most that appearances were deceiving.

They spread out in the kitchen, which didn't have much to offer other than thick dust. Next to the fireplace was a nook where firewood likely had been stored. Now there was nothing but a rusted axe, discarded under a layer of ash.

On the counters were tarnished tin salt and pepper shakers. Lola picked up the salt and shook it, hearing the soft susurration of shifting grains. It was still partly full.

Gael paced the perimeter of the room. "Walt, this place is incredible. It's nearly exactly as it must have been a hundred years ago. You could turn this into a museum."

"Oh, yes, my parents would love that," Walt said, his face darkening. "Letting the riff-raff traipse through our home, pawing at our history? Never."

"That's disgusting," Nix said, her eyes narrowing at Walt.

He flung his arms wide. "I don't agree with it! But that's how it is with them. They're not..." His voice faded away, and Lola tried to imagine what words he was looking for. *A proper family? Kind?*

"Well, I think it's creepy that you ignore a huge part of your house, letting it just fall apart." Nix wrinkled her nose and turned away as Walt's jaw set tightly, closing off whatever he was going to say to defend himself.

"I think it's cool," Gael said.

"I do as well." Lola put a hand on Walt's shoulder. "All families have skeletons in their closet, right? The fact that you had servants living in your home is hardly unusual. Fairly common back in the day."

Nix found an unopened cupboard and pulled it open. A half-century's worth of dust puffed out from inside. She backed away, coughing, waving her hand in front of her face.

Within the cupboard were wooden blocks and a child's wooden pull toy in the shape of a duck. "What's this?" she asked.

"It looks like some children's game," Walt said, though he seemed reluctant to touch anything.

"No way!" Gael reached into the cupboard, bringing out a plank and blowing dust off the top, revealing the symbols scribbled over it. Gael placed it on the table, and Lola came over, wiping her hand over the dust to better read the lettering.

Once she realized what it was, she nearly fell as she scrambled to get away from it. "A Ouija board!"

"It looks like one of the original ones," Gael said. "Here's the mover thingy." He put the wooden block on the dusty board like a game piece—it was shaped like a moth, with a hole cut in the centre.

Lola's chest tightened. "It's called a planchette," she said, the words falling flat out of her numb lips.

Moons and stars were painted along the sides, with the alphabet and Roman numerals in black slanted script. In the top corners were the words YES and NO, and at the bottom was an ominous GOODBYE.

Spirit boards were designed to communicate with the world beyond this one. But sometimes other creatures used them as a door.

"I used to have one of these," Gael said, grinning at the memory. "We used to play with Diego. Walt, do you remember?"

Walt's thin face flickered into a smile. "Yeah, only you always moved the planchette."

"Did not!" Gael chuckled. "Well, not all the time. But it freaked Diego out so much we gave it away."

"But what's it doing here?" Nix said. "Were your servants a bunch of Goths?"

"It was probably really normal to have one," Gael said. "Spiritualism was big in the 1920s."

"How do you know that?"

He shrugged. "I read. Apparently after losing so many men in wars, people wanted to find ways to communicate with the dead. The occult was huge, and contacting the beyond was a big source of entertainment."

"There's nothing entertaining about it," Lola said, her voice thin and high like the hiss of a kettle.

Memories from the last time she'd seen a Ouija board in use, led by a misguided witch, flooded back to her. Lola had laughed, drinking blood and wine with Beau, as a demon possessed the woman and ripped through the humans in attendance. It had been amusing then—when she had been the most horrifying thing in the room.

"What's wrong with you?" Nix nudged Lola, who hadn't moved, her gaze riveted to the board. "Don't tell me the former vampire is afraid of a silly game."

"It's not a silly game," she said through gritted teeth. "You shouldn't mess with the occult. You have no idea what you can summon. Please put it back."

"It's not real...right?" Nix asked, her voice quieter than usual as she glanced at Lola.

Gael's eyes hardened. "You can't be serious, Lola. You don't actually believe in this, do you?"

"How can you not? You've seen the Otherworld. Of course there's more to it than children pushing a game piece around."

"But it *is* a children's game. Made by businessmen wanting to make a buck off the spiritual craze of the Victorian age. It's not real." He rapped his knuckles on the wood, and she winced.

"Things like this don't stay harmless for long," Lola said, her voice barely above a whisper. "Spirits can latch onto objects or even toys—"

"Spirits?" Nix cut her off. "You mean like ghosts?"

"Wait, do ghosts exist?" Walt asked, his eyebrows pinching together. "I thought they were just a human construct, a hopeful wish that the afterlife exists."

"What are you talking about?" Nix gave him a mystified look.

"We should use it," Gael said and settled himself on a chair, his fingers hovering over the planchette.

Nix gave him an assessing look, then sat next to him. "I'm in."

Walt sat down with them, setting the candle next to the plank. The dusty wood gleamed faintly in the light, the symbols etched into its surface feeling more like warnings than decoration. "It's just a game. Haven't they found that even when nobody tries to move the planchette, their subconscious mind takes over? It's harmless." He cast an eye on the board, then put his fingers on the planchette. "We can see what our subconscious wants us to know."

"Traitor," Lola muttered.

"Come on, Lola," Nix said. "Gael will probably move the planchette like he always does, the big cheat."

"I won't," he said. "This time," he added under his breath.

He leaned forward, the candlelight casting ghoulish shadows over his face, his lazy grin a dare. "Sure you don't want to miss out on any messages from the beyond?"

Sometimes Lola wondered about those in her life who had been left behind—her real life, the one Jacquotte had stolen from her. Against her better judgment, she approached the table, holding Gael's gaze as she accepted his dare and placed her fingers delicately on the planchette.

His smile was sharp as a razor with a dangerous edge as his fingertips brushed hers, sending a flash of heat up her arm.

"Nix?"

The red-headed girl stared at their hands as though mesmerized. Lola's fingers trembled, waiting as though aching to move, but the planchette stayed still. Finally, Nix reached out and placed her fingers next to Lola's.

"Now what?" Nix asked, her voice unusually quiet.

Gael's grin widened. "We ask it something. Like...who's here with us?"

The planchette jerked under their fingers.

Nix gasped. "That wasn't funny, Gael."

"It wasn't me," he said, though his grin faltered as he glanced at the candle. Its flame had shrunk to a wavering thread of light.

"Stop playing around," Lola whispered.

A spark crackled up her fingers. She gasped and looked at the others; each was frowning at the board. She tried snatching her hands back, but it was as if they were glued to the wood.

"Wait..." she said, but the planchette began to move. Not slow and shaky, but in quick, sharp moves. A leaden silence stifled them, thick with unspoken dread as the planchette spelled out its message.

E...V...I...L...H...E...R...E...

FOUR

The planchette hesitated over the final E, then fell still. The room seemed to exhale all at once. Whatever had kept Lola attached released her, and she jerked her hands away, flexing her fingers. They tingled like they'd been plunged into ice water.

Nix's chair scraped as she pushed back, eyes wide. Across the table, Gael shook out his own hands, his smirk erased by a darker expression. "What the hell does that mean?" he muttered.

"Evil here." Lola's voice was flat, glaring at Nix, certain she was responsible. "Very funny."

But Nix snickered. "Not bad. Even I got spooked. Who did it?"

Walt picked up the planchette, flipping it over to see the underside. "Fascinating," he said.

"Put it down." Lola's words were harsher than she intended. She couldn't bear to see it move again, those jerky, unnatural twitches. Tension built up inside of her like something was on the verge of crossing over.

Then it came: a sound like the wings of a trapped bird inside a chimney. A blast of scorching wind whipped through the kitchen, bringing with it a scream—a primal wail of rage and despair that melded with the rushing wings. Lola clapped her hands over her ears, stifling the scream building in her own throat.

"What the hell is that?" Nix hunkered down against the gale.

"Probably just a draft," Walt said. "Old houses, you know."

"That wasn't a draft," Lola said, her voice trembling. "That was something *Other*."

Gael's voice was low. "Evil here. Is that a warning—or a threat?"

Nix crossed her arms, her earlier humour replaced with a pinching scowl. "Come on, someone's messing with us. Good job, whoever it is." She paced the room, her movements jerky. Her gaze kept darting to Walt.

The planchette clattered as it fell out of Walt's fingers, and Lola jumped.

"Careful with that," Nix snapped.

"Sorry," he said, blinking at her tone. "Are you okay?"

"Fine," Nix said, though she wrung her fingers together as her steps quickened. "I just feel...weird. Like I could run a marathon or something."

"That's weird, because your normal activity is beating up other girls with sticks."

Walt's dig at her field hockey playing was a constant source of friendly ribbing between the two of them, but now his teasing fell flat. Nix's dark glare silenced him. The energy in the room was off-kilter, like a radio tuned to the wrong frequency.

An odd, blank look settled over Nix's face. With swift, sure footsteps, she moved towards the giant hearth, which loomed like a cavernous maw.

"Something's not right here," she said.

Lola joined her. No cobwebs adorned the corners of the chimney, and the floor seemed to have been recently swept.

Nix dropped to her knees and started running her palms over the flagstones.

"What is it?" Lola asked.

"This one," Nix said, groping like a blind person trying to decipher the braille message. "It's not level with the others." She traced a barely perceptible outline.

"How did you notice that?" Lola stooped down beside her, inspecting the stone. "It's not even a quarter inch raised."

Nix shrugged her shoulders as though something itched at her back. "I don't know. It just caught my eye, I guess. What do you think it is?"

The rock was cool as a tomb under Lola's fingertips. "A hiding place," she said, noticing faint grooves worn into the edges. "But it hasn't been opened in ages."

Gael stood over them, holding the candle, his face lit up like a child given the keys to the candy store. "You found a secret hiding place?"

"The house is supposed to be full of them," Walt said, with less child-like wonder. He seemed tense, like this was exactly what he had been afraid of. "Maybe we should leave it alone."

"No, we have to open it," Gael said.

Lola and Nix, crouching inside the fireplace, gripped the edge of the rock with their nails and tugged upwards. After a long minute, it shifted by a fraction.

Lola braced herself on the floor, and holding Nix's gaze, the two of them heaved at the stone together. With a grinding noise that caused Lola's teeth to grit, it pulled free of the floor with a swirl of ages-old ashes rising from the cavity beneath.

Both girls fell back onto the blackened flagstones. The treasure hunter inside Lola perked up, on the scent of new bounty.

A hole gaped in the ground, dark as sin. Nix hesitated over it, as though unsure she wouldn't be bitten by whatever was concealed in the depths, then held her breath and plunged her hand in. She came out with a leather-bound book, its cover cracked and brittle.

"How could you possibly—?" Gael stared at his friend, a

frown marring his face. "That's not normal." He shot an accusing look at Lola as though this was her fault.

A stirring of air blew past them, the creeping feeling of the Otherworld surrounding them like a fog. Nix stared at her soot-filthy hands, holding the leather-bound tome.

"What did you find?" Lola asked softly, as though approaching a wild animal. The wild-eyed look Nix gave her reminded her of prey ready to flee, and the room seemed to be cloaked in eerie silence.

"I don't know how, but I just knew it was there," Nix said, inspecting the book. "It *feels* right. Like finding an old friend."

The oppressive air thickened as Nix laid the book out on the table and unlatched the front clasp. The book opened on a whisper of fragile parchment.

Inside was a scrawl of thin, spidery words, the ink faded and hard to read in some places. As Lola's gaze darted over the words, she sucked in a breath. "It's a diary," she said, her pulse quickening.

Diaries, especially ones hidden away in secret recesses, were the best place to uncover ancient truths and potential treasures. She itched to read through the crumbling pages, the delicate script that lined each page. "Dated May 1921."

"My God, Lola, it's nearly as old as you," Nix said, but the smile she gave was brittle. Her hands shook as she flipped to the first page.

Lola leaned closer, squinting in the flickering candlelight to read the faded script, when Nix slammed the diary shut. The candle extinguished in a rush of air, plunging the room into shadow. Only the thin light from the windows provided any illumination.

"We shouldn't read this." Nix's voice was a harsh whisper. "It's private."

The hallway filled with the slow, deliberate creak of heavy foot-steps. Faint light danced along the hallway, growing stronger with every ominous step, as unsettling shadows crawled along the walls.

"Walt, who could be down here?" Lola whispered urgently.

His face was paler than the ivory curtains that drifted in the half-light around them. Walt shook his head, his lips pressed together in a desperate grimace, and cold dread washed over Lola. She leapt towards the fireplace and placed the flagstone back in place, hiding their discovery.

Nix cringed back near the counter, and Gael moved forward to stand in front of her.

The footsteps paused just outside the threshold, and Lola swallowed back the whimper that wanted to be let out.

The figure stepped into the doorway, haloed by his lantern's cold glow. For one heart-stopping moment, he seemed to materialize from the past. His face was a perfect echo of the portrait in the study, the first Walter Seabourne, his expression severe and unyielding.

"And who do we have here?"

The voice broke the silence, and the man coughed once. Not a ghost, she realized, though he bore an uncanny resemblance to the portrait that hung in the study. This man wore a three-piece business suit, and his lamp had an LED bulb shaped to look like a gas lantern. This must be Walt's father; the genes ran strong through the Seabourne line.

"Walter?" Mr. Seabourne said, his voice a cold whisper. Walt looked frozen, a deer caught in a hunter's sight. His fists clenched tightly, but his shoulders slumped, a silent surrender as his father scrutinized him.

Mr. Seabourne took a step forward, and Lola felt a desperate urge to keep his attention away from his son. She moved to intercept him.

"I'm sorry, it's my fault. I really wanted to look around down here. It's so cool!" Her voice was bright and jaunty, a giggly schoolgirl on an adventure. "I was just curious."

Mr. Seabourne's gaze flickered to her, then to Gael and Nix. "And how did you know about this place unless Walter has been bragging about family secrets?" His voice was cultured, delicate even.

Lola's heart sank as she realized she hadn't saved Walt at all.

"That's right," Walt said, raising his chin to face his father. "I thought I'd impress them. What's the point of having special things if we can't show them off? Isn't that right?"

Mr. Seabourne assessed his son for a long minute, and every second that ticked by, Lola's skin crawled a little more. Walt's father seemed to be promising a reckoning, soon.

Finally, he cleared his throat. "We keep this section of the house off-limits for a reason; we're not sure about the structural integrity. You should all leave now."

None of them needed further encouragement. Lola caught a flicker of movement as Nix slipped the diary into a drawer, her hands trembling. For a heartbeat, Lola thought Mr. Seabourne's gaze lingered on the fireplace, his eyes narrowing, and her pulse quickened. Did he know about the diary?

They filed down the corridor towards the staircase. Passing the mirror, Lola gave an involuntary shiver. The pale, hollow-eyed figures reflected there looked like strangers—ghostly, fragmented versions of themselves.

The door to the study was propped open, and they piled through. Gripping their bags in their arms, they all headed to the front entry without being told. Their time at Seabourne Estate was finished.

In the front parlour, Mayor Seabourne was perched on the edge of a tufted chaise lounge. On the table beside her stood an oversized martini with three olives. She watched as her husband hustled the group of them towards the door.

"Oh really, Arthur, is that necessary?" She drawled as she took them all in. "They're just children. A study session hardly warrants all this fuss. You'd think they uncovered state secrets."

"It's getting rather late, I think." Mr. Seabourne's smile was sharp as diamonds. "I think it's for the best if everyone went home. Do you disagree, Adelaide?"

Mayor Seabourne's gaze flicked between her son and her husband. "Whatever you think is best, Arthur. I'll have Cook make up your favourite prime rib; I had her go to the market today."

He gave a distracted nod. "Fine. But first, I'll have a word here with Walter about appropriateness and sharing family secrets."

Mayor Seabourne's placating smile froze on her face.

Walt's jaw tensed, but he turned to Lola, Gael and Nix. "I'll see you guys at school tomorrow." Though he seemed to be trying for a jovial tone, his words had a hollow ring. "Thanks for the study session."

"I trust you can find your way home safely." Mr. Seabourne gestured them towards the door.

As they were ushered out of the house, Lola stole one last look at Walt. His jaw was tight, his shoulders squared as if bracing for a blow. Behind him, his mother turned her face away as she reached for her drink, her gaze as cold and unreadable as her husband's. Then, the door shut firmly behind her.

FIVE

"What just happened in there?" Nix asked, glancing back at the house. They clustered at the gates, the wrought-iron bars cold to touch.

"Gael?" Lola asked. "You know the Seabournes the best. Was that...normal?"

Doubt flickered over Gael's face. "I didn't notice it much when I was a kid," he admitted, his voice quiet. "But looking back, I think there was always something about his father that I didn't like."

Walt's forced bravado replayed in Lola's mind—the way his shoulders stiffened as his father spoke, the barely concealed terror in his eyes. Mr. Seabourne didn't need to shout or threaten; his presence alone was enough to crush the air from the room.

The manor loomed behind them, its gables and balconies etched against the moonlight like jagged teeth. Even in its elegance, the house exuded an air of secrets, the ivy clinging to its walls like ghostly fingers. Perched on the edge of a windswept cliff, it watched over the restless sea beneath.

Lola shivered, her breath visible in the cool air, and tightened her scarf as the waves below crashed in rhythmic defiance. "Do you think he'll be okay?" she asked.

"Walt?" Gael said. "Yeah, he'll be fine. Mr. Seabourne's just like that. He thinks he's some kind of nobility in the town, like we're all his peasants, but he's mainly just talk."

Still, Gael's face held an ounce of unease that did nothing to settle Lola's fears.

"I couldn't imagine growing up in a place like this," Nix said, shivering.

"My mom did tell me one story about the house," Gael said. "It has to do with the original Walter Seabourne, the one who built it."

"The rum-runner," Lola said.

"Right. Walter Seabourne made a fortune smuggling liquor through the cliffs during Prohibition. But one night, in a fog thick enough to swallow ships whole, he didn't make it back. His boat struck the rocks, and by the time the mist cleared, there was nothing left but debris. His wife waited for him on the widow's walk for three days, drenched in rain and grief. The next morning, she disappeared. Some say she went to join her husband; others say her spirit never left."

"Tragedy surrounds this place," Lola said. She chewed her lip. "Does anyone else think it was weird Mr. Seabourne was down in the Belowstairs? I mean, Walt said nobody ever went down there. How did he know we were there?"

"Maybe his mom told him?" Gael said.

Lola shook her head. "She didn't seem like she wanted him to be caught by his father, which says a lot."

"He could be up to something," Nix said finally, her voice a cold whisper. "You hear things about Mr. Seabourne, how maybe not all his business dealings are on the up and up, you know?"

"I'd believe it." Lola looked out to sea. The moonlight reflected off the waves, moving with a mesmerizing rhythm.

A phantom ache stirred within her, a longing for the power she used to wield, the affinity for water that had once defined her. The pull of the ocean was still there, faint and teasing, like a whisper she could no longer answer.

A fog was rolling in from the east, just like in Gael's story. For a moment, she thought she caught the glimmer of lights from a ship. She blinked and it was gone, just like in the tales of ghost ships that saturated the Maritimes.

Lola turned away from the Atlantic. After everything they'd experienced in Seabourne Estate, she was seeing ghosts everywhere she looked.

"The Belowstairs is interesting, like a time capsule buried inside the house." She turned to Gael. "I wonder if there might be something your mom might want to use for her book."

Gael's mother, Anita Smith, was a Bolivian archeologist who'd fallen in love on Duchesne Island, or *with* Duchesne Island; Lola could never figure out which it was. Since the Smiths had found a significant amount of pirate treasure on their property, she retired from cleaning houses and was working hard to write a book documenting the history of the island.

Gael shrugged. "My mom would probably love the idea of it, although she might not want to have anything to do with the estate. She worked here when we were little. After school, Mum would bring Diego and me over to the house while she cleaned, and that's really how I met Walt. I was the help's son. Mr. Seabourne didn't like it, so when we got a bit older, he'd come over to my house instead. The mayor would send a staff member to pick him up at the cottage."

"It was kind of Anita to take him in like that."

"I think she worried about him. Maybe she knew something about Mr. Seabourne, even back when I was too young to realize. Now that I see him, I wonder if I could have been a better friend."

"Don't say that; he's lucky to have you." Lola reached out instinctively, her hand brushing Gael's arm.

For a moment, his eyes met hers, searching, but then he

stepped back. The warmth between them dissipated, leaving her hand cold as he turned towards the path without another word. He strode away from them, Lola reeling in his wake.

"Wow, that was awkward," Nix said.

Lola shot her a dirty look, but Nix just shrugged. "It's never not going to be weird, you guys wanting to be together and yet refusing to be together. I'll walk you home?"

"It won't be awkward forever," Lola said as she hooked her arm through Nix's. "Soon we'll be able to be friends."

"You keep on telling yourself that," Nix said. They descended the path together. Seabourne Estate sat on top of the cliffside, looking down over the town of Port Despardoux. Rather like Walt's parents did to the residents there.

"Where do you think he's going?" Gael's silhouette had already been swallowed up by the shadows of the woods that surrounded the winding road.

"Probably to Lost Souls. He's been hanging out there a lot. With the hyenas," Nix added quietly. "They've really embraced him. In part because he's on the baseball team, and in part because of...other stuff."

"Is that other stuff how he has money now?"

"A bit." Nix shifted away, not meeting her gaze. "And also... Cassidy."

Cassidy McFarland. Lola's insides tightened. She was the beautiful, bubbly girl who had thrown herself all over Gael that summer, and while he'd been under a desire spell, he'd returned her advances.

"I see." Lola tried to sound nonchalant but inside was a riot of emotions. "Are they dating?"

"I mean, Cassidy would really like that; she's not shy about how she feels. But as far as I know, no. Not yet."

"Right." Lola swallowed hard. She was the one who broke up with Gael. She was the one who'd kissed someone else, and not under the influence of any spell. She didn't get to tell him who he could see, no matter how much it hurt.

She gave Nix's elbow a gentle shake. "How are you, by the way? That Ouija board thing seemed to freak you out."

Nix snickered. "Oh, Lola, for a centuries-old demon, you are so gullible. *I* moved the planchette."

"And you spelled out *Evil Here*? How very horror queen of you."

"You were all so freaked out," Nix teased, but her voice lacked its usual brightness. Lola studied her friend out of the corner of her eye. Her laughter was weak, her gaze avoiding the house behind them. Something had rattled her in the Belowstairs, even if she wouldn't admit it.

As the fog crept in, Lola stole a final glance at Seabourne Estate, its windows dark and unyielding. Somewhere inside, Walt faced his father. The thought sent a chill skittering up her spine. Secrets clung to this house like the mist on the cliffs—and she had a sinking feeling they were far from done with it.

Six

"Okay, Ms. I've-Done-It-All. What do you think of high school so far?"

Lola stared at Nix, trying to come up with an answer that could cover everything being thrown at her. She hadn't thought it would be a big deal. She'd been through so much, had dined with kings and killed their servants, had partied with the rock stars of the 60s and brought their exquisite highs to the next level as she fed on their blood.

Lola thought she *had* done everything, but entering into a modern high school as a junior was brand new.

She was overwhelmed by the crush of bodies brushing against hers, the plaid of the girls' uniform skirts and the sparkle of accessories, the chatter and the laughter, the perfume and the makeup reapplication and the sports guys' chest-bumping in the hallway. There was something to see around every corner, and she wanted to see it all.

A slow smile crept across her face. "I think I might love it," she said.

"Ooh, good, keep that attitude because we're about to jump

into English Lit, and Mr. Heinzen is a real jerk. Gael's in the class, just so you know."

"Thanks." Lola smoothed her hands over her skirt. She shouldn't be nervous to see him, but she couldn't help how her stomach flip-flopped at the thought.

With Nix as her guide, they made it to the second-floor class and tucked themselves into desks near the windows. The room was drowsy-warm from the early autumn sun, and spirals of dust whorled through the beams coming in from the window. Glancing outside, Lola caught a flash of the ocean. It soothed her jangled spirit, and she let out a breath.

Turning to Nix, she noticed deep shadows stretched out under her eyes. "Are you okay?"

The redhead rolled her eyes. "I wish everyone would stop asking me that. I just had trouble sleeping, is all." Then she caught a glimpse of something over Lola's shoulder, and her face shuttered.

Reiko Frost entered the class with her usual swagger, her piercing gaze cutting through the room like a blade.

She had chopped off her blonde tips, leaving an inky black pixie cut. Piercings cuffed both ears, and her eyebrow held a silver bar. She paused for a moment when she caught sight of Lola.

Lola held her gaze. Even with the brand that marred her collarbone hidden, Lola was hyper-aware of the girl's allegiance to the demon-hunting Order.

At some point, the two of them needed to have a proper conversation.

Reiko moved to her desk on the opposite side of the class. Behind her, Gael entered the classroom, chatting with Cassidy.

Seeing them together caused Lola's stomach to plummet.

The worst part of it was they looked so good together. Gael was designed to rock a uniform. His tie was loosened and the first button undone, giving a tantalizing glimpse of the brown hollow of his throat. And Cassidy was the perfect co-ed, her skirt hiked up to nearly criminal, her auburn hair in its bouncy ponytail.

Seeing Gael lean towards Cassidy, his tie askew and his casual laugh rippling through the air, felt like watching a lifeline drift just out of reach. He used to feel like home to her. Now, he was a reminder of what she'd given up.

Gael caught sight of Lola immediately, but all he did was raise an eyebrow before he went to sit between Nix and Cassidy. Lola felt the distance like a blow.

A small man in an ill-fitting suit came into the classroom, and everyone started taking their laptops out of their bags. Even Nix, who'd never had so much as two pennies to rub together, pulled out a battered Chromebook.

Lola had only brought a notebook and pen and immediately realized she hadn't done nearly enough to prepare for high school.

Nix snickered at her notebook, and even the girl sitting behind Lola took notice. She had long brown hair shaved on one side.

"Are you...new here?" she asked.

"Um, yes, just started," Lola said. "I don't have all my equipment yet. Um, my old school believed in traditional materials."

"Poppy, this is Lola," Nix said to the girl. "She's from Europe and went to a boarding school." Her cheeks puffed out as she tried not to laugh.

"That's cool," Poppy said. "I knew a girl from Sweden who did that. Did you travel around to see all kinds of historical places, that kind of thing?"

"Something like that." Lola thought of the locations her treasure hunting had taken her: the jungles of Cambodia, the steppes of Peru. "It was an interesting education. Not a lot of tech in the field."

"It must have been amazing," Poppy gushed.

"I don't know." Gael leaned forward, joining their conversation. His shirt sleeves were rolled up, and Lola's gaze flew to his forearms braced on his desk. "Sounds like a crap school to me. Do you even know how to do math?"

His words stung, all the more so when she heard Sam and Cassidy titter behind him. While she'd had decades to read all the books and knew she'd excel at English Lit, she had shared—in confidence with Gael—that she didn't have the faintest idea how trigonometry worked.

"That is so wicked," Poppy said, entirely missing the tension between them. She called to the front of the room. "Mr. Heinzen, we have a new student. She's from Europe."

Lola's cheeks heated as all eyes swung to her, and an insect-like buzz of gossip rose from the crowd. It was possible some rumours were floating around about her, based on everything that had happened since she'd arrived on the island. She lifted her head as Mr. Heinzen turned to her.

His sour look was not improved as he took her in, and he puffed out his scruffy cheeks. "Right, I heard about our late newcomer. Ms. Monteux from Paris, is it? And why is it that you've cared to join us weeks into the semester? Having too much fun with your snails and frog's legs?"

Lola tried not to scrunch up her shoulders at his hostility. "I prefer the baguette and beret stereotype myself. And I was attending my father's funeral. I worked it out with the administration."

Mr. Heinzen didn't seem to have a counterpoint to that one, so with a pointed glare, he turned to his computer. All his notes flashed up on the screen and he began his lecture.

"Man is condemned to be free because once thrown into the world, he is responsible for everything he does."

Poppy's hand shot up, and Mr. Heinzen let out a barely disguised sigh. "Yes, Ms. McCann?"

"*Humans* are condemned to be free," she said firmly.

Mr. Heinzen's eye twitched. "Yes, humans," he said after a long pause. "Can anyone tell me who wrote this?"

Lola tried not to smirk. She'd once spent an evening smoking in a café with Jean-Paul Sartre and his wife, Simone de Beauvoir, hearing their thoughts about freedom and life. The famed literary couple had belonged to an element of people who sought out the macabre and thought they could brush the forces of darkness while remaining in the light themselves.

They were interesting, though. Lola had enjoyed them enough to let them live.

Mr. Heinzen was struggling not to curse the class. "Anyone? Did anyone do the reading? How about you, Mademoiselle Baguette? Any chance the French system somehow actually provides an education?"

"It was Sartre. He supposes that freedom is a bad thing, though we say we want it. He thought free will was a burden."

He paused. "And? What do you think?"

"That we are condemned to be free?" Her classmates watched the interplay with bored gazes. Lola let out a long breath, feeling as though this was a test, though she wasn't sure what she was being marked on. "No, I don't. Freedom is everything. Our choices in how we live our lives are the only thing that makes them worth living."

Everyone stared at her, including Mr. Heinzen. She cleared her throat. "He was a bored man, Sartre, and thought life was the greatest curse to endure. His wife was more interesting."

Poppy let out a whoop, and the class came to life again as some of her classmates made derisive noises.

Nix shook her head. "Always with the philosophizing."

One boy raised his hand. "Will this be on the test?"

Mr. Heinzen cleared his throat. "I disagree with Ms. Monteux's assessment. I suppose something can be said for having done the reading, though. Perhaps I'll add more philosophers to our list."

A groan rose from the students. Sam raised her hand. "Mr.

Heinzen, just because some dork knows boring stuff doesn't mean we all should have to suffer."

"Suck up," someone said loudly, and others snickered. Cassidy shot a look of triumph at Lola while Gael tried to hold in his laughter.

Lola held herself very still, trying not to sink into her chair as she wanted to. She couldn't imagine why her classmates' mockery would bother her, but it did.

A sharp rap at the door interrupted the rabble, and a young man entered the classroom.

He leaned against the door frame, his tousled hair falling over his forehead. He wore jeans and a tweed blazer with elbow patches as though attempting to look both professorial and cool.

He couldn't be much older than his early twenties, and most of the girls sat up a little straighter as he smiled. "Knock, knock," he said, and Mr. Heinzen rolled his eyes.

"Ah, yes, more newcomers. You might as well come in, though we had discussed a later time. Class, this is Matt Vernon, the new editor of the *Duchesne Daily*. He's here to…I'll let him tell you."

Mr. Heinzen sat back in his chair and picked up his phone.

"Hey, guys." The editor had a smooth voice that matched his appearance, attractive with a sharp finish, but there was something about him that put Lola off. He was trying very hard to put off a certain vibe; she hadn't decided whether he'd succeeded or not.

"Call me Matt. I'm way too young to be Mr. Vernon." There were some ingratiating giggles, and Matt's smile sharpened like a shark's. "I'm here to talk to you about the revival of the *Port Despardoux Tribune*. Your high school newspaper."

"We don't have a paper," someone said.

"Correct." Matt pointed at him. "But you used to, and you can again. I was hoping to help start things up. Let me tell you a bit about myself. For the past several years, I've been working as an investigative journalist. I delve deep into one specific story for a long time, covering a range of topics in crime or injustice. Digging into a story in that way takes patience and courage, and an understanding of humanity and history."

It sounded a little like treasure hunting. Lola, intrigued, made some notes in her book. Instead of a pile of gold, you uncover the truth, although she didn't know which was more valuable.

"Why did you come to Duchesne, then?" she asked.

The class's attention was riveted to him. "Well, after my latest scoop, where I went undercover with a Montreal biker gang, I found myself needing a change of pace. The *Duchesne Daily* had an opening, which was fortuitous."

Fortuitous for Matt Vernon, maybe, but not for the unlucky former editor. Richie Dawgsby had been torn apart by werewolves, though Lola refrained from bringing this up.

"Anyways," Matt continued with his smarmy grin. "I would like to set up the *Tribute* again, and I'm looking to see if there's enough interest from the student body to make this work. I'll need all levels of involvement: reporters, photographers, copy editors, designers...the works. It's interesting, practical work, and, of course, it will look great on your university applications." Matt winked. "Is anyone interested?"

Lola raised her hand; so did Gael. In a flash, Cassidy's hand shot up as she giggled, and Lola forced her eyes to not roll back in her head.

Nearly a third of the class raised their hands. Matt rubbed his hands together.

"Excellent. We'll meet after school to discuss." He paused, then smiled, his white teeth blinding. "Let's see what we can dig up together."

SEVEN

After class, Lola watched as Reiko rushed out of the classroom as if she had an appointment to keep. Seeing an opportunity, Lola threw a breezy "See you later" to Nix and ducked out of the class after the mysterious girl.

Reiko was already down the hallway, and Lola sprinted after her, dodging other students as they disgorged from their classrooms at the same time. Reiko turned down a less busy hallway, and Lola was able to catch up, grabbing her by the elbow.

Reiko spun, arms up and every muscle tensed, as though her hunter instincts had taken over. When she recognized Lola, she sneered but straightened and rolled her shoulders back as though forcing herself to relax.

"What's the rush?" Lola asked, carefully backing away a step, though not far enough away they couldn't have a quiet conversation. Reiko was far stronger than she was. Lola didn't have the same supernatural strength she once did, and Reiko had been trained to fight, likely from childhood.

"I don't have time for this," Reiko said, rolling her eyes and trying to push past Lola.

Lola let her go, calling after her, "What's the Order of Hanta Cythraul?"

Reiko's mask slipped for the briefest moment. Fear, or maybe something sharper, flickered in her eyes before she shoved Lola against the lockers hard enough that her breath came out in a whoosh.

"You don't know what you're talking about," Reiko hissed, but her voice wavered.

"Secret society of demon hunters. Sound familiar?" Lola shifted, trying to get Reiko to ease off the pressure on her chest.

Reiko glanced around, realizing they were drawing a crowd, and let Lola go. With a suffering sigh, she let her backpack slip to the floor. "I don't know how you know about that, but you've never heard of it and will never mention it again."

For all her nonchalance, Lola could see she'd gotten under Reiko's skin. Her eyes kept flicking around the hallways—not at the students, Lola realized, but at the ceiling. Where cameras might be placed.

"Are we being watched?" Lola asked. Worry fluttered at her breast; how sophisticated was this Order?

Reiko gave a tiny shake of her head. "No. I don't think so. Tell me who told you about Hanta Cythraul." Her voice dropped to a whisper.

"The thing I've never heard of and will never mention again?" Reiko's glare promised murder, so Lola relented. "I have my sources. According to them, you're a secret organization that hunts demons, although not as secret as you might think. How am I doing so far?"

With pale skin even whiter than normal, Reiko clenched and unclenched her hands. "You don't know what you're getting into," she said. Her voice was strangled.

"Then enlighten me."

"Listen." Reiko met her gaze, deep distrust shading her eyes. "You need to back off. You have no idea what you're up against."

"*You* don't know what you're up against," Lola said. She brought a finger to Reiko's face. "This is *my* island, and I need to know what you're doing here."

"*Your* island?" Reiko's snort was full of scorn. "You barely got here before me."

"What—" Lola froze mid-sentence, the weight of Reiko's retort landing like a sudden blow. It was true; Lola had only arrived on Duchesne a few months before Reiko. But still, the certainty of her own claim buzzed in her chest, insistent and immovable. "Doesn't matter. You come to my home and hurt my people, so I will do what I need to figure out why you're here."

"Is that a threat?" Reiko pulled herself to her full height, several inches taller than Lola.

But Lola was in no mood to be intimidated. "No, it's a reality. I don't know where you come from, but I'm willing to go head-to-head with your little Order."

Reiko shook her head, her astonishment at Lola's words seeming to edge into admiration. "Who the hell are you? No— *what* are you? You're *something*."

"How flattering. Why don't you take out your little device and find out?"

"My little device?"

"The thing you were flashing all over the carnival. A little pagan technology? Reading some kind of paranormal measures? What does it do, Reiko?"

Reiko smirked, though threads of dark worry flashed in her eyes. "I have no idea what you're talking about. But whatever you are, stay out of my way."

"Don't cause any trouble, and I'm sure we'll be just fine." Lola gave Reiko a falsely sweet smile.

"Hey," came a small voice next to them, breaking through Reiko and Lola's face-off. Nix held her books in front of her, hurrying up to Lola. "What are you doing?" Her shoulders were squared and she refused to look at the other girl.

Reiko immediately lost her intimidating stature, shuffling her toes on the linoleum floor. She stared up at the ceiling, whether to check for surveillance equipment or to avoid looking at Nix, Lola wasn't sure.

Lola turned her back on Reiko. "Nothing. We're done here." She started down the hallway. Nix grabbed her arm in an iron grip and marched her to the nearest bathroom.

Once inside, Nix cast a glare over the other girls fixing their hair at the sinks before whispering to Lola, "Spill."

"Spill what?"

"What did Reiko want? What did you say to her?" She paused. "Did she mention me?"

"I just wanted to get some of my concerns out in the open," Lola said, then smirked. "And she didn't mention you, but I swear she nearly fainted when you came up."

"What! Why? What?" Nix was bruising her arm.

"Listen, I still think it's safe to say we need to stay the hell away from her. But I get the sense she doesn't feel good about how things went down over the summer."

A few months ago, at the Carnival of Fools, everyone in town had been snagged by a supernatural spell that fed on their most basic desires. Reiko and Lola were the only two in town who had protection against the enchantment.

The fact that Reiko hadn't been under a spell meant she had no excuse when she targeted Nix for a nasty prank. Then afterwards, she befriended her to get close to Lola, taking advantage of Nix's crush on her.

It was all the worse because it was the first time Nix had opened up about her attraction to other girls, and it steamed Lola just thinking of it. "Reiko is a snake. You should stay away from her, Nix—she's not worth it, okay?"

Nix looked as though she wanted to argue but finally gave a sharp nod. "Fine. Not worth it. As long as you don't get into trouble mixing up with the Order of Hanta thingy." Nix scrunched her nose. "Leave it alone, Lola."

"Why would I go messing with that kind of thing?"

Nix's gaze met Lola's innocent face and she snorted. "You are so stunned. Like, straight-up reckless." Nix shook her head, muttering under her breath. "Why do I even try?"

EIGHT

The new journalism club was an unexpected clash of the school's hierarchies. Lola slipped into the classroom at the end of the day, scanning the students scattered around the desks. Overachievers leaned in eagerly, jocks lounged near the back, and a cluster of hyenas sprawled in their usual dominance at the centre.

At the heart of the crowd sat Violet Wynn, her sharp gaze flickering over the room like a queen appraising her court. Flanked by Cassidy and Sam, she ruled with a lazy smirk.

Lola's stomach tightened. Violet had antagonized her since she'd set foot on the island, and her role in Nix's summertime prank was still fresh.

But for all Lola didn't want to forgive her for her cruelty, she couldn't shake the sense that Violet's knife-sharp edges came from somewhere dark. Something Lola could relate to.

Violet's on-again, off-again boyfriend, Ethan, was nowhere to be seen. Good. Lola had bad blood with the school's golden boy, and she'd seen enough of his entitled grin and self-serving charm to know it hid something twisted inside.

Violet caught Lola's eye and arched a brow, her expression

unreadable. Lola refused to look away. The blonde girl might rule Port Despardoux High, but Lola had faced worse. With a measured step, she crossed the room and slid into a seat near the edge of the group.

The chair beside her screeched as someone sat down. Lola stiffened.

Reiko.

"Why are *you* here?" Lola hissed, keeping her voice low.

Reiko didn't look at her, her face placid as she unpacked an expensive-looking camera from her bag. "I like photography. Is that a problem?"

Suspicion prickled at Lola's scalp. The camera was probably all kitted out with supernatural spells if it came from the HC, as Nix called it. "Are you here undercover as a high schooler to spy on us, and this just provided you with the perfect excuse?"

Reiko's lips twitched with a warning smile. "You think too highly of yourself. This will look good on my CV. Being trans-ferred to the middle of nowhere isn't helping my application to Oxford."

"Cry me a river," Lola said. "What, does Oxford not accept hunting demons as acceptable extracurriculars?"

Reiko's gaze sharpened, a reminder of just how easily she could wipe the floor with Lola if she felt inclined. But before Lola could push her further, Gael entered with Matt trailing behind him.

Gael grabbed a seat next to Cassidy, who immediately leaned in to whisper something in his ear. Gael smirked, then caught Lola watching.

Her face flamed, and she stared straight ahead, her chest aching with phantom pain.

Matt took centre stage, cutting off her thoughts. "Greetings, truth-seekers." He'd ditched the blazer and stood in front of them in jeans and a faded T-shirt, looking more like a college kid than a teacher. "It warms my heart to find such interest in our school paper, the *Port Despardoux Tribune*."

He brought out a stack of papers and put them on the desk, a fake grimace playing over his face. "I'm going to date myself, but here are some copies of the paper from when I was editor a million years ago. Or, maybe not quite that long ago." Again, the shark smile. Lola looked away from him. She couldn't pinpoint it, but something about him felt off. Like he was the only one in on a private joke.

"I encourage you all to come up and check out what used to be news. It might give you story or column ideas, but I also want you to come to me with new stuff. What matters to you, right here, right now?"

Everyone else seemed captivated by his energy, leaning forward like he was handing out secrets. Lola sat back, arms crossed, refusing to be swept up.

Violet raised her hand. "Aren't we ignoring the totally obvious? A school paper is, like, completely outdated. Nobody reads print anymore."

He flashed his predatory grin. "I'm a dinosaur, so I'm going to disagree with you on that, but you have a point: People consume their media in many ways. Who are you?"

"Violet Wynn." She flipped her hair back over her shoulder.

"Congratulations, Violet Wynn. You're the new web editor."

Violet pursed her lips, as though the conversation hadn't gone the way she wanted, but she gave a begrudging nod.

He didn't stop. "Let's keep the ideas rolling. Who's interested in working behind the scenes on copy-editing and design?"

Several students raised their hands, and Matt began divvying out roles for the paper. Lola volunteered as a reporter, as did Gael and Cassidy.

When Matt gathered his writers at the front, she kept a careful distance from them, her cheeks heating when she caught Gael's eye. To distract herself, she flicked through one of the old papers, full of photos of young smiling kids, each of them confident that the world was made for them. It made Lola feel unaccountably sad and she set it aside.

"Okay, reporters." Matt leaned in conspiratorially. "Don't tell anyone else this, but you're the most important part of the team."

That sent a titter of laughter through the gathered students. "You say that to everyone," Cassidy said with a simper.

"That doesn't mean I'm wrong." Matt smiled. "The stories you write are the lifeblood of the paper. You are the reason why people are going to pick up the PD Tribune, understand? What are we going to want to put in there? Remember, there are no dumb ideas."

"Obviously the major events that are going on," one boy dressed all in black said. "The upcoming student elections, sporting events, competitions, that kind of thing."

"Great, all good stuff."

"What about the school dances?" Sam perked up. "We need announcements for homecoming court and when to purchase tickets for the winter ball."

"And, of course, tons of photos to showcase it all," Cassidy joined in.

"Excellent stuff. Everyone wants to see themselves in the paper, and they want to read about what's going on, the stuff that matters to them personally."

"What about classifieds?" Gael said. "You know, lost and found, job postings, messages to other students. Maybe charge for ads, give us a budget."

"Entrepreneurial thinking. I like it." Matt tilted his head, inspecting Gael. "I would expect nothing less from the famous treasure hunter of Duchesne Island."

Gael reddened and glanced at Lola before he could stop himself. He had been the face of the treasure hunt with the media. Since the treasure pit had been on his land, it only made sense. But Lola knew that the attention made him uncomfortable and wished she could shield him from it. She pulled a grimace of sympathy, and he looked away.

Oblivious, Matt shifted gears. "This is all great stuff. I was also hoping we could dig deeper. The island's unique. We should explore that. Local mysteries, even."

Lola's eyebrow raised. Investigating the island? Sounded like Matt's job as editor of the *Duchesne Daily*. Was Matt using the student body to get dirt for his paper?

Her hand shot up. "I'm interested."

"Yeah?" Matt looked at her fully for the first time. "Are you willing to seek out the truth?"

It's what I live for.

The realization hit her with startling clarity. She'd always loved research, the thrill of untangling ancient mysteries, then plunging deeper to uncover secret truths. It felt like being at sea in a storm, knowing she would make it through if only she could hold her course.

"I can handle it," she said mildly, but inside, her heart thundered.

"Would you be intimidated by interviewing the police?"

Lola hid a grin. Intimidated, no. Not so much as she'd be worried that the head of the RCMP on the island would throttle her. She couldn't imagine what Sergeant Greyson would say if she asked for a quote, considering he was still suspicious of her in regard to several murders on the island. It would be interesting.

She shrugged. "We have a working relationship."

"Sounds intriguing."

"If we're going to talk about the island, maybe we could look at some of the island's haunted history," Gael said. "Like all the ghost stories and paranormal rumours."

Lola shot him a piercing look. What was he playing at? Gael knew nobody could know the truth about the Otherworld. Just the fact he was aware of its existence put him at risk. And now he wanted to publish stories on it?

Reiko was also glaring at Gael, holding her probably-magical camera. At least Lola and Reiko agreed on one thing: Gael was being reckless.

Matt wrinkled his nose. "I'm not interested in the fairy tales your moms told you when you were going to sleep," he said. "We're here to uncover facts. Duchesne is a fascinating place without the creepy crawlies."

"What about articles on the island's non-haunted history?" Lola asked, thinking of the Belowstairs and the diary Nix had found. "Maybe some stuff that goes into what life was like?"

Matt pulled another face. Clearly, there *were* dumb ideas. "That's not what a newspaper is about. We want stories about things that affect us now, today."

Lola twisted her lips. Ancient history was her favourite thing to dig into, especially since that's where the answers to buried treasures and unsolved mysteries were usually found.

The meeting wrapped up with a flurry of assignments. Lola was tasked with covering the student elections—a far cry from treasure hunts, but at least it wasn't sports.

Lola was already scheduling time to track down the hopeful student candidates when she heard a hiss from the doorway. Walt and Nix waved at her to join them.

"How was chess club?" she asked, joining them.

"Lame." Nix rolled her eyes.

"Only cause I beat her." Walt nudged Nix with his elbow. Their tension from the night before had eased, so Lola took a chance.

"Do you think we could study at your house again?" A flicker of guilt licked through her at asking, but she really wanted to take a look at the diary. Something told her it was important.

Colour stained Walt's pale cheeks. "You would want to? After what went down yesterday?"

"Only if it's okay. I don't want to get you into trouble."

He gave a shrug as though it was no big deal. "Shouldn't be a problem. My dad left again this morning, so we wouldn't have to deal with...that."

"I was hoping we could go back to the Belowstairs." Lola lowered her voice. "I want to check out the diary Nix found."

"That dirty old thing?" Nix gave a sneer of disgust. "I think we should use it as kindling."

"Nix, you pulled it out of an ancient hiding place after the Ouija board went crazy. I think there's something there."

"Well, yeah, maybe..." Walt cleared his throat, tugging the sleeve of his blazer over his wrist. He couldn't quite hide the ring of dark bruises marring his skin.

"I'm sorry, let's not," Lola said immediately. "It was stupid to ask."

Walt looked at her, then straightened. "It's my house too. I'm in if you are."

His gaze was caught by something over Lola's shoulder, his face reddening even more. Lola turned as Violet approached their group.

"What's the freak squad talking about?" she asked, her eyes on Walt.

"Absolutely nothing that concerns you, Vi." Walt finally met her gaze, and a long moment stretched between them.

Matt called out then, interrupting the showdown between the two. "Hey, guys, we've gone into overtime. You're all free to leave, but good work, everyone. I'll be back on Friday afternoon, and you better be there too. Showing up here today means an unbreakable contract that you have signed on for the year." He let out a bark of laughter. "Just kidding. Not really. Now get out of here."

Students started to mill around them, heading into the hallways. Gael stopped to fist-bump Walt.

"We're going back to mine this afternoon if you want to join," Walt said.

"Yeah?" Gael's gaze flicked to Lola, then back to Walt. "I'm busy, but thanks for the invite."

Gael joined the hyenas without looking back, his easy laugh already blending with theirs. Walt shifted beside Lola, his shoulders slumping just enough to break her heart a little. She watched the distance grow—not just as Gael walked away, but within their group itself.

NINE

"Why are they so great?" Nix asked, kicking a stone as they wandered the manicured path leading to the front entry. "Why does everybody want to spend time with them?"

The autumn wind howled around the edges of Seabourne Estate, making the towering mansion seem alive—leaning into them with malevolent intent. The wind slashed through Lola's scarf, and the damp chill settled in her bones.

"You mean the hyenas?" Walt said, unlocking the massive French doors. They opened with a creak into the darkened entrance hall beyond. "And by everyone, you mean Gael."

"Well, exactly." Nix shivered as she stepped over the threshold of the house. "Although to be honest, I don't know why *I'm* here. I'm not into all this creepy stuff, either. And you'd think *you* would have had enough of it," she added to Lola.

"I guess it's something that you never get out of your system," Lola said.

The distant clatter of pans echoed unnaturally, the vastness of the house distorting every sound. Despite the evidence of others moving through the rooms, the manor seemed yawningly empty.

"How do you handle it, Walt?" Nix gazed around the dark panelling that penned them in despite the ceilings that soared two storeys above them. "It's pretty creepy in here."

"You get used to it," Walt said, but he ducked his head in a way that made Lola think he never had. Loneliness clung to him like a cloak, here with his cold house and even colder family. She could see why he'd turned to the warmth of Gael's small cottage.

Only Gael wasn't with them now. She wasn't sure which of them missed him the most.

"So, we're going back into the passageways, right?" Nix asked, her eyes gleaming as they made their way to the study.

"Sure," Walt said with a studied nonchalance, even as his shoulders crept towards his ears. He glanced behind him as though waiting for someone lurking there to jump out and berate him.

Lola understood what it was like to always be on guard around your family, hyper-vigilant of setting someone off. Of course, Lola's family had been a crew of murderous vampires, but she suspected Walt's experience hadn't been much easier.

"Is your mom here, Walt?"

"She's probably still at city hall," he said. "She works late on weekdays. And weekends, to be honest. It's just us and the staff. We can do whatever we want." He set his jaw in a way that felt rehearsed, as though he'd done this many times before to convince himself and others that he was fine.

His voice was low and even, but the slight crack betrayed his nerves. "Let's go to the Belowstairs."

In silence, they filed through the study. It seemed as cold and majestic as ever, a massive space dedicated to books and rare arti-facts, like something in a museum. It was a beautiful room, but Lola wondered if anyone truly enjoyed it.

Walt closed the door behind them, ensuring the latch made no sound to give away their presence.

Lola's gaze immediately went to the bookshelf that hid the

passageway. As she took it in, the groaning began again, and a chill shuddered down her spine.

As Walt approached the secret passageway, Lola noted which book activated the doorway. The gold embossing spelled out *Treasure Island* in swooping cursive.

Walt's hand lingered on the book, his shoulders tense as though the house itself was watching. His eyes darted towards the shadows, searching for threats only he could imagine as he pulled the lever.

With a whoosh of air, the shelf creaked open, revealing the dark corridor beyond.

The musty air hit Lola first, a sickly mix of mildew, candle wax, and something coppery, like old blood. It pressed against her chest, making her breath shallow. Even the walls seemed to crowd closer, the dark wood gleaming like wet skin.

"Eegh," Nix said. "It smells like something died down there."

A loud thud echoed from somewhere deep in the house. Nix froze mid-step, glancing at Walt, whose hand tightened on the door frame. "Just the wind," he said, but his voice wavered.

He moved into the darkness first. His fingers tightened around his phone, the beam of light swaying unsteadily along the dark passage as he made his way down the stairs.

Nix and Lola exchanged a look, then followed their friend. Lola took up the rear, and the door fell shut behind her. Lola turned and saw no door handle, just a blank wooden panel.

Sandpaper dryness coated her throat. This fear was ridiculous: She'd faced death, darkness and monsters, but now, her vulnerable human body betrayed her at every step. The fragility was maddening.

"Walt?" she called out, her voice a hoarse whisper.

"What is it?" Walt came back up the stairs.

"How do we get out? From this side, I mean."

"There's a catch here." Walt pointed out a wooden lever built into the door frame; he gently pulled it down, which released the catch and opened the door by an inch, and Lola released her pent-up breath.

The stairwell creaked under their footsteps, and the darkness took on an extra shade of black as they descended into the bowels of the house.

As she made her way down the corridor, the scratching started again: hushed, like a light sawing. Certainly not rats. Lola turned to stare at the wall, where her dim reflection had frightened her so much.

As she approached the mirror, the scratching stopped, and all the hairs at the back of her neck stood up.

Decades of grime coated the reflective surface; it was a miracle anything could be seen through it at all. Wiping a hand across the glass, she froze as light flickered in the corner of the reflection—alive and dancing, but when she turned, the corridor was empty.

Her breath fogged the surface, but no matter how much she rubbed, the light in the corner of the mirror grew stronger—alive, flickering like a heartbeat.

The smell of candle wax was stronger. The scratching started again, more frantic than ever. She could hear distant crying. Horror rolled through her as the wail twisted and grew until it erupted into a scream that roared past her like a freight train, blowing into her like a physical force.

The air turned rank, the smell of decay overwhelming her senses.

Her eyes filled with tears against it, and her own screams mingled with the horrible sound. She crouched, her hands clutching at her ears as the agonized wailing passed over her.

Then, it was gone.

Lola cautiously glanced up, the silence deafening after the scream from before. She let out a sobbing breath as she saw two lights bobbing towards her, the white beams of phones, not phantom candlelight.

"Lola, what happened?" Nix asked.

"You guys didn't hear it?" Lola scrabbled to find her phone while Walt came to her side and helped her up.

"Hear what?"

"The screaming," Lola said, her voice faint.

"Are you having visions again?" Walt asked. "Like last summer?"

Lola wrapped her arms around herself, trying to shake off the nausea. "Maybe. Walt, I think something bad happened down here."

In the stark light, shadows stretched out Walt's expression. "Based on everything I know about this house, it wouldn't surprise me at all."

"So, what do we do?" Nix asked. "Do we keep on going?"

As if there were any other choice. "Of course we keep on going," Lola said. "We need to figure out what happened."

"Why is it always us?" Nix said, her face half-lost in shadows. "Why can't we, for once, leave the scary things alone? Why do I think Lola was the kid who poked things with sticks, just to see what would happen?"

The thought unexpectedly warmed Lola, making her smile. "Maybe I was. But something tells me I *need* to find that diary and figure out what's happening. You guys don't have to come, though."

"Oh, we'll come," Nix said and looped her arm through Lola's. "Try to keep up this time, alright?"

Her friend's flaming courage lifted her, and Lola continued down the passage, making it to the kitchen without incident. Through the narrow windows near the top of the wall, a hint of daylight trickled in, casting the entire room in blueish-grey light.

The diary was the first thing she saw, sitting at the centre of the long plank table. "Did you take it out of the drawer already?" she asked.

"What?" Nix released Lola, leaning against the wall and

crossing her arms over her chest. "No, we didn't make it this far before you started wailing back there."

Lola's pulse quickened. The diary shouldn't have been there. It was as though the house itself wanted her to find it. She set her bag down next to the Ouija board, still laid out on the table, and shot the planchette a distrustful look as she reached for the diary.

It seemed heavier than its size warranted. As she flipped through the pages, each one whispered faintly, like dry leaves brushing against stone.

In the dim light of the kitchen, she could barely make out the writing, but she turned her flashlight onto the page and squinted. "This writing is so faded, but here on the first page, you can see the ink: This diary belongs to A...Alice, I think. Mc...Cullough. Alice McCullough."

"McCullough?" Nix came to read over her shoulder.

"Yes, Alice McCullough. You can just make it out here." Lola pointed at the looping letters. Nix stared, then shook her head.

"How can you even read that?"

"Well, it's not as hard as Sumerian," Lola said and chuckled. She glanced up to see them staring at her. "Well, it isn't."

"You read Sumerian?" Walt asked.

"Sometimes." Lola felt defensive. "I like languages; it's all about getting into the rhythm of it. Like this." She delicately leafed through the pages of the diary. Each was overflowing with words; whoever Alice McCullough had been, she'd enjoyed writing. "It seems illegible now, but you get to know the form of the letters she uses, the symbols of it."

As her fingers passed over the ink, a thrill passed through Lola, an emotion entirely outside of her own. There was a flutter of excitement or anticipation. She frowned as she flipped through the pages, going further into the diary. As she passed through each month, the feelings she channelled changed, getting more disturbed, more frantic. Dread seemed to seep off the pages.

Lola slammed the diary closed with a gasp. She looked up to find the other two staring at her.

"Lola, your nose," Walt said.

She brought her hand to her face; it came away wet with blood. Walt handed her a clean tissue without a word. "Thank you," she said, a little hoarsely, as she dabbed at the blood.

"You had a vision?"

"Not so much a vision, more like…I could feel the emotions of the writer. Of Alice." She stared at the diary. "That was weird."

"Well, we can all agree that this diary is evil, and we should probably burn it," Nix said. Her tone was joking, but her eyes were narrowed in unease.

"No, it's not evil. She was excited at first, hopeful. But then, something scared her." Lola reached for the diary again, bracing herself, but nothing happened when she touched it.

"Why do you need to know? The book just gave you a nose-bleed; that's a sure sign you should just walk away."

"Stop trying to get rid of the thing. Why were you interested in the name McCullough?" Lola pinned Nix with a glare.

Nix shifted her weight back and forth as though she couldn't settle. "McCullough is my mother's maiden name. I wonder…what if she's related?"

Lola stilled. It was too big of a coincidence. "What if we found the diary of your ancestor? It would make sense why you were drawn to it. You might be connected."

"Like, on an Otherworldly level? No thanks." Nix took a step away from the diary. "I can't be sure it's a relative."

"Anyone in your family named Alice?" Lola asked.

Nix snorted. "Only like a thousand. They were all Alice or Mary. Or Mary Alice."

"Your mom really went sideways with Arabella," Lola teased, using Nix's given name, grinning when her friend's scowl flickered into a reluctant smile.

"Actually, it was my grandma. She named my mother Florence,

which was unheard of at the time. It was probably because my mother was the sixth girl, and you couldn't name everyone Mary Alice. Not that they didn't try."

"We should ask your mom about Alice. Get more information."

Nix's eyes lingered on the diary. "I'm still not sure whether we should keep a book that gives nosebleeds."

"How about I take it? You don't have to touch it at all. Just ask your mom if she'll talk to us. Maybe we can find out what happened to Alice McCullough."

TEN

"Order up!" Faye called, sliding a grilled focaccia sandwich onto the counter.

Lola swept in to grab the plate, her mouth watering at the smell of roasted vegetables and melted cheese. She didn't officially work at the Pain Perdu anymore—after her short-lived attempt to run Faye's ice cream shop over the summer, they'd agreed she was better off paying rent for her room upstairs. But that didn't stop her from helping out during the afternoon rush.

Balancing the order, Lola wove between tables, delivering plates with a quick smile. "We're slammed today," she called to Faye, whose cheeks glowed pink as she flipped another sandwich on the grill.

"Blame the weather," Faye puffed, adjusting her apron. "The tourists are sticking around longer than usual. They're supposed to leave by now and go admire the mainland foliage, but no. They just can't resist Duchesne in the fall."

As she delivered the last sandwich, Lola's gaze flickered towards the oak forest that ringed the town of Port Despardoux. Autumn leaves painted the island in fiery hues, but lately, Lola had avoided wandering the quiet paths.

The massive oak that stood at the centre of the island, the Tree of Life, had once been her refuge. It had embraced her, even when she was a vampire. It was as if the tree had known her destiny. But now, when she visited, the tree seemed...aloof. Its roots, reaching all the way down to the Well of Souls, seemed to hum an unspoken question, one she wasn't ready to answer.

She forced herself back to the present, glancing at the sunlit brick buildings. "Your food probably doesn't hurt, either."

Faye flashed her a grin as she popped another sandwich out of the grill and sashayed over to deliver the order in her sky-high heels. To Lola, Faye had always invoked the allure of Parisian women, with her cloud of perfume and red lipstick. Somehow, the baker had always felt like home to her since she'd stepped foot in the café.

But as Faye passed from one table to the next, flirting outrageously with the customers, her laugh was piercingly high. Lola wondered if she was throwing herself into the work at the café a little too hard. Perhaps it had something to do with the absence of Sergeant Greyson. He'd made himself scarce after they had fought during the carnival while in the throes of the enchantment cast on the townspeople.

Lola's heart twinged with guilt. Despite Faye's obvious feelings for the sergeant, they had fought over her and were no longer speaking. Lola would be thankful forever that Faye had stuck by her, but she hadn't wanted it to cause her pain. Although she certainly didn't miss Greyson's nosy questions.

The bell over the door jingled and Lola left off her musings. Nix bustled in with her mother, Florence. With their tiny frames and curly red hair, the resemblance was obvious. But while Florence's eyes were a warm brown, her daughter's sparkled blue like the Atlantic on a sunny day.

"Over here!" Lola waved to the pair, bringing them to a table near the back, one of the few that wasn't taken. "How are you, Mrs. Nix?"

"I told you, it's Florence. It's lovely to see you again, dear."

Florence pulled Lola into a hug, and she grinned. Mother and daughter had more in common than their hair; Nix had inherited her mother's warmth and easy affection.

"It's lovely to see you again too. Thanks for coming in today."

"When Nix told me she'd babysit for the rest of the week if I took some time off to go for coffee, I nearly fainted." Florence smiled at her daughter, brushing a tendril of hair away from her face. "I'm barely ever off my feet. This was too good an offer to miss out on."

"What can I get you?"

"You are a doll. I'll take one of those pumpkin spice thingies everyone is talking about."

"Make it two." Nix grinned as she settled in next to her mom, unravelling a bright scarf from her neck.

Lola rushed to prepare the order. With a gesture of her head, she asked Faye if it was okay if she joined them, and Faye gave a distracted nod.

Reaching under the counter, Lola pulled out Alice McCullough's diary as well as the printed pages of the translation she'd been making, deciphering Alice's handwriting.

Alice had been a maid at Seabourne Estate, and her journal was rich with descriptions of what life was like back then, especially for the working poor. Lola tucked the book and pages under her elbow and carefully carried over the drinks.

"Here we are," Lola said, placing drinks in front of them, then slipping into the open chair. "Florence, I don't know how much Nix has told you about what we found."

"Just that it had something to do with the McCullough family. Ooh, that is nice." Florence took a sip of the sweet drink and her eyes drifted shut. "It's going to keep me up till midnight and I don't even care."

"We found a diary from 1921 of a maid who worked for the Seabourne family. Her name was Alice McCullough."

Florence's face turned ashen, her fingers tightening around her mug. "Alice McCullough?"

Lola's excitement spiked; they were onto something. It was like finding a clue on a treasure map. "Yes! Does that name mean something to you? She wrote exceptionally well, and was clearly very intelligent, although she had scathing descriptions of the family she worked for."

"Walt's family?" Nix gave a snort of laughter. "That tracks."

"They did seem pretty terrible. Although Alice was friendly with their daughter."

Florence stared into the swirling foam of her drink, frowning as though it had turned bitter on her. "It's been years since I've thought of her," she murmured, her voice tight. "Did you say 1921?"

Faye bustled up just at that moment. Lola had to shake her head; she would swear up and down that Faye had some kind of enchanted hearing when it came to gossip. "What's going on, Flo? Are these girls bringing you down?"

"Oh, no, it's nothing, Faye. Not their fault. They couldn't have known. It was just a startle to hear after all these years." Florence stared at the diary, her head bowed, a curious blend of intrigue and shame washing over her features. "Alice McCullough. She was my grandmother's aunt."

"What happened?" Faye breathed, trembling from the possibility of discovering a secret.

"Ach, I shouldn't. It caused great shame and embarrassment to my family. My grandmother spoke of it as something evil that had happened."

Lola's heart skipped. *Evil here.* The Ouija board's message flickered in her memory. Could the reappearance of Alice's diary be connected?

"It sounds awful." Faye put her hand on Florence's shoulder and squeezed. It looked as though she was comforting the woman, but Lola knew she was just loosening her up. "Why don't you enjoy one of my chocolate croissants?" Faye's voice was a croon, nearly a lullaby, rocking Florence into complacency. "They just came fresh out of the oven. On the house."

The corners of Florence's mouth curled up. "That does sound nice."

"Now you just wait there. And don't spill a word until I'm back." Faye glared at the girls in warning.

Lola bit back a grin. Nobody could make a person talk like Faye. If café proprietor ever didn't work out for her, she could pick up a career as an interrogator.

Lola and Nix whirled on Florence, but the red-haired woman only sipped at her coffee. "I need to get my thoughts in order. You really sprung that one on me." She gave her daughter a chiding look.

"But I didn't know this was scandalous. How could I? You never told me about secret family shame." Nix glowered at her mother as though she'd been holding out on her.

Her mom glowered right back. "There was no need for you to know, though I suppose it will come out now."

Despite having to ring through three bills, Faye returned within moments, chocolate croissants still steaming. "Now," she said, faintly out of breath, "what was that story you were going to tell?"

Florence leaned away from her, disconcerted by her intensity, until Faye smiled and grabbed her hand. Florence's smile fluttered back to life. "It's just, my grandmother always told me never to speak of it."

"Such a shame," Faye murmured, leaning closer, her voice unusually soft. "Secrets like that weigh a family down. My grandmother always said secrets were bad for the soul. She was French, you know."

Florence exhaled slowly. "Maybe it's time, then. As I heard it, Alice McCullough was the only daughter in a large family with no great means."

"Sounds familiar," Nix muttered, but Lola elbowed her to keep quiet.

"Alice was educated along with her brothers and showed great potential. She read whatever she could get her hands on. She worked at the Seabourne Estate as a housemaid and, from everyone's account, was a dedicated, hard worker, a girl to make her parents proud. But she wished for greater things than her lot in life. She had a yen to travel to the mainland."

"That's what the diary says," Lola broke in. "She wanted to have adventures and see the world."

"Yes, well. On a late October night in 1921, Alice McCullough disappeared without a trace. And with her, some of the family's legendary jewels, including a sapphire tiara the family was so proud of. Mr. Seabourne himself came to the family homestead to accuse them of raising a thieving daughter. It was assumed that she skipped town with her ill-gotten gains, sold them and went on to follow the life of adventure she'd always wanted.

"Nobody ever heard from her again, but the family had to live with the disgrace. My grandmother spoke of the sadness that lingered in the home for years. I understand Alice had been a joyful, passionate girl, well-loved by her family. Her betrayal broke her father's heart. He died of a heart attack a few years later, but my grandmother always said he really died from missing her."

"That's terrible," Lola murmured.

"Yes, what she did was just awful."

"I meant that your family suffered for it. It's not their fault that she took the jewels and ran." Lola chewed her lip. "It doesn't seem like her."

"What, like you knew her?" Nix's confrontational tone snapped Lola out of her contemplation.

"Obviously not. I've just been reading her diary, and she doesn't sound like a thief." Lola winced at how feeble that sounded. "You're right, though. What do I know? Do you want to look at the diary, Florence? It seems like it should belong to you.

I've deciphered the first part." Lola shuffled through her papers, but Florence waved her away.

"No, I don't want to see it. That diary likely contains the nail in the coffin of her guilt."

"I'll let you enjoy your coffee, then." Lola gathered up the papers, realizing the café had quieted down and Faye no longer needed her help.

Through the window, Lola spotted Reiko walking briskly down Main Street, her satchel slung over one shoulder. She rarely saw the demon hunter outside of school.

But now, as Reiko disappeared around the corner, she thought it might be useful to see where the girl spent her time.

"Well, if you don't need me anymore, I have something I need to do," she called to Faye. "It's a project I'm working on. Nix, walk out with me?"

Nix glanced up, bemused by Lola's change in demeanour, but Lola jerked her head with an intense look, indicating they should hustle. "Oh, yeah, Mom, I gotta go watch the littles. Enjoy some downtime."

Nix jumped from her seat, grabbing the leftover chocolate croissants, and together, they ducked out of the Pain Perdu.

ELEVEN

Outside, the air was damp and heavy, clinging to Lola's skin like sea mist, the faint tang of salt lingering on the edge of the chill wind. Overhead, clouds skipping by on the stiff breeze cast whipping shadows along the brick buildings.

"What are we doing?" Nix demanded, her voice cutting through the quiet.

"Shh." Lola tugged her friend's arm and quickened their pace. Lola's gaze swept over the shuttered shops and dim alleys, scanning for the silhouette she had glimpsed moments ago. A weathered sign creaked as it swung in the breeze.

At a cross-street, Lola froze, her breath hitching. There was Reiko. When Nix saw her former crush, she jerked to a stop, her face flushing scarlet.

"Lola," she muttered. "What are we doing?"

"I want to see where she lives," Lola said. Putting a finger to her lips, she continued to follow Reiko at a distance.

They made their way down Main Street to the wharf, then turned into the wind as they passed a row of broken-down townhouses that marked the end of the nice part of town. Here, down by the docks, the streets were emptier, the lights dimmer. The buildings leaned inward like they whispered secrets to each other.

When Reiko reached a sagging wooden apartment complex, she turned. Her coat flared briefly in the wind before she disappeared inside, swallowed by the peeling paint and rusted iron railings of the building's façade.

"This is where she lives?" Nix asked. "Not a swanky place."

"Not a nice place to live at all," Lola said, assessing the dive.

"But why does this matter?" Nix turned her back on the shoddy apartment. "She's a back-stabbing bitch. Not to mention a demon hunter."

"Who does she live with?" Lola asked, running through the questions that had been bothering her. "Are her parents with her? What do we really know about her?"

"Who cares where she lives or what she wants? Honestly, Lola, why are you so obsessed with her?"

"I just like to know about the people who could become problems." Lola took note of the crooked apartment building, then turned and started walking back towards the wharf, her boots echoing on the cracked pavement. "Besides, if she's living all the way out here, this close to the docks...that says something. She can't have much money, and I suspect she's alone."

Nix glanced at the gloomy surroundings. "Well, don't think I'm going to start feeling sorry for her."

"No, but it's more information than we had before. So, what do you think?"

"I told you, I think she's a bitch."

"I mean, about your Aunt Alice."

"Oh, yeah." Nix's eyes went wide as she thought about it. "Who knew my family was hiding such a dark secret?"

"Is it such a dark secret? I mean, sure, she stole something from the Seabournes, but they were rich and powerful, and she was obviously poor. Why would it cause *such* distress? They probably had insurance for the jewels. I bet the tiara belonged to the

Seabourne's daughter, a cosseted little rich thing who never even wore it and only missed it when it was gone."

"Lola, I'm not sure if you got the whole moral compass thing when you became human, but stealing is wrong."

"I did spend the last eight decades grave robbing."

"Not to mention murdering people to stay alive."

Lola huffed out a laugh. "So, in the grand scheme of things, was it really that bad? The Seabournes didn't need their jewels. However, Alice had no money and a big life to live. I'm not going to fault her for that. Maybe it wasn't right, but I'm having a hard time condemning her for it."

Nix's face darkened, her jaw tightening. "I don't love the idea my ancestor was branded a thief."

Lola hesitated, her eyes searching Nix's face. "Are we even sure she was a thief? It sounds like no charges were pressed. The only evidence is Mr. Seabourne coming to accuse a family at the time their daughter disappeared. He sounds like a big bully."

In fact, he sounded like the current Mr. Seabourne.

Nix let out a bitter laugh, her voice rising. "But that's what everyone ended up thinking, and on an island like this, what everyone thinks is fact, whether or not it's the truth!" Her voice cracked on the last word, and she turned away, blinking quickly.

"I don't like that." Lola lofted the diary into the air. "I think there's more to this story, and I'm going to figure it out."

"I don't think you should read the diary. Not after my mom got all upset like that."

"Why not? It might give us a clue about what happened."

"What Alice did—"

"Allegedly."

Nix hugged herself tightly as though bracing against a storm. "Whatever. She messed things up for the family."

Lola considered this, but she wasn't going to let it slide. She had felt the girl's emotions as she'd flipped through her diary; she was too invested in Alice's story now. "How about we don't say another word about it? *Unless* I find something that would exonerate her."

Nix stared at the diary. "It would be nice to find proof she wasn't a thief."

"Secrets are bad for the soul, you know."

"What, did your French grandmother tell you that too?"

"No idea." Lola let out a little sigh.

"Oh, yeah. Sometimes I forget you're like an orphan. Sorry about that."

Lola gave a rueful smile and Nix took her arm. "So, what graves have you robbed?" she asked.

Countless scores of jewels and coins flashed through Lola's mind. "Nix, if I told you, I'm fairly certain somebody would have to kill you." She said it as a joke, but when the words came out of her mouth, suddenly they were less funny.

"Just kidding," she said, her words hollow to her own ears. Nix had stiffened, but she wasn't even paying her any attention. She stared over Lola's shoulder to the Victorian house on the corner of Main Street and Wharf.

The sign above the entrance read *McInnes' Tea Shoppe*, with smaller letters beneath: *Psychic Readings by Appointment Only*. The words shimmered faintly as if they caught a light that wasn't from this world.

Nix's gaze darted towards the tea shop's window and her jaw tightened. "Let's go," she said, her hand gripping Lola's arm.

Lola followed her line of sight. Mrs. McInnes stood silhouetted in the glass, her pale face sharp and unyielding. She'd only spoken to the mysterious woman once, and that had been enough to know that McInnes was a witch, through and through.

The older woman's gaze fell on her, and Lola's head swam, the world tilting as if she stood on the edge of a pinwheel. The psychic parlour blurred before her eyes, and then—

She was somewhere else.

She watched a scene play out behind a thick veil. The room

was familiar, but it took a moment for her to figure out where she was, as it was out of context.

It was the servant's kitchen in the Belowstairs, now alive with motion and sound, a stark contrast to the dusty relic it was now. The hearth roared with a merry fire, sending flickers of golden light across polished counters and laden tables. It smelled of fresh bread and sharp apple cider.

Someone played the fiddle, and people—dressed in plain clothing from a century ago—clapped and danced to the beat, laughter ringing out bright and carefree.

Lola's focus was drawn to a thin figure standing apart. A girl, wiry and watchful, her red hair tucked under a kerchief. *Nix.*

Nix's gaze darted over the crowd, birdlike, then she slipped out of the kitchen. Dread unfurled in Lola's chest, cold and consuming. The mirth of the kitchen faded, replaced by a low, guttural wail. She tried to follow, but an unseen force held her back as if the veil between worlds had turned to iron.

She reached out, desperate to break through—

And snapped back to the present with a gasp. The cold pavement pressed against her palms, her cheek.

"Nix," Lola whispered, reaching out blindly.

"Lola!" Nix's voice cut through the haze, her hands gripping Lola's shoulders. "What happened?"

Lola blinked up at her. "I saw you." Her breath hitched. "You were in danger."

Before Nix could answer, a prickle ran up Lola's spine. She straightened, leaning on Nix for support, as the faint clink of wind chimes sounded from the psychic parlour.

McInnes glided towards them, like a river in no rush to arrive at its destination. She held her back unnaturally straight, her white hair falling back like a ghostly veil.

Lola was rooted to the spot as the woman inspected her, her presence heavy like the centre of gravity. Finally, McInnes offered a linen handkerchief.

Lola accepted it, bringing it to her nose, to find it dotted with blood. If these visions continued, she was going to have to invest in her own handkerchiefs. "Thank you."

"You must learn to shield yourself against the onslaught," the woman said in her whispery voice. "The Otherworld seeks you out, and if you let it, it will take over."

"But I saw—"

"You saw what you needed to, but at what cost? You are open, far too open."

"I don't mean to be," Lola said grumpily because she never asked for any of it. "They just come to me." Her head was pounding now, like the mother of all migraines setting in.

McInnes lifted her slender fingers and ran them over Lola's forehead. Cool relief from the pain rippled through her like a healing stream.

Lola's eyes fluttered shut in relief. "Thank you," she said.

The witch's lips curved slightly, though it was more knowing than kind. "You have a hard path to follow. The island is inside you now, and it can be powerful. But the power demands a price, and you must be ready to pay it." Intensity flickered behind her placid grey eyes, flickering like a flame. Lola shied away.

"Enough," Nix stepped between them, her voice shaking. "Leave her alone."

McInnes tilted her head, her expression unreadable as though deciding whether Nix's outburst was amusing or tiresome. "I only offer what is needed."

"She doesn't need anything from you," Nix retorted, tugging Lola back with a protective fierceness.

McInnes's smile deepened, faint and mysterious. "She will. Come see me for a reading, little vampire, and we will go from there." With a final lingering look at Lola, she turned and melted back into the shadows of the street, leaving a ripple of unease in her wake.

Lola allowed Nix to tug her away, the witch's whispering voice still echoing in her mind. She nodded faintly but said nothing, her thoughts too tangled to untangle just yet. McInnes knew exactly what she had been and seemed to know what was going on as well.

In loaded silence, they made their way along Wharf Street. Upbeat music was playing nearby, and Lola realized they were close to Lost Souls, the bar that jutted out over the water. She took in a deep breath of briny saltwater air, clearing her head.

"I hate that woman," Nix finally said.

Lola peered back over her shoulder, but the tea shop was lost behind a cluster of buildings. The cryptic warning had jangled her nerves. "What happened between you and McInnes?"

Nix turned away, staring glumly down the street. Towards the lighthouse, Lola realized, where Nix lived with her sprawling family. "McInnes is just a weird old lady."

"But you don't like her, and it seems personal. Why?" It was more than that; it seemed as if Nix was afraid of her.

Nix's look was far away, staring out over the waves lashing the rocky shore in the sunlight. "It was a few years ago. I went to get my fortune told. Everyone does it eventually. McInnes will only read for you once, and they say she's never wrong. I thought it would be fun, or exciting." She paused. Lola didn't interrupt, waiting as Nix's fingers fiddled with the edge of her sleeve. "I saved up for months—every dime from babysitting, birthday money, anything I could scrape together, to hear my destiny."

"And you didn't like what the fortune teller told?"

Nix's shoulders hunched. "It's not like that. Listen, I'm sure it's just a sham and nobody can predict the future, but when you're there, and she's telling you things that will happen, it doesn't sound like some stupid horoscope. It sounds like...your fate, laid out in front of you. Like she *knows*."

A hush in the wind allowed the words to hang between them like a portent.

"Nix, what did she tell you?"

"That I would never leave Duchesne." Her voice cracked on

the last word. "There was other stuff there as well, but that was the biggie. I'm stuck here for good."

"That's crazy, Nix. Of course you'll leave the island. Even if you settle here, you can go other places."

"I've never left Duchesne, Lola. Not once. Never stepped foot on the mainland. Every single time I've had a chance to leave—class trips, vacations, anything—something happens, and I'm not able to go."

Nix's look was solemn, so Lola grabbed her hands and looked her full in the face.

"Nix, I promise you this. You will someday leave the island. You will see the wonders of the world and have big adventures. If I have to move heaven and earth to change your destiny, I will make that happen."

Nix's grin was lopsided. "What, are you a fortune teller too?"

That reminded Lola of the vision she'd had, of Nix in trouble, somewhere inside Walt's family mansion. She pressed a hand to her forehead in memory of the pain.

Nix's face fell. "Sorry, Lola, I guess you kinda are a fortune teller. What did you see?"

Nix had been so despondent about her destiny that Lola didn't want to tell her she'd seen her in the vision. So she told her the half-truth. "I was in the Belowstairs, except it was different. People were dressed differently, like from a long time ago."

"Sounds like you saw something that already happened. A memory?"

"I think so. The servants were having a party, and everyone was happy. But then...I got a sense that something horrible was going to happen."

"Something horrible happened at Seabourne Estate? You don't need to be psychic to tell me that."

Both girls turned their faces upwards, looking at the looming silhouette of the estate sitting far above the townsite, looking out to sea. A sharp wind blew against them, causing them to stumble.

They shivered together, and then Nix giggled. "This whole day is freaking me out. Listen, I do have to get back to babysit. Are you okay with the whole..." She waved her hand around her nose.

"Oh, yes." Lola dabbed at her nose again with McInnes's lovely handkerchief. "I guess I might have to talk to McInnes at some point about these visions if this keeps on happening."

"Don't." Nix's eyes were serious. "There's something about hearing the rest of your life like that. It...kills your hope. I don't want that for you."

"Okay, I'll stay away from the creepy old lady."

"Good. Now, try not to be blown away in this squall."

Nix was shouting over the stiff wind that had blown up as she made her way up the rocky path towards the lighthouse.

When Lola turned around to go back through the town to the Pain Perdu, though, she came to a halt. Panicked, she ducked behind a decrepit shed as she caught sight of Gael, standing outside Lost Souls, far too close to Cassidy.

TWELVE

Gael and Cassidy lounged against the railing; their faces turned to each other in a way that made it seem like everyone else was just background noise. The sight twisted something deep inside Lola. She couldn't let them see her, not like this, shaken up and bloodied-nosed as she was.

Heart pounding, her gaze darted to an alternative path, a rocky one winding steeply up the hillside. Without hesitation, she veered towards it and began the arduous climb, deciding a walk might clear her head.

She couldn't think of Gael now: not about how he had moved on and certainly not about how she had nobody to blame but herself. Those thoughts could spin around her head for hours, dragging her down without offering a way out.

Instead, she turned her mind to her vision. What did it mean that she was being shown the past instead of the future?

More importantly, why was she having these visions, and who was sending them to her?

That Nix had been in her vision made her profoundly uneasy. All of her senses told her that her friend was in danger, but she had no idea how to help.

The wind whipped at her as she climbed, pushing at her. She gloried in the sting of the salt and the power of the ocean calling out to her. The sea had always been her constant—her freedom.

Relishing the burn in her legs, she crested the hill, and the Atlantic spread out before her like a restless, glittering expanse. Her hair was flung about her face, and she laughed with delight, pushing the strands away.

The island was a wild, magical place and felt more like home to her than anything in her past. Eight decades adrift with Jacquotte and her vampire crew, and after all that, this rock was where she found her haven.

She didn't want to hear what destiny had in store for her. It seemed too much like a trap, taking away the freedom she'd fought so hard for. A destiny clung to you like an anchor, bearing you down.

Below her, Port Despardoux spread out, the streets twining around old brick buildings and homes painted cheerful pastel colours, every path threading inevitably to the water. Beyond the town, beyond the beaches, the oak forest spread across the island, now dotted with crimsons and yellows like a tapestry. The Tree of Life towered above it all.

The sight of its massive crown made her heart quicken. Closing her eyes, she could almost feel its pulse thrumming in her own veins. When she had found her soul under its roots, she'd forged a connection with it. She concentrated on that kinship.

She drifted in her mind's eye and started to slip away, into the roots, into the earth and the life water that ran beneath it.

Like she *was* the island.

She ripped herself out of her reverie with a sharp gasp. Her imagination was playing tricks on her. All the talk about destinies and dark secrets was getting to her. Shaking her head, she kept on walking, ignoring the trembling that played out in her hands.

Seabourne Estate reared above her, crouched like a great spider on the hill. The iron spikes of the widow's walk seemed to scrape the sky, and its shadow stretched unnaturally long over the rocky ground.

A circling seagull shrieked overhead, the sound jolting right through her. Looking westward, she spotted the jagged shoals where countless ships had met their end over the centuries. Local legends whispered of ghost ships and doomed souls who sank into the crashing foam, their pleading still echoing on stormy nights.

The setting sun was just kissing the line of the ocean, creating a shimmer of light. Shielding her eyes from the brightness, Lola thought she could see the outline of a schooner. Its outline wavered on the hazy horizon, almost too faint to be real.

"Some kind of place, isn't it?"

Adrenaline flooded through her, and Lola spun, stopping herself from falling into a crouch and baring fangs that didn't exist anymore. Her hair tangled in her face, and she batted it away, trying to see who had sneaked up on her.

"Sorry, did I scare you?"

She finally made out Matt Vernon's form, as she blinked away sunspots. Her journalism teacher was grinning at her reaction.

"You can't just creep up on people out of nowhere!"

Heart hammering in her chest, Lola stumbled a few feet away from him. She didn't miss being a vampire, for the most part, but sometimes she wished she could have kept some of her hunter's awareness of the world around her. It seemed now she stumbled through the world deaf and blind, surprised and disconcerted by what she found coming at her.

"I called out." He gestured towards the path. "Guess you didn't hear me. It's Lola, right?"

"Right." She exhaled slowly, calming her racing pulse.

"That place would make anyone edgy." Matt nodded his chin towards Seabourne Estate. "Do you think they ordered the 'gothic mansion that's clearly haunted' package when they built it?"

"It doesn't quite match the charm of the rest of the town."

Lola looked down at Port Despardoux, the candy-box-coloured homes.

"You find it charming? I find it...small."

Lola bristled. "It's a lovely place."

He shrugged. "Guess it depends on what you're looking for."

She started to walk away, but he kept pace.

"I don't mean to insult it. I heard you were from Paris, so I thought you might feel the same. Doesn't it feel quiet compared to that?"

"If it's so *small*, why are you here?"

"I knew Richie, actually, the former editor of the paper? We went to journalism school together. The guy was eccentric, always had his conspiracy theories, but we kept in touch. He had such interesting stories about Duchesne. I'll admit I was curious. I was shocked to hear about his death and, at first, applied for the position to see if I could figure out what happened. But it looks like it was just an animal attack."

Lola's stomach twisted. Richie's death had been anything but a simple animal attack. "Why stay, then?"

"Because this place is weird." His face lit up, and for the first time, he seemed genuinely interested. "Weird stories, weird people. I want to figure it out."

He took out a vape pen and puffed for a moment. Lola wrinkled her nose at the sweet cherry-flavoured smell.

"Awful, isn't it?" he said with a self-deprecating grin. "I picked the most ridiculous flavour so I'd hate it enough to quit. It hasn't worked so far, though."

"You should try marshmallow," she said. "I bet that would work." She continued up the hill towards Seabourne Estate.

"Ha, probably." Matt trailed behind her, and the skin at the back of her neck prickled. Why was he following her? "So, have you been in there?" He gestured to the mansion.

Lola glanced at the lifeless windows. "A few times."

"What's it like?" His tone was casual, but she caught the sharpness in his eyes as though he tucked the answers away for later.

"Kinda like the outside." She was tired of being drilled for information. "What's it like running a paper with zero staff?"

"Challenging. I'm trying to update the whole system and bring the paper online."

Lola glanced at him. "The people here like their paper."

"Maybe I'll put out a weekly print version."

"The weekly *Duchesne Daily*?"

"Something like that. I can't keep up a daily rag on my own."

"Is that why you're using the student body of Port Despardoux High to find stories for you? Mining us for information?"

His eyes crinkled and he let out a bark of laughter. It made her like him just a tiny bit more. "Figured that out, eh? I guess I'm not very sneaky. But yeah, it's always a good idea to keep your ears open for any source of story."

"Is that why you're here?" She gestured towards the woods behind him. He didn't seem like the outdoorsy type; he seemed like he'd be reading Kerouac in a dimly lit pub.

Matt nodded. "There's been chatter about strange lights off the coast over here. I wanted to see this place from a higher vantage point."

"They say Duchesne is haunted. Are you sure you're not looking for the spirits of those lost at sea?"

Matt's snort was derisive. "Ghost stories, hardly. Every unexplained phenomenon has an explanation. I want to be the one to discover the truth."

Lola nodded to the mansion. "How about the Seabournes? What truths have you discovered about them?"

"Besides that they live in a creepy house? They're your typical wealthy family in a place like this. You know: big fish, small pond. Their Harvest Ball is apparently epic, though."

"Harvest Ball?"

He pointed his vape at her. "If you can get into that party, do it. Every year, the Seabournes put on a banger, no-holds-barred joy ride. That would be some kind of scene." He gazed at the estate, his expression half-amused, half-intrigued.

"I should go now." Lola wondered if he would follow her, but he seemed content to remain where he was.

"Nice chatting with you, Lola. Keep your ear to the ground."

He said this with an ironic smirk. She left him in a cherry-flavoured cloud, staring up at the mansion. But when she glanced back, she could see him climbing over the ridge, towards the cliff-side, determination drawn over his face. She wondered if she'd misread him entirely—had he been following her, or something else?

"Interesting," she said to herself. She half-thought about following *him*, when she spotted a dark figure further down the path, staring out to sea.

Sergeant Greyson stood motionless at the edge of the cliffs, his trench coat whipping in the wind.

She slowed. Matt had mentioned chatter about lights off the coast—police chatter? Was that why Greyson was here? Had Matt been trailing *him* instead?

That was too much traffic for one lonely cliffside on a haunted island. Lola turned down another path so she didn't have to pass by Greyson. But she wondered what exactly everyone was looking for that evening.

Thirteen

"Why are we going to the library?"

Lola tugged Nix by the wrist as gusty wind nudged them along the cobblestone path. The vision of Nix had haunted her all night. It didn't make sense, but it seemed to tell her that the past could somehow threaten the future. Her dreams had been filled with wailing and Nix's tear-streaked face. She needed to know more.

"Research," Lola said.

"Research what, exactly?" Walt asked. He hadn't needed much convincing to tag along.

"I had a vision about the Belowstairs, but from the past. That's never happened before. I want to look into the history of Seabourne Estate, see if we can turn up anything interesting."

"Blood-curdling family secrets?" Walt's mouth thinned at the idea.

"Don't act like you're so special," Nix said, waspish. "I have a jewel thief in my family tree."

"And my family?" Lola raised her eyebrows. "Definitely worse than yours."

Walt nodded. "Noted. Fine, let's dig into my gruesome family history."

"But why can't we just do this online?" Nix said.

"Because the library's better."

Lola hadn't yet mentioned the witchy town librarian with a connection to books, who could give them Otherworldly insight no search engine could touch.

"Still don't see why I need to come," Nix grumbled, pulling free from Lola's grip.

"Fine, then. Don't." Lola sighed, unable to meet Nix's eyes, disappointed that she would blow her off.

Nix wasn't the only one, either. Lola had texted Gael to see if he'd join them, but he didn't respond. She couldn't count how many times she'd stared at the *read* notice, nor how much it pinched her heart that he couldn't even be bothered to respond to her.

Nix hesitated, her gaze flickering over Lola's face, before continuing towards the public library, a beautiful sandstone building. "No, I'll come."

"Good. I want you guys to meet someone."

Lola felt a shiver of happiness as they stepped out of the wind and into the warm library, surrounded by the dusty smell of the wooden shelves. Most of her happiest moments had been in buildings like this, chasing down clues for her next hunt. Researching Seabourne Estate felt very similar.

"It's a nice place," Walt said, looking as though seeing it for the first time. "It seems more substantial than I remember."

"I haven't been here for years." Nix clutched her elbows, inspecting the shelves suspiciously as though they were full of strange and potentially boring things. Nix preferred to be outside as much as possible, always moving. A quiet building designed for curling up on a chair for hours at a time was not her place.

To Lola, however, it was a harbour in a tempest.

A book thumped onto the floor above, making them all jump. Lola's smile widened.

"Is someone there?" Marissa emerged from the back office, her tweed skirt and round glasses giving her an old lady look at odds with her nineteen years.

"Lola!" A smile brightened the librarian's face. "You're back! I can't wait to show you my latest project—bottling light to recreate sunshine in the dark." Then her eyes widened as she took in Lola's companions, and she coughed. "Ahem...for our Dungeons and Dragons group, of course." She narrowed her eyes and hissed, "You brought friends?"

"As discussed previously, it is a public building. But don't worry about them. They *know*. Marissa, this is Walt and Nix."

"They know *what*?" Marissa clipped her words.

"About magic and the Otherworld. And vampires."

"Oh." Marissa blinked. Her hands played over the counter. "And how do they feel about witches?"

Marissa was a fledgling witch, only recently coming into her magical powers, but some of her talents were unique. Books with information she needed would jump out at her...literally. The library's silence was broken by thumps and bumps at all hours as the books responded to her requests, falling off their shelves to get her attention.

"They are just fine with witches," Lola said before Nix could jump in.

"We are?" the redhead said under her breath.

"She's very good at finding info on the Otherworld. And right now, we need information. I had another vision."

"Wait." Nix threw her hand out. "Library girl knows about your visions? I thought this was an exclusive club!"

"Marissa helped me figure out what was going on at the carnival while the rest of you were partying your faces off. She's the reason none of you are pigs right now."

"Happy to have you aboard, then," Nix said, her face paling.

"Yes, well." Marissa seemed unsure about the pixie-bright redhead but turned back to Lola. "What kind of vision?"

"It was something that happened in the past at the Seabourne Estate."

"The Seabourne Estate? There's a place with a colourful history. There's been all kinds of stories about the original owner, not to mention the house itself..." Marissa trailed off, her excitement building as she tied her hair into a bun. "What are we looking for?"

"A theft that happened on the estate in 1921." Lola caught Nix's stabbing glare and shrugged. "It might not be connected, but it seems like too big of a coincidence that the diary showed up right before I got my vision."

"Fill me in on the diary and I'll get you set up." Marissa clip-clapped in her Mary Jane shoes, leading them upstairs. She ignored the books tumbling down around her as she set up the microfiche reader with old copies of the *Duchesne Daily*.

Another thump sounded, and finally, Nix let out a disgruntled huff. "What's going on? It sounds like a staggering drunk loose in the library."

"That would be unfortunate." Marissa's smile was unconvincing. "Lola, a word?" And she swept out of the room, leaving Lola to follow.

Three stacks over, Marissa bent to pick up a book. She glared as Lola came around the corner. "You told your *friends* about the Otherworld?"

"I didn't have much choice," Lola said. "I met them when I was a vampire, and they were in danger."

Marissa sniffed, her face pinched. "And the Order of Hanta Cythraul? Do they know about that?" She whispered the words.

Marissa had discovered the name of the Order that Reiko belonged to after finding a journal with their symbol in her father's personal effects. Her father had been travelling for months, but they suspected he was a member of the Order as well.

"They know as much as I do, which is next to nothing."

Marissa's face dropped. "You didn't find anything on the mainland?"

"Not much. Only that they're a society of demon hunters, very hush-hush. It appears their life's work is to rid the planet of all Otherworldly activity. Their mantra is essentially that all demons are evil."

Marissa pursed her lips. "I wonder how *they* feel about witches?"

"Or about ex-demonic types," Lola added. "They don't seem very nuanced. Like a stab-first-ask-questions-later kind of organization. I've been watching the Order member here; she's also at the high school, though I'm not sure why. She appears to be living alone, though she did suggest the school might be monitored by security cameras."

"They're using modern equipment," Marissa said. "Interesting. One of the few references I've found about the Order is that they blend magic with technology, which means they use Otherworld power even as they try to destroy it."

"That might explain this." Lola took out a small metal device. Roughly the size of a music box, the object was filled with a dizzying array of dials and coiled wires. "I found this at a shop for esoteric magic. The HC's insignia is carved into the bottom, but I don't have a single clue what it does." Lola had been too intimidated to mess around with it.

"The HC?" Marissa asked, distracted, as she turned the box over in her hands, playing with one of the gears.

"That's what we've been calling the Order of Hanta Cythraul."

Marissa looked up with an arched brow. "You're calling it the *HC*?"

"Less of a mouthful, you know?"

Marissa's disgruntled look told her she absolutely did not know. She refocused on the device. "Could I keep this for a while?"

"It's yours. I've been staring at it for weeks and it's done nothing for me. Have you heard from your father at all?"

At the mention of her father, Marissa puffed out a breath and set the box aside. "He's been in touch, mainly to let me know where he's going next. I believe he's in Patagonia now, but I'm not clear exactly why. And no, before you ask, I haven't asked him if he's a member of a secret society and why he never told me."

"I get it. It's an awkward conversation you might want to have face to face. But when is he coming back?"

Marissa sighed. "I don't know. He's always pushing me off. I could really use some of his insights right now. I feel like we're drifting on our own."

"We're not on our own; we have a magical library."

"The whole place gets jumpy when you walk in. It's like all the books want to talk to you." Marrisa lifted the book in her hands. "Oh look, this is about supernatural phenomena. What a surprise. What haven't you told me about the case, Lola?"

"Something creepy is happening at the Seabourne Estate. There's paranormal activity in a secret passageway. I've had some spooky encounters, and with my vision of the same place, I think something's trying to get my attention."

"Like what?"

Another book tumbled off the shelf in front of Lola and she caught it. On the cover was a skull, the title in black scrawled across: *Spectres and Ghouls: A Study.* "I'm going to guess a spirit. You have a very large selection of occult books, did you know that?"

Marissa puffed out her breath. "It comes with the territory." She grabbed the books spread around her, and they made their way back to the research room. "You think you'll find anything in old papers about ghosts?"

"Depends on who the editor was," Lola said. "If Richie was involved, then definitely."

Marissa's smile was sad. "He really did love all that stuff." Marissa had been friends of sorts with the late editor of the paper.

"Did you know there's a new editor now? Matt Vernon. He's teaching at the high school too."

"I met him. Matt came in to look through some historical books on the island." To Lola's surprise, Marissa's cheeks coloured at her words.

Did the tightly wound librarian have a crush on the journalist with the shark smile? Lola couldn't resist pushing. "What do you think of him?"

"He's pretty confident, isn't he? Richie was never like that. Matt seems to know what he wants." No mistaking the burgundy flush that crept over her face now.

"He does seem assertive." Lola forced herself not to tell Marissa immediately that she didn't trust him. "He used to be an investigative reporter."

"I wonder why he came to this little island? I suppose we do have an unusually high murder rate." Marissa chewed on her lip as though it just occurred to her.

"Maybe it's a blip."

"Maybe it's you." Marissa turned to Lola with uncharacteristic directness. "Things have gotten worse since you came to Duchesne."

Lola looked away. Her fault. The werewolf witch Otsana had told Lola that an Otherworldly gate had been opened, and Reiko warned her a surge of energy from the island around the same time was now driving Otherworld activity towards it. All of it coincided with Lola's arrival on Duchesne.

"I didn't mean to," she said quietly.

Marissa shot her a look from under lowered lashes. "I never assumed you did. But still."

Lola's guilt followed her as she returned to the research room, where tension hung thick.

Nix glared at Walt, whose face was pale and strained. "We

haven't found too much," he said, turning to Lola with relief as she entered. "Just an article about the theft and a missing woman. As you suggested, it made front-page news back then. I printed it off."

"It was a lovely article," Nix said, her words diamond-sharp. "Where my family is cast as lowlife criminals and the Seabournes here are all goodness and light." A furious scowl played over her face as her hands clenched into fists. "It's not true!"

"Nix! Are you okay?" Lola stepped between the two of them and grabbed Nix's shoulders.

Nix blinked as though startled. Her face, just seconds before lined with fury, softened. "What? I...I don't know what just happened."

"You were furious with Walt."

Nix nodded and swallowed. "I didn't mean to. I haven't been sleeping really well...sorry, Walt, that was really weird of me."

Walt's face was still pale, but he eased back in his chair. "Don't worry about it."

A book thumped somewhere in the stacks, and Nix shot a look of pure irritation. "Why does that keep happening?" She rubbed her hands over her face and sighed. "Sorry, I'm no good cooped up inside. I don't think I'm your girl for this, Lola." She glared at the research room.

Her eyes were rimmed with redness, and dark shadows pooled beneath them.

"I think we have what we need, anyways," Lola said, watching her with concern. "Let's call it a day."

As they passed the front desk on the way out, Lola paused to speak to Marissa. Piles of papers were spread out in front of the librarian.

"I did a quick search and found some articles about work being done on the Seabourne Estate," Marissa said. "Renovations back in 1921. Mean anything to you?"

"Maybe?" Lola took the outstretched copies. "Thanks for this."

Marissa's gaze was bleak. "Be careful, okay? I'll keep on looking and see what the books tell me."

The trio left the library, and Walt paused outside on the steps, clearing his throat. "This might not be the best time to ask." His gaze flicked to Nix and away again. "But my family does this party every year."

"The Harvest Ball," Nix said immediately.

"You know about it?"

"Walt, it's the biggest party of the year," Nix said, rolling her eyes, but the exasperated look she gave him was affectionate. "Of course I know about it. Everybody does."

"Well, I want to invite you guys. It's a dress-up thing."

Nix's cheer returned for a moment, a grin briefly flashing over her face. "Really? Like we'd party with all the celebrities and important families on the island?"

"And their kids," Walt said.

"The hyenas." Nix's lip curled.

"That's the downside. But if you guys were there, it wouldn't be so awful for me."

"Enough, Walt, you're embarrassing us." Nix nudged him with her elbow and he relaxed. Lola suspected Nix's outburst had upset him far more than he had let on, but it seemed like all was well again. "We'll come to your fancy-pants party. Right, Lola?"

Lola thought back to what Matt had said about the ball; how it would be the place to be. "I wouldn't miss it."

"Good. I mean, great. It's next weekend."

"Walt, did you think we wouldn't come?" Lola asked.

"Well, after everything that's happened there, I thought you might want to...avoid it."

Nix checked her watch and hissed. "I gotta go, guys. Walt, I'd never avoid your creepy house, but I'm outta here." With a wave over her shoulder, she took off at a jog down Main Street.

Both Lola and Walt watched her go in silence. Once she was far enough away, Lola turned to him. "I'm worried about her. She's been acting strange."

He looked down. "Like towards me? I thought I was the only one to notice, but I think she's starting to hate me."

"That's the thing; I *know* Nix doesn't hate you. But she's being erratic, like she's not entirely herself. Also, the vision I had? Nix was in it."

"The vision from a hundred years ago? That's...odd."

"Right? I have no idea how something that happened in the past can be tied up in all this, but everything is telling me that Nix is in danger." She gave him a hopeful look. "I'd like to go back in."

"To the Belowstairs?"

"I know we're not supposed to go poking around down there, but if there's something down there that's trying to hurt Nix..."

"If it's to help her, we'll do it," Walt said. His face showed nothing but calm determination. "Let's go right now. But what are we looking for?"

"To see if anything pops out at me." Lola swallowed. "Hopefully not literally."

FOURTEEN

Seabourne Estate was in the process of a massive transformation. As Lola and Walt approached the front gates, a hive of workers swarmed the grounds, ferrying in crates of supplies and towering decorations.

Lola halted as a crew in overalls brushed past them through the front door, laden with gilded vases, extravagant golden feathers drooping over the rims. She blinked at the sight of flats filled with champagne being wheeled in by the dozen.

"Is this all for the Harvest Ball?" she asked.

Walt sighed, a cringe settling over his features. "It's always like this. My parents make sure it's *the* event of the season. They pour everything into it so they can get coverage in Toronto design magazines. Big shots from the mainland would do anything to get an invite, which does loads to help my father's business."

"And his business is...?" Lola asked delicately. Everything about Walt's father suggested *handle with care*.

Walt shrugged, dismissive. "He buys and sells things. I'm not sure exactly what, but it's enough to keep the caviar flowing."

Lola gave a low whistle, watching heavy cases of the delicacy being unloaded from a truck. "You weren't joking. I've seen parties in my days, but this is going to be *extraordinaire*."

"That's not even the half of it," Walt said, a flicker of humour returning to his eyes. "Come inside. I'll show you."

They stepped into the grand front hall, where chaos reigned. Boxes overflowed with faux fur and feathers, women with clipboards barked orders into headsets and teams of tech specialists adjusted cameras and lighting equipment.

"The theme this year is the Roaring Twenties." Walt flicked her a look. "I know, not very original, but it plays up the house's history with rum-runners. They've hired actors to re-enact scenes from that era. You know, gunfights between gangsters and flapper girls having affairs, that kind of thing. The scenes are filmed in black and white and projected in hidden corners throughout the house. Not everyone gets the same experience, and it becomes a treasure hunt to find them all. Guests spend half the night talking about the secrets they uncover and the other half bragging about it online. By the next morning, mainland blogs are buzzing, and my father's name is everywhere."

"Walt, that's...unspeakably cool." Lola grinned. "I can't believe I scored an invite."

He flushed and ducked his head. "It'll make the party tolerable for me, at least. Let's go to the study."

The room had barely been touched by the decorators, likely because they could hardly improve on it. A gleaming art deco liquor cart near the desk caught Lola's eye, though.

"This is beautiful, Walt." She ran her fingers over the sunbursts etched into polished chrome, the mirrored surfaces reflecting the crystal decanters filled with spirits of rich ambers and gold.

"It's original from the 1920s, in near perfect condition. Dad loves showing it off."

Lola had seen many parties that glorified the Roaring Twenties but remained unconvinced it was a time that should be remembered fondly. It was a time of decadence and flash while the world dangled between two disastrous wars. She'd been born then, though she didn't remember it.

Returning to the task at hand, she set Alice McCullough's diary on the desk, smoothing the leather cover. "Everything seems to lead back to Alice, somehow."

She'd spent late nights translating the spidery script, more and more admiring Alice's sharp wit and biting observations, at times making Lola laugh out loud. Altogether, it painted a picture of a bright, defiant woman—a stark contrast to the scandal that defined her in the island's history.

"She wrote about Irene Seabourne," Lola said, glancing at Walt. "The one she allegedly stole from. But the diary suggests they were close friends. They were both intelligent women and educated for their time. Apparently, the friendship started when Alice stumbled over Irene in the study, who was crying because she had taken apart her father's new radio and she couldn't put it back together."

"Irene Seabourne was my ancestor," Walt said.

"Well, she sounded interesting. Reminds me of someone." Lola nudged him. "The diary goes on to show how they would discuss technology of the future—at the time, that is. They were fascinated by electricity, and Irene would share her books with Alice. At one point, Irene went to a lecture on the mainland given by Edison and brought back her notes for her. They even had a secret alcove for their exchanges."

Lola could just picture it: two bright young women, sharing ideas and dreams of what their life would hold.

Walt frowned, his gaze fixed on the portrait of Walter Seabourne the First. "Alice must have wanted out of her life as a maid," he finally said.

Lola sighed. "I mean, can you blame her? It does seem to point to her taking the jewels and running." She glanced up at Walt. "I want to find that alcove. It must be Belowstairs."

Walt cracked his knuckles. "Let's go in, then."

"I seem to be attracting Otherworldly activity to me. Things could get spooky. Are you sure you're up to it?"

"Lola, I've known my house was haunted since I was little," Walt said. She got the sense he didn't mean haunted by ghosts but didn't push any further.

Lola pulled a flashlight out of her bag. Today, she came prepared to explore the darker side of Seabourne Estate.

The door to the study swung open. "Walt?" His mother's pinched voice startled them both as she appeared, her sharp gaze zeroing in on them. "What are you doing here?"

"Studying," Walt said immediately as Lola swept the flashlight into her pocket. "I mean, it's a study, right?"

"I'm not sure your father would approve of you being in here now," she said, her voice clipped. "Anyways, the tailor is here. You might as well get your final fitting done now; I don't want him to have to come back. That man can talk; it gives me a migraine being around him. Come, we'll get this over with."

"But Mom, I have a guest."

"She can entertain herself." Her icy glare skewered Lola like she was a street urchin ready to pocket their treasures. "Without touching anything."

"I'll just sit here and study." Lola took a tentative seat on a puffed leather chair and pulled her file of papers towards her. As Walt was ushered out, he glanced over his shoulder and mouthed *wait for me.*

Lola waited for the door to shut before letting out a breath. The room felt different when she was alone, quieter. The muffled sounds of construction on the other side of the door seemed to fade away.

She leafed through the files Marissa had copied for her, not that there was much in them. There were some articles that mentioned the Seabourne family had taken a last-minute trip to Europe over the fall of 1921 and gave their staff an impromptu holiday, though it seemed the original Mr. Seabourne remained behind, probably to manage his thriving rum-running business. Marissa had even managed to find an invoice from that period for a delivery of bricks to the estate, including careful tallies at the bottom, seemingly done by Mr. Seabourne. A cryptic note was dashed on the side: *Took care of Irene's little problem.*

Lola circled this twice. What was Irene's little problem?

A whisper cut through the stillness, causing goosebumps to ripple up her arms. The whisper grew to an excited murmur, urgent and layered.

She turned slowly to face the bookshelf that concealed the passageway. "Hello?"

The whispers dropped to a low moan, resolving into one single mournful word.

"Help."

Lola's heartbeat took off as she approached the bookshelf; she couldn't pretend it was just a draft. She ran her finger along the spine of *Treasure Island*. She should wait for Walt, she knew. It would be the right thing to do. But what if, in the meantime, his mother decided that she needed to leave?

Casting a guilty glance over her shoulder, she tugged on the book, letting the mechanism slide into place. Walt would come find her.

The bookshelf swung open with a guttural sound, like a dying man, as musty air rushed past her. Despite the pit in her stomach, she stepped into the cool landing of the stairwell.

The door clicked shut behind her, causing her breath to seize in her chest. All the sounds from the house were hushed, as though she had entered a different world.

The air was thick with the dust of ages and mildew rotting the wood. She braced her trembling hand on the banister and clicked on her flashlight, seeing nothing but the wooden staircase heading into darkness.

The Belowstairs might be home to evil spirits, yet she knew this was where she would find answers, hopefully before something terrible happened to Nix. With that in mind, she descended into the gloom.

The stairwell seemed to go on longer than it should, the walls pressing in on either side as though she was moving back into the past with every creak of her boots on the wooden steps.

She reached the bottom of the stairs and took a deep breath, bracing herself against the panic that wanted to roar up inside of her.

"*Merde*," she whispered and took a few unsteady steps. "Get yourself together, Lola. It's just a hallway."

A flicker of warm light appeared further down the hallway. Somebody was down here with her. Lola forced herself to remain frozen in place as the light wavered for a moment, then strengthened.

It flickered in the shadows, golden and warm, like a candle held at eye level, though the cast light didn't illuminate a form.

"Wait," she tried to call out, but her voice was nothing but a trembling whisper. She steeled herself. She couldn't fall apart now. The light began moving away from her.

Lola followed until the unmoored light arrived at the place where the mirror hung in the corridor. The place where Lola was sure she'd seen a face. The candlelight disappeared.

"What was that?" Lola directed her flashlight over the wall, the dull mirror picking up the light.

That's when she noticed a thin seam in the wall. She ran a fingernail along it, trailing it in a rectangle all around the mirror.

A hidden door. How had she missed it before?

Dust motes spilled out in curlicues as she dug in her nails at the seam and braced herself. To her surprise, it began to shift immediately in a shower of grime.

A door of thick brick peeled away from the wall, opening to a closet-like space. It was shoddily made compared to the fine building of the rest of the estate, but she supposed they must have cut corners in the servant's quarters. The shadows inside were so dark they seemed to drink up the light.

A walled-up alcove? Was this the space Alice had written about in her diary, where Irene would leave her books, where the young women would meet up by candlelight to discuss the grandiose ideas of the early twentieth century?

With the thrill of discovery as heady as ever, Lola entered the space.

Her hand felt along the side wall, pressing, trying to find the secret place where Irene would leave books for Alice. Excitement bubbled in her chest. Perhaps Alice wasn't a thief; perhaps the jewels had been hidden in the Seabourne Estate the whole time. She could vindicate Nix's ancestor.

Above her, she saw only cobwebs and the skittering of spiders who had never seen the light of day. Her knee bumped against something. Heart in her throat, she directed the beam of light down.

Her flashlight sputtered and went out, plunging her in suffocating blackness.

Lola backed out of the alcove.

But firm bricks met her back. The door had closed.

"No."

Panic swarmed her like locusts. It tingled to her fingertips as she spun and slammed her palms against the wall, trying to force it open. She scrabbled at the door, trying to find a handle or hinge. But there was nothing but a solid brick wall.

FIFTEEN

Lola's fists banged against the brick until her knuckles bled, her calls swallowed by the darkness. "Is anyone there?" she rasped, her voice cracking. "Help!"

She ripped at the wall in animal-like panic, but the rough brick and mortar was unrelenting, scraping off the skin of her fingers.

The air was damp, the kind of cold that seeped through bones, thick with the scent of decay and rot.

Falling back, she clutched at her arms. She needed to calm down; this wasn't getting her anywhere.

"*Petite imbecile*, you've gotten yourself trapped in a secret chamber," she said out loud, if only for the comfort of her own voice. She'd been in worse situations. She'd gotten in here; she could get out.

But somehow, this felt different; she had the oppressive sense that something was watching her. Waiting.

She needed to let Walt know what she'd done and where she was. He wouldn't be happy she'd gone in without him, but at least he wasn't trapped in here with her. She scrambled for her bag, but she'd left it back in the study, with her phone.

Closing her eyes, she took a steadying breath. She'd have to find her own way out.

With delicate fingertips, she explored her prison, probing her surroundings and found a little bench in the alcove. Blinking back tears of dread, she sat, the wall behind her rough and cool against her shoulders.

Walt would come down here eventually looking for her, but would he know where to look?

A wisp of hair brushed stickily over her face, and she jerked back with a gasp. She struck out, but nothing was there.

"A cobweb," she breathed. It had to have been that.

She was alone in this space, wasn't she?

Frantic, she searched for the seam of the door that she had entered by. There had to be a release mechanism, just like the other secret passageway. Every door could be opened.

But no matter how many times she ran her fingers over the wall, all she found were rough bricks joined together with sloppy mortar. There was no door, no seam, no exit.

A sound reached her then, faint at first, but as she focused on it, it grew louder.

Scritch, scritch, scritch. The scratching sound.

She held her breath. The sound was all around her.

Scritch, scritch, scritch.

Horror flooded through her as she realized what the sound was.

Stifling a whimper, she ran her nails over the bricks. *Scritch, scritch.* The noise was nails scratching at the stone.

Somebody else was trapped in the walls—somebody who wanted to be let out.

Someone sniffled. They were crying. Sobbing. *Scritch, scritch, scritch.*

Lola doubled over, sinking to her knees, heaving. The sobs and scratches filled the alcove, vibrating in her skull.

Someone was in the space with her, though she couldn't see them.

Her terror overwhelmed her until she no longer felt as though she was a person.

She reached out for anything—any shred of strength she could find.

And then she felt it; a familiar pulse underneath her palms pressed into the floor.

As she focused on that faint beat, her awareness pushed out beyond the alcove. She could sense the earth beneath the floorboards, the roots of trees and the mushrooms that grew underground.

The loamy smell of soil surrounded her as she felt the vibration in her fingertips, the thump, thump of the tree that sat in the centre of the oak forest, whose roots stretched all the way down to the Well of Souls and beyond.

What had McInnes said? The island was inside her, and it could be powerful.

The Tree of Life grew from the source of magic on this island. Lola was connected to it, somehow, and trapped as she was, she reached out for it.

Lola sunk her spirit into that source of energy, pulling in one steadying breath after another. The power felt green and alive as it filled her, soaking into every cell of her being like a cool wave.

Opening her eyes, she found the absolute darkness had retreated from a glimmer of light. It came from underneath the wooden bench, glowing like the phosphorescence in the Well of Souls. Following the source of light, Lola felt the rough wood underside of the bench, her fingers scraping against splinters. There, at the back, was a built-in shelf. The place where two girls used to hide books and messages for each other a century ago.

Reaching further in, her fingers brushed against something brittle. Papers. She pulled them free, the glow casting flickering shadows over the yellowed pages. A final goodbye from Alice to Irene? As she pulled them out, the sobbing intensified, and every hair on her body stood straight up.

The power from the Tree of Life still filled her. What did it mean? That she could access its Otherworldly power? McInnes had warned that the power demanded payment.

She couldn't think about that now. Nothing was worse than being trapped behind this wall. Whatever this connection meant, she would use it to save herself.

Following the sense of magic all the way to its core, Lola pulled it inside of her until her skin was glowing with the same green light. Placing her hands against the wall, she gathered up all that power inside of her and, with a wail of rage at being trapped, she slammed it into the bricks.

They exploded under her hands with a resonant boom, then staccato cracks as individual bricks were pulverized under her hands. Debris flew in all directions, ricocheting off the walls around her.

The wall collapsed, and she tumbled out of the alcove onto the wooden floor of the Belowstairs. She crouched there, sucking in breath, trying to steady the trembling in her limbs from the expenditure of power.

She turned to survey the damage she'd caused. Surely an explosion of that size should have alerted the entire construction team upstairs that something devastating had just happened. Lola might have compromised the entire foundation of the estate; everyone should be getting out.

But the entire world seemed to focus on a single pinpoint. She stood, shaking, as her flesh crawled with the realization.

The wall was perfectly intact, the mirror sitting innocently at its centre. There was no door, no alcove, no hole. For a moment she wondered if the stress was getting to her; was her sanity crumbling under everything she'd been through over the past months?

"No," Lola said aloud. "It *was* real."

She stared into her own reflection, at her dirt-smeared face, the tear tracks along her cheeks, the wide, hollowed-out eyes.

The mirror flickered, and Lola realized she wasn't seeing her own reflection. It was a girl on the other side of the mirror, on the other side of the wall, crying as she slapped her hands against the wall. Her eyes rolled in fear, tears and snot running down her face as she soundlessly pleaded.

Lola banged against the wall, mirroring the girl's image. "Who are you?" she cried. "How can I help you?" Her hands were bleeding from the abuse they'd taken but she couldn't stop. The girl was so desperate, so scared.

The girl stopped, suddenly, as though she'd heard Lola. She turned to face her, staring at her behind the tangle of her curls.

She looked just like Nix.

Hatred burned from her gaze as she stared directly into Lola's eyes.

The doppelganger in the mirror screamed, shattering the silence like a pane of glass. An invisible force slammed into Lola's chest. She flew back, her head cracking against the wall with a sickening thump.

"Lola!"

Footsteps pounded towards her, a flashlight beam bobbing. "Lola, what happened?" Walt crouched next to her, grabbing her arms. "Are you okay?"

"I heard a voice, and I followed it," Lola said, her voice cracking from the strain. "I found the alcove."

"The alcove?"

"It's behind the mirror. It's...someone is there. They're trapped, and I was trapped there, and they are so very angry." She thought of the face in the mirror, Nix's face, boiling with rage.

Walt frowned, his flashlight dancing across the untouched wall. "Lola...there's nothing here."

"Not now, but there was."

He hesitated. "Let's get you upstairs and figure it out."

She grabbed his arms as he tried to pull her up. "Did you hear me? Somebody is trapped inside the walls."

He was watching her with concern. "Did you fall? Maybe hit your head?"

Lola put her hand to the back of her head and winced. "I did, but only because the ghost hit me. Kind of."

"Right." Walt lifted Lola up onto her feet. "Can you walk?"

She nodded, then wished she hadn't, as the world spun and her stomach tried to heave. Walt put his arm back around her, taking some of her weight. Together, they shuffled down the hallway and up the stairwell back into the study.

The normal world around her seemed so different from the horrors in the Belowstairs, Lola felt like she was waking from a nightmare.

"Walt, I don't think Alice ever left the estate. I think she's still here." Her voice was a horrifying whisper, and Walt grimaced.

"Let's look at this rationally. You hit your head; could you have dreamed it?"

It was as though he was reading her mind, but she forced herself to shake her head. "No. Walt, there is an alcove. I found it. I think I went into a pocket in the Otherworld."

Walt's look was skeptical. "It's dark down there; you might have just gotten scared."

Lola thrust her chin out. "Don't gaslight me. *I* used to be the thing that scared people in the dark. I know creepy, and this was beyond anything I'd experienced. There is an alcove down there, and a ghost who's trapped."

"Listen, I believe you believe this happened, but how can you be sure?"

Lola held up her hand, the packet of yellowing papers still clutched in her bloodless grip. Her fingers were bloody with scratches. "Because I found these inside it."

"What are they?" Walt stared at the brittle papers as Lola delicately laid them on the desk.

"I would bet a sack of gold these are letters passed between Nix's ancestor, and yours."

Sixteen

Wearily, Lola stepped through the front door to the Pain Perdu, the little bell jingling as warm air, rich with the scents of fresh bread and brewed coffee, wrapped around her like a blanket. The café buzzed with low chatter and clinking cutlery and the hiss of the espresso machine below that.

Lola wanted nothing more than to take a hot shower and dig into the papers she had earned in her trial in the Belowstairs. But she hadn't taken two steps inside before Faye's voice cut through the din, sharp enough to turn a few heads.

"Lola! What happened to you?"

Lola's hands flew to her face, wondering what she looked like to cause Faye to leave the busy counter and bustle towards her. Faye wiped her flour-dusted hands on her apron, then placed a warm hand to Lola's forehead. "You're pale as a ghost. Come, sit down."

"I'm fine, Faye—" Lola tried to protest but was tugged into the kitchen area, away from the clients, where Faye pushed her into a chair.

"You don't look fine. Have you even eaten today?" Faye tsk-

tsked as she hurried over to one of the massive fridges and returned with a ham and cheese croissant. Within moments, a steaming mug of chamomile tea had joined it.

"Eat," the baker ordered, her hands on her hips.

"Really, Faye, I just want to get upstairs."

Faye's eyes narrowed as she took in her charge. "You're getting skinny," she said. "Wherever you've been travelling to, you haven't been taking enough care of yourself, but now that you're under my roof, you're going to get some proper meals. Understand?"

Resigned, Lola picked up the croissant. Her appetite was nonexistent, but she took a bite to appease Faye.

The baker's voice softened. "You're pushing yourself too hard, you know. Whatever's going on, it can wait until you've had a proper meal and some rest."

Lola nodded, grateful Faye was there. She made her feel cared for—an experience that was entirely new for her.

Once she'd eaten enough under Faye's watchful eye, she begged to get upstairs for an early evening. Faye finally relented after noting several times how tired Lola looked.

She was right. Lola could barely get one foot in front of the other as she trudged up the stairs and had to muster the energy to collapse on her bed, the soft cotton bedspread brushing against her skin. From there, she surveyed her little bedroom.

She'd made an effort to put more of her personality into the space. She'd used the print she'd loved by the werewolf Conri she'd met over the summer. He'd been a talented artist, and she'd fallen in love with his interpretation of predators chasing through swirls of colours. She'd used the painting, in purples, greens and golds, to influence her choices. Since it reminded her of Mardi Gras in New Orleans, she found some impressionist paintings of the French Quarter and some lovely half-masks that decorated her walls now.

She'd also hung a framed photo of herself with Nix, Gael and Walt, laughing on the boardwalk in the summer before the carnival had come to town and everything had changed. It was her favourite thing in the entire room. On a whim, she reached into her drawer and pulled out another photo she'd had printed, one of her and Gael.

Sitting cross-legged on her bed, she held the photograph between her fingertips as though it might crumble into ash. The image captured Gael leaning in, his warm brown eyes on hers, a quiet smile curving his lips. The summer sun cast a golden glow on his face. Her thumb brushed the edge of the photo, a small unconscious moment, as though she could reach into the past and touch the boy who used to look at her that way; she could almost hear their carefree laughter.

She slid the photo back into the drawer. She didn't have a right to display that one now, but she couldn't seem to let it go.

The muted sounds from the Pain Perdu could still be heard from downstairs. It was too early to actually turn in; she still had so much to do. First, she texted Nix that they needed to get together to discuss what she had found: the alcove and the letters and the ghost. It wasn't something she could just throw out in a text. Nix was already weird about the Belowstairs, and she wasn't sure if her friend would believe her.

Walt still didn't entirely believe what had happened to Lola, though he couldn't explain how she'd found the papers. Lola didn't take it personally; Walt didn't like things that didn't have a rational explanation, that he couldn't see with his own eyes. He *really* didn't like the Otherworld: Of all of them, he had the hardest time with the dangerous world Lola had brought to them. Still, he was as supportive as he could be while always trying to come up with the most logical explanation.

Her fingers hovered over her phone, wondering if she should text Gael. He was the most open-minded; he'd always been the first to back her up. And yet, since she'd broken up with him, their friendship had withered too. Not that she should have expected otherwise.

Her fingers lingered over his name. Thinking of him was tender pain, like a bruise she couldn't stop pressing.

Her phone dinged, and for a moment, she thought it would be Gael, that he could sense she was thinking about him. But it was from Walt.

You okay? You don't have to come to the Harvest Ball next week if you don't want to.

She smiled.

I wouldn't miss it, she responded. She'd be damned if she wasn't going to get to the bottom of what was going on at Seabourne Estate.

At that thought, she sat up, groaning, and moved to her desk, bringing with her the papers she'd found in the haunted alcove. They were as aged as Alice's diary, the ink faded, held together with a black silk ribbon. Her lamp cast a golden glow over the papers she'd found in the haunted alcove, their edges crumbling like autumn leaves.

The scent of musty aged parchment mixed with the faint smell of lavender she had tucked into her dresser, creating a comforting mix of past and present.

Her hand trembling from exhaustion and foreboding, Lola untied the silk ribbon, soft and frayed at the edges as though it had been constantly handled.

Separating the papers one by one, she was relieved to find that the lettering was still clear after all this time. The bundle had probably sat undisturbed in the walled-off alcove for decades; it was a miracle the letters hadn't been destroyed by mould.

Holding her breath, she held up the first one to the light.

Dear Alice,

Your thoughts on the use of the vacuum amplifier in radio broadcasting were most illuminating. I've hardly been able to sleep these past nights, thinking of the significance. I must tell my tutor of your thoughts; he will likely be grumpy that someone else is able to reason beyond his limited capacity.

I have included the latest serial in James Joyce's Ulysses. *I've just read it and can't stop thinking about it. Please read this so we may discuss; I am eager to hear your take.*

Meet me where we rendezvous, the usual time. I'll be waiting.

Letters from Irene Seabourne to her maid. The last line had been underlined, the ink darker as though Irene's pen had lingered there.

Most of the letters were similar: Irene writing to Alice about books and ideas they were discussing. The girl's handwriting was crisp and elegant, a refreshing break from Alice's loopy scrawls in the diary.

Irene had an analytical way of expressing herself. In comparison, Alice rambled on in her diary. She was an idealist, longing for the greater world outside the confines of Seabourne Estate.

Despite their differences, the two girls seemed very much aligned and, if Lola wasn't mistaken, rather sweet on each other. The packet of letters seemed to be every correspondence Irene had sent Alice, gathered and tied with silk, like a precious treasure. A silk ribbon would have been expensive for a maid in the 1920s, something she would have used for the letters from her sweetheart.

Every letter from sensible Irene ended with her signature and a faint X inscribed next to it, barely there, as though the writer couldn't believe her daring. As though she knew she wasn't allowed to feel the way she did.

Lola traced her fingertip over that X. How romantic, and how tragic. The two never ventured out into the world together, hand in hand as they would have liked. She ran her finger down the front cover of the diary, the silk ribbon lying next to it. She wanted very badly for these two to have had a happy ending, though it wasn't possible. In the 1920s, two women could never live together openly.

As far as she knew, Irene Seabourne spent her life on Duchesne Island. She needed to research the history of the Seabourne family; an important family like that would likely be documented somewhere. Perhaps Walt knew of some kind of memoir or biography of some of his relatives.

At the last letter, Lola paused. Irene mentioned she was preparing for their great undertaking. *Nearly all the elements are in place*, she'd scrawled, her writing loopier than usual as though great feelings were passing through her pen to her words.

Lola opened her laptop and began typing out Irene's letters. It was easier work than deciphering Alice's diary, but she was bleary-eyed with exhaustion as it was. She made notes to herself as she went: What was this great undertaking the girls were planning? And why did it never happen?

As for Alice, she remained a mystery, one that was wrapped up in the Belowstairs. Had she betrayed Irene's trust, taken her jewelry and run for it? Or had she never left Seabourne Estate?

The thought made Lola shudder. She wasn't going to stop until she figured out what was going on, even if it meant facing down the ghosts of the past and present.

SEVENTEEN

Lola readjusted the plunging neckline of her costume for a final time before she made her way up the front path of the Seabourne Estate. It had only arrived the day before, and she was enamoured with the black and gold flapper dress: the way the fringe of beads twirled around her knees and the fabric swished over her hips as she strutted up the path.

Seabourne Estate was dazzling. The front entrance had been transformed into an autumnal dreamscape: the harvest season with the opulence of the 1920s. Garlands of fall foliage wrapped around the grandiose double doors, nestled with white pumpkins, lanterns and fairy lights leading the way up to the entry.

She shivered, unsure if it was nerves or excitement. Despite the horror of what had happened inside the walls of this mansion, all anyone had spoken about over the past week was the Harvest Ball: Who was invited, what celebrities were going to be there from the mainland, what new tricks and treats the Seabournes would come up with this year. It was hard not to get caught up in the hype.

Walt had asked her to come early before the bigger names arrived and things started to get crazy. She knew he meant before the hyenas descended on his house. It had been nearly half a year since Walt had turned his back on his old clique, preferring the company of his old friend Gael, and Nix and Lola. He'd also cut off the hyenas' access to his family's wealth and outrageous parties.

But in this case, he couldn't control the guest list, and now the hyenas would be present; they could turn on him. Lola smoothed her faux-fur wrap around her shoulders. She would be there for her friend, whether or not a hateful ghost haunted his house.

Still, she hesitated. The pumpkins cast distorted shadows over the steps, and she feared something would jump out at her. The air seemed to grow colder the closer she approached the front door. Was she truly ready to face whatever it was that hid within these walls?

She fiddled with her invitation, elegant with creamy paper that Walt had handed her at school yesterday. "They won't let you in without it," he had said with an eye roll. "Thanks for coming, again, after...everything."

He still wasn't sure what to make of Lola's account of his haunted servants' quarters, but he knew she had been shaken. His concern for her was touching; she wouldn't let him down.

Squaring her shoulders, she strode up to the mansion. Gas lanterns flickered along the porch.

The snap of a twig behind her sent her spinning around with a gasp, hand at her throat, wondering if the ghost who wore Nix's face was following her.

"Lola? You okay?" A very normal voice called out. Gael approached, strolling up the path.

She put her hand over her eyes and let out a trembly laugh. "It's you." Her breath came out shaky. His warm hand cupped her shoulder.

"I spooked you, hey?" Gael gave her a gentle squeeze and released her, his half-smile almost apologetic. "Bet you're not used to that."

Gael filled out his pinstripe suit well; it suited his broad shoulders, though he kept on tugging at the sleeves. His black waves had grown long enough to get caught in his collar.

Mon Dieu, he was beautiful, dressed up like this. Good enough to eat.

"Not used to it at all." She swallowed. "I'm a little on edge, is all."

Gael nodded. "Walt told me what happened. Or his version of what happened. He said you had a panic attack."

"I did not!" Lola straightened in outrage. Her fear fled in face of her indignation. "I was walled up with an angry spirit. I would like to see Walt handle that!" She was about to continue her rant when Gael held up his hands, laughing in mock surrender.

"I said it was *his* version. Lola, I believe you. About everything."

"Oh." Lola deflated. "Thanks."

"I mean, spooky things happen around here. I'd be a fool not to believe you. Tell me about it."

In the light of the lanterns, Lola gave him a short version of the whispers, the candlelight, the door and the alcove. She didn't tell him about the power she'd found within herself to break free because she didn't have the faintest idea how to explain.

"And you found the letters there?"

"All the letters were addressed to Alice. This seems to circle around Nix's family, and I'm worried about her. Maybe she shouldn't be here tonight."

"I don't think we can stop her. She was going on and on about her costume yesterday in math."

"We'll have to take care of her, then. Keep an eye on her, make sure she's okay."

"It's a deal." Gael gave her that lopsided grin she loved, and it neatly broke her heart in two once again.

To distract herself, she gestured to his bow tie hanging limply around his neck. "Are you going for the undone look here?"

"I tried tying it. Disaster."

"Need a hand?" Her voice wavered, her fingers brushing against the untied bow tie before she fully realized she'd moved closer.

"If you don't mind." His voice was low, intimate. "I've given up."

How many times had she performed the very task with Beau before they entered a glamorous party like this one? Her hands trembled as she worked the fabric into complicated knots, the heat of Gael's skin seeping through his shirt. She could feel his eyes on her, hungry.

She took a step back to admire her work. "All done. You look very dapper."

He smiled at the old-fashioned word and ran his hand through his hair. "Thanks. You look dapper too; I mean, the girl version." He huffed out his breath and his voice softened. "I mean, you're a knockout, Lola."

The air between them scorched as they looked at each other for a moment too long; long enough for her to imagine trailing her hand down his forearm—bringing it to circle her waist, him tugging her in towards him...

He cleared his throat. "So, Seabourne Estate is *actually* haunted." He looked up towards the attic of the gothic house looming over them. "When I was a little kid, I would sometimes hear noises in empty rooms or get that sense that somebody was watching me, but nobody was there, you know?"

Lola nodded. "Something weird is going on here."

Gael snorted. "That should be our town motto."

She smiled. "Ready to dive in?"

"With you? Always."

Lola tried to ignore how his voice lingered over the word as he pressed the bell.

The door opened, an army of servants in black and white behind it. A gloved butler took their invitations on a golden plate and ushered them into the house. Lola's wrap was whisked away as they were guided through the Seabourne mansion.

Every table was topped with golden candelabras, surrounded by white flowers that draped to the floor. The flickering light danced in time with the lively strains of jazz music that floated through the air.

As they passed by one of the corridors, a lick of ghostly white movement caught her eye, and Lola froze. Was it the spirit who trapped her?

Gael peered over her shoulder. "Cool!" he said. "You found one of the hidden videos." They ventured down the hallway, which led to a pantry. There, the video of a flapper girl giggling and beckoning towards them played out on the wall. The way she flipped her skirt around suggested she was looking for a private rendezvous. Her black-and-white face was heavily made up and overly expressive, like the silent film stars from the era.

Lola and Gael watched until the figure disappeared, the video finished. Lola let out a whistle. "They really thought of everything, didn't they?"

"Yeah," Gael said. "I've heard about this party for so many years. It's awesome to finally be here." His jaw was tensed, though, as if he was on edge being in the estate. Was it bringing back old memories for him?

"It means a lot to Walt that you're here for him now."

Gael gave a tight nod and jerked his head. "Let's go find him, then."

EIGHTEEN

A candlelit path led to the ballroom, which spanned the back half of the Seabourne's sprawling home. The black and gold floor was polished to a mirrored finish. Light cascaded from chandeliers like frozen waterfalls, catching on gilded mirrors that seemed to double the room's opulence.

A handful of expensively dressed guests gathered around a seven-piece jazz band playing on the raised stage in the corner. At the centre was a champagne fountain, inlaid with mirrors to refract the candlelight.

Floor-to-ceiling windows lined the entire back wall, where doors opened out onto a terrace. From there, the view over the Atlantic, still sparkling in the red light of the setting sun, was uninhibited.

"*C'est magnifique*," Lola breathed.

"I'm glad you approve," came a voice from behind her. Lola turned to see Mr. Seabourne in a glossy tuxedo bearing down on them. This time, it wasn't with an angry edge in his eyes; rather, he was all charming smiles as he approached Lola and Gael. "What a marvellously attractive couple. I want to pay you to just stand there, looking at each other like that."

Lola's cheeks flushed pink as Mr. Seabourne gave a chesty laugh. "Oh, we're not..." she faded away in embarrassment.

"Now, who do we have here?" Mr. Seabourne barrelled over Lola's discomfort, looking her up and down. "I thought I knew everyone on the island, and I feel like I'd remember you."

Clearly, he did not remember ordering her from the Belowstairs when he had caught them down there, and Lola wasn't going to remind him. "I'm new. Lola." She extended her hand to shake it, but he grasped it and brought it to his lips. She forced herself not to snatch her hand back.

"*Enchanté*," he said with an oily smile, then turned to Gael. "And who is this strapping young lad?"

"Gael Smith, Mr. Seabourne."

"Eh? The cleaner's son." He eyed Gael blearily. Clearly, he'd started the evening several cocktails ago.

"That's right." Gael jammed his hand into his pocket, his jaw tightening as he stared down Walt's dad.

"I heard you found some luck down there in the dirt." Mr. Seabourne moved in closer, and the ripe smell of bourbon washed over them. "Find any other trinkets down there? Is it worth opening the hole again?"

Gael's nostrils flared, and Lola was about to tug him away when a voice rang out over the polished floor of the ballroom, sharp and cool as diamonds. "Darling."

Mayor Seabourne tapped towards them on sky-high T-strap heels. Walt came in behind his mother, frowning as he saw his father crowding his friends.

The mayor wore a drapey black art deco gown with intricate beadwork and elbow-length evening gloves. Her hair was curled under an elaborate jewelled turban, and she held a martini glass aloft, the liquid barely sloshing though the glass was filled to the brim.

In a three-piece suit, Walt looked as elegant as his mother. Unlike Gael, he seemed used to formal wear, moving with confidence. It added gravitas to his gangly frame, making him seem older.

"You look amazing!" Lola said, wondering if Walt was aware. She kissed him on the cheek, careful not to smear her lipstick, and admired him for long enough that Gael cleared his throat.

"Walt, who are your guests?" Mayor Seabourne asked, her eyebrows raised as she took in Lola.

"Mom, this is Gael. And Lola, she's a friend from school." His voice hardened when his father's gaze dropped to Lola's neckline.

"I think I'll head on over to the bar," Mr. Seabourne said.

"Darling, don't you think you've had enough for now?" Mayor Seabourne's stare could cut glass.

"I think I know when I've had enough. Not like this limp noodle you've been raising." Mr. Seabourne gave a small chuckle as he playfully punched Walt's arm, who looked away, fists clenched.

"And here I thought you were nothing but," Mayor Seabourne said airily before turning to Walt, ignoring the furious flush on her husband's face. "Now, I think it would be best if you were to get upstairs to the games room. It's better for all." Her gaze flickered towards Mr. Seabourne, telling them everything: *Go away before things get worse.*

But Lola was watching Mr. Seabourne. Something had caught his eye across the ballroom. His flushed face quickly faded to pallor, and for a moment, his mouth sagged open. "Dammit, not now," he muttered under his breath. He cleared his throat and gave a weak attempt at a smile. "Must mingle, you know."

Curious as to what had shaken the conceited man, she peered in the direction Mr. Seabourne was heading. A tall man in an over-sized fedora had entered the ballroom, taking up most of the entryway.

In his 1920s suits, he could have been an actor hired to play a gangster. But that didn't explain Mr. Seabourne's reaction when he spotted him. The businessman's steps were much less confident as he approached.

What caught Lola's interest the most were the man's eyes, a deep blue so intense they seemed to shimmer. When he turned his head her way, they glimmered like the waves of the ocean catching the light. She whipped her head away before he caught her staring.

Who was he, and why was Mr. Seabourne so upset to see him? Had Lola seen the Otherworld shining in his eyes, or had it been a trick of the candlelight?

"Yes, I'm looking forward to seeing the rest of the house," Lola cooed, giving a large fake smile to Mayor Seabourne as she grabbed both Gael and Walt by the arms, guiding them out of the ballroom.

"Walt, your parents know how to put on a show," she said under her breath.

"Yes, they like to go all out in all things," he said. "Has anyone seen Nix?"

"Let's go find her." Lola tugged the boys away from the freezing hatefulness of Walt's parents.

They took a different way out of the ballroom, away from the strange blue-eyed man, passing through a dining room where a sumptuous feast was being laid out by a team of sweating caterers.

"This way," Walt murmured, leading them down a narrow corridor to a hidden pocket door. "It will take us to the front entry again."

"How many hidden doors does your home have, Walt?"

His smile was thin. "It's been a while since I've counted."

"I used to love exploring this place when I was little," Gael said. Lola smiled up at him, aware she was still holding on to his arm, feeling the warm muscle underneath his suit jacket. Suddenly her palm was scorching hot, so she let him go, finding herself clinging only to Walt, and she dropped his arm as well.

They paused to look at Lola, who mercifully caught a glimpse of Nix at the other end of the corridor. "Look, there she is!" she cried, thankful to interrupt the awkwardness. But as she approached, Nix disappeared in a glitch and reappeared again. It was another black-and-white projection.

Lola froze. How could the actress look just like their friend? This girl wasn't wearing garish makeup and costume; rather she wore a simple dress with an apron over it. Her eyes were wide with terror, raising her arms up to protect herself as she backed away, cringing from what appeared to be an oncoming blow. Her mouth opened in a silent scream before she disappeared.

Lola's skin crawled. "That was...dark."

The icy terror she'd felt in the Belowstairs returned, making her feel weak in the knees. Horrible things lurked in this house.

Walt was staring where the video had disappeared, brow furrowed. "Usually they go with things that are fun and glamorous. You thought it was Nix?"

"I did...I mean, the actress looked a little like her, right?"

The three of them shared troubled looks, just as a voice called out: "Seriously, what are you guys doing? This place is a maze!"

The real Nix appeared at the end of the corridor, where her doppelgänger had disappeared moments before. "There you are! One of the butler guys said you'd be here. What's wrong?"

She noticed them all gaping at her and came to a stop. Lola flashed an uneasy look to Gael, then approached Nix. "It's nothing. We just caught one of the projected videos. Let me see what you're wearing. You look incredible."

Instead of a dress, Nix wore a tuxedo, fitting her perfectly to give the illusion of long legs and a pinched-in waist. Her long curly hair had been pinned back to look like a bob, her features accentuated with a faint trace of makeup.

"Isn't it great?" Nix flushed pink up to the roots of her hair. "Mom found it in the kid's section of her shop and tailored it for me."

"It's stunning. And very you."

Nix glowed. Lola grabbed onto her hand, feeling a sudden need to protect her. "We were just on our way upstairs."

"What about the ballroom? I heard it's amazing."

"Overrated, trust me." Lola raised her eyebrows. "I'm curious to see the rest of the house."

"Yeah, we're going to have fun," Gael said. Lola wasn't entirely sure if his enthusiasm was faked or not; he still seemed shaken by the disturbing scene they'd witnessed.

Walt's look was openly bleak. "Let's just try to survive this thing."

Nineteen

After sneaking through the hidden door, the four of them found the front entrance crawling with guests, with more coming up the front steps. The Harvest Ball had started in earnest, and servers with trays of champagne mingled with the beautifully dressed people, ushering them towards the ballroom.

They twisted through the crowd to the sweeping marble staircase that would take them to the second storey. The banister coiled with green foliage and white pumpkins, elegant and derelict, as though nature was laying waste to the property, beautiful in its decay. Lola shook her head, trying to get the image out of her head.

"So where's the party, Walt?" she asked. "Or did you just want to get away from your parents?" She didn't mind leaving the dysfunction behind them, but it seemed like everyone else was heading towards the ballroom.

"The games room. It's where the kids go." The bitterness hadn't faded from his tone.

"The kids' party? Why do I feel we're going to be force-fed chicken nuggets?"

She nudged him, and Walt smiled at her attempt to cheer him

up. "That's just what it's been called. It used to be an expensive babysitting service—every year, I'd be kept upstairs with a group of nannies and kids my age, bobbing for apples. Of course, things have changed now."

A set of gilded double doors were on the opposite side of the staircase, flanked by two burly men in suits. Walt nodded at them, and they opened the doors to a long parlour that stretched along the back of the house, directly above the ballroom. The room was swathed in shadows; the dancing light of the candles and the heady scent of incense made the atmosphere feel thick.

Windows along the back wall opened to a balcony overlooking the ocean, and a gleaming pool table was set near the end of the room.

"It's like stepping into an old-fashioned bar." Gael whistled as he took in the over-the-top decorations. Tables were set with elaborate platters of food that seemed far too fancy for a kids' party. A crystal bowl of punch was surrounded by chilling beer, bottles of wine and an array of liquor.

"They were going for a speakeasy style," Walt said, his voice brittle. "For a little bit of excitement."

"Clever." Lola eyed the alcohol, wondering how messy things were going to get that night; clearly, the intention was for the teens to get drunk. No wonder the hyenas had been so mad when Walt cut them off; the parties at this house were indeed epic.

"But who ordered the séance?" Nix asked, pointing at a long table set along the windows. Draped in heavy midnight-blue velvet, metallic thread wove mystical symbols over the tablecloth. A crystal ball sparkled at the centre of it all, with a set of tarot cards lying to its side.

A strange thrill ran through Lola at these symbols of the occult. At least the old Ouija board hadn't made an appearance.

"Séances were popular in the 1920s," she said. "People would host them and knocking parties to contact the beyond."

Nix frowned, suddenly stern. "But that's not possible, is it?"

Lola shrugged. "They were mostly charlatans. In my experience, the realm of the living and the dead are separate; the divide between the two is far too great to bridge."

Although, that wasn't entirely true. When Lola went to the depths of the Well of Souls, she'd gone to a place where nothing material existed. It was where a piece of her soul had been hiding for eighty years.

With her soul finally intact, she had been granted humanity and allowed to live out her mortal life. However, that place was like none she had ever encountered before. It was a place beyond all that she understood.

Shaking off the thought, she stepped out onto the balcony. From here, she could survey the terrace outside the ballroom, now milling with guests enjoying the air as things heated up inside. Lola leaned on the railing, squinting at the people below her, trying to catch a glimmer of the Otherworld among them. Everyone shimmered with gold and jewels, making it difficult to determine what was magical and what was just wealth.

The sea air outside dripped with humidity, and as the air cooled, mist formed along the ground, creeping up the walls like spectral fingers claiming Seabourne Estate. Lola shivered.

"How are you doing?" a voice said behind her. Lola turned to see Nix. "About being back at the house? After, you know, nearly being eaten by it."

That surprised a low laugh out of Lola. "I won't lie. I'm a little tense. Something evil is stirring, but I can't figure out what it is."

"Are you going to go back to the Belowstairs?" Nix's eyebrows raised.

Lola shook her head. "Too many people here tonight. I just want to keep an eye on things."

She wanted to add, "and keep an eye on *you*" because she was certain Nix was somehow entangled with the Seabourne ghost.

A squeal of laughter caught their attention, and both looked back to the entrance of the parlour. Guests had begun to arrive, including a large group of girls dressed like flappers. They entered the space in a cloud of feathers and perfume, giggling and clutching each other, exclaiming in high-pitch shrieks as they took in the spiritualist décor and, most of all, the speakeasy's bar.

She recognized many of them, while other elaborately dressed teens must have come in from the mainland. Most grabbed champagne flutes and hung in tight circles, gossiping while shooting glances around the room.

Boys arrived, too, decked out in suits with loosened ties, shedding their jackets as soon as they entered. Lola spotted Ethan's golden crown of hair as he raised his fists in the air.

"Come on, people, let's get hammered!" he bellowed.

Music began to boom, and one of Gael's teammates, Ross, stepped behind the bar, pouring copious shots that guests started knocking back. The energy in the room shot up to the stratosphere.

Cassidy entered the room, arm in arm with Sam Lynch. Both wore dangerously low-cut dresses with dangling strings of pearls and feather headpieces. Cassidy scanned the crowd; Lola suspected her target was Gael. Sure enough, she steered towards him, leaning in as she approached, her breasts close to spilling over her neckline.

"At least she's not trying to be obvious about it," Nix said next to her.

Lola smirked at her dry tone as Cassidy poured herself over Gael.

"You okay?" Nix's voice was far too kind.

"It would be unfair if I wasn't."

Knowing that didn't help, though; didn't mean Lola wasn't feeling hollowed out on the inside like a jack-o'-lantern. "What really bothers me, though, is how he's embraced the hyenas. I mean, hanging out with *Ethan*."

Ethan had terrorized Lola over the summer, and it was hard to stomach seeing Gael laughing with him. Gael had been the one to warn her Ethan was a psycho, and now it appeared they were tight friends.

Nix glowered. "Back when it was just the two of us, I knew it was only a matter of time before someone noticed how hot he'd gotten. And then you came." Nix gave a wise nod as she watched the scene play out in front of her, Gael being embraced by the bright, shiny people. "It's your fault, really. You came, and you noticed because obviously you have eyes, and that set everything off, like dominoes falling."

Reiko emerged from the crowd, and Nix stiffened. The demon hunter wore a black dress with thin straps; elegant but simple. Her black hair was scraped back into finger waves.

Despite her heels, Reiko moved like a predator in a crowd of prey. Her dress showed off toned arms, as well as displaying to full effect the brand at her collarbone, the mark of the Order of Hanta Cythraul.

"Can you see the mark at all?" Lola asked Nix in an undertone. Reiko usually wore high-necked shirts and had never shown off this amount of skin. Lola had only caught glimpses of her brand beforehand, but here it was on display for the world.

With her brows furled tight, Nix's gaze travelled over Reiko's body. "No idea what you're talking about."

Lola squinted at the mark. It gleamed, just like Otherworldly things did for her sometimes. Since she'd come back from being a vampire, she had another level of sight: one that allowed her to sense the Otherworld.

Reiko raised her chin, then, and caught sight of Nix. Her face remained a cold, perfect mask, but her eyes glinted with something sharper.

Nix looked mutinous, eyes shining, before she looked away. "I need a drink," she said, striding back into the party. Lola followed behind her, the blast of the music and the heat and smell of alcohol and sweaty people hitting her like a fist. She caught Nix's hand.

"Nix, just be careful," she said. "There's still something evil here."

"Yeah, yeah, the story of our life." Nix took a champagne flute and raised it in a mocking salute to Lola before taking a big sip as she danced away.

Alone, Lola perused the bar. Surrounding everything were hundreds of white flowers; it appeared almost as if the table were covered with snow. The effect was beautiful, though Lola suspected lost on the surrounding crowd.

Hidden in the foliage at the back was an expensive brand of sparkling water. Standing to the side, she sipped the water, pretending she wasn't watching Gael from the corner of her eye.

"What's going on between the two of you?"

Lola startled; she hadn't noticed Violet sidle up as she stood there.

"What do you mean?" Lola deliberately turned her back on the crowd, taking in Violet's dress, a backless ballgown in sparkling silver. With a beaded headdress over her blonde waves, she looked like a goddess next to the other girls, sophisticated next to their childish costumes. Lola couldn't help thinking how well she matched Walt with his detached elegance.

"Oh please, you so clearly can't keep your eyes off Gael."

"We're just friends."

"It doesn't bother you at all that Gael just shoved his tongue down Cassidy's throat?"

"He did not!" Lola whirled around. Gael had moved a safe distance away from Cassidy, destroying a plate of charcuterie with some of his teammates.

Violet smirked, her look saying *gotcha*. "Right. Just friends."

Lola smoothed her hand over her hair. "It's a work in progress."

"Well, FYI, Cassidy is fully into making him hers entirely. She practically has, like, a dream board on the go. And she might look sweet, but that girl is deadly when it comes to getting what she wants."

From the way Cassidy stared at Gael, Lola believed it. She couldn't help the vicious thoughts that popped into her head: *She's only with him for his looks; she wants to wear him like an accessory.* "As long as he's happy," she said faintly.

Violet snorted. "Since when do you let others stomp all over you? You know, when you first arrived in town, I thought I'd have some kind of competition."

Lola tilted her head. "Sounds like you respected me more when I was pouring a drink over your head."

"Maybe I did. You certainly were more interesting."

Lola took a sip of water. "Interesting is overrated. I'm tired of being talked about."

Violet's eyebrows arched. "What did you expect? You showed up on the island out of nowhere, started fights and found treasure in like a week."

"Does it bother you that I'm stealing your thunder?"

Violet looked amused more than anything. "I can hold my own. You're, like, far too chaotic to be any kind of threat."

"I'm just trying to live my life like everybody else," Lola said, the girl finally starting to get under her skin. "I appreciate the real talk, but what happened between Gael and I was my choice."

Violet took a long swig of her drink, whiskey fumes wafting around her. "As long as you know that."

"Violet!" A voice across the room caught their attention. Ethan, with narrowed eyes, was watching them near the pool table, gesturing for Violet to join him.

"Are you being summoned?" Lola asked archly.

Violet gave her a withering look before stalking away from her, away from Ethan, to the bar to refresh her drink. Her look was murderous enough that people jumped out of her way. From the set of his jaw, Ethan clearly did not like to be disobeyed.

Then Lola caught Walt watching Violet, too, and her smile

slipped. Walt would do best to stay away from the girl; her sharpness would cut him a thousand different ways.

Cassidy had been whispering with Sam and some of the other girls, their bobbing feathers giving the impression of a flock of exotic birds. The gaggle broke apart in giggles. One girl turned the music down as Cassidy took the centre of the floor.

She clapped her hands, her laughter filling the room like champagne bubbles. "Alright, everyone, gather up—we're going to play Spin the Bottle!"

TWENTY

Cassidy's announcement was met with groans and scattered boos.

"What are we, ten?" someone muttered, but the protests were half-hearted. Violet rolled her eyes so hard that Lola thought they might pop out of their sockets.

Stifling a laugh, Lola watched as the glittering girls took their places in a circle at the room's centre, drawing in the rest of the crowd like moths to a flame.

Nix knocked back the rest of her champagne and joined the circle, glaring in rebellion at anyone who would dare tell her she couldn't join.

Reiko's expression was guarded, but she entered the circle as well. Why she'd want to join in the teenage games, Lola could only guess. In her hands was her camera. She'd been taking photos all evening, but the brass knobs on the device gave it away as another one of her magical instruments, courtesy of the HC. Lola's hands itched to grab it, to take it apart and see what Reiko and the Order were up to.

Gael wiped his hands and avoided the circle until one of Cassidy's friends dragged him in. He followed, laughing—a little too easily, in Lola's opinion.

Even Walt took his place, face devoid of emotion. She wondered if he was used to this crowd's silly games or understood it was easier to go with the flow than stand out.

The crowd hushed in anticipation, the only sound from the strings of the gothic rock song playing over the speakers. As the scent of incense grew heavier, Lola fought off a moment of nausea.

She glanced up to catch Ethan's look burning into her.

"What, you're too good for us? I thought the French were all about kissing."

The entirety of the party turned their attention to Lola. Though her heart pounded at the confrontation, she feigned disinterest. "Yet ironically, we avoid the frogs."

A chorus of "oohs" and laughter sounded, and Ethan's face hardened. "I think you're scared."

"I think you're boring," Lola retorted.

Violet glared at Lola as though this was her fault and knocked back her drink before grabbing Ethan's hand and entering the circle. "If Lola doesn't want to be kissed, she doesn't get kissed. Now, who's going to get this thing started?" Without a word, she handed her empty glass to the boy next to her and waved him away. He immediately scampered off to fetch her a new one.

"Me!" Cassidy announced. A table had been placed at the centre of the circle. Pausing for dramatic effect, she placed an empty gin bottle down and gave it a half-hearted spin. The bottle wobbled and came to a stop.

It pointed in the general direction of her girlfriends, all of whom dove out of the way with screeches of laughter. The only person left in the general vicinity was Gael, blinking helplessly.

"Well, hello there." Cassidy approached him like a wolf stalking a lamb, smoothing her hands up his chest to his shoulders. She pressed against him as she stood on tiptoe and took his mouth with her reddened lips, kissing him thoroughly.

Lola looked away, ignoring the sharp twist in her chest. It

didn't matter that seeing him kiss Cassidy felt like being gutted with a fishing hook; it had been her choice.

After a stunned moment, Gael's hands wrapped around Cassidy and everyone started shouting.

Finally, Cassidy rocked back on her heels, holding on to Gael as though she would topple over. Gael's mouth was smeared red, his face flushed, and he seemed embarrassed by the amount of cheering.

"Your turn," Cassidy purred.

Gael stumbled into the circle, and Lola found herself hoping the effect was from overindulging in gin, not Cassidy. He spun the bottle, landing on a girl from Lola's English class. The reaction was more subdued, and though Gael gave her a chaste peck on the cheek, it still earned her a glare from Cassidy.

And so it continued. Lola quickly tired of the game. She caught Reiko surreptitiously capturing moments on camera, and Lola had half a mind to try to catch what she was doing, knowing it would be impossible to sneak up on her.

Then, the crowd fell silent. It was Violet's turn to spin, and she stalked into the centre of the circle. She paused, aware all eyes were on her, before giving the bottle a sharp spin. The bottle fell directly on Walt.

A few hushed giggles sounded as Violet slowly raised her eyes to his. Lola wondered if she would refuse to kiss him. From the way Walt flushed, she suspected he believed the same thing. But he raised his chin and held her gaze like a dare.

She paced towards him, bringing her hands up his neck and kissing him full on the mouth.

After a beat, a few people let out whistles. Then her eyes closed, and Violet softened the kiss. Walt shifted forward and took her waist in his arms, kissing her deeply. Lola wondered if they remembered what had happened when they were in the Maze of Desire at the carnival. Walt and Violet had been dancing around each other ever since.

The whistling faded away, and Lola heard someone mutter, "Oh shit." Because the kiss was hot.

And Ethan looked ready to explode with rage.

After a breathless moment, they broke apart. Walt appeared stricken, while Violet's eyes burned into his. Somebody cleared their throat while a few others let out nervous titters.

Violet seemingly became aware that everyone was staring at her and, for once, didn't appreciate the audience. She spun, glaring at anyone who met her gaze, and left the circle.

Walt blinked, seeming to realize he still had a part to play. Almost robotically, he spun the bottle, and Lola gasped when she saw it landed on Reiko.

With her ferocious glare, it didn't seem certain whether she was going to kiss Walt or stab him in the heart. Her intriguing camera was nowhere to be seen, and her jaw was a tense line as she angled her face up and brushed her lips over the side of Walt's mouth. Walt spun and left the circle, his gaze flicking to Violet as though he couldn't help himself.

On her own in the middle of the circle, Reiko looked unsure of herself for the first time since Lola had met her. She seemed out of her element, eyes wide like she couldn't quite figure out how she had gotten there. The hard rock song playing in a disturbing minor key built up to a thundering crescendo as she spun, the bottle taking extra long to finally wobble to a stop.

On Nix.

Reiko slowly met her gaze. Nix's face was blank, but she stepped into the circle as though in a trance.

For once, nobody laughed or cheered as the two girls met, arms going to each other's waists.

Reiko tilted her head, dark eyes searching, asking a question that hung unspoken between them. Nix's cheeks flushed, her lips parting as if to answer—but instead, she nodded, a quiet surrender.

Their lips met, and Nix's and Reiko's arms wrapped tighter

around each other. Reiko pressed Nix into her at the small of her back, and Nix's lips turned up in a tiny smile even as she kissed Reiko back.

For one moment, not a single person moved.

Then, the room exploded.

The electric lights flickered, then flared with a blinding flash and went out, while the music cut out with a buzz like a dying wasp. People shrieked as the room darkened, now lit only by the candlelight on the tables.

The crowd swarmed from the circle as though seeking shelter. Reiko had thrust Nix behind her as if to protect her, her hunting knife in hand, though Lola was mystified where Reiko stored her weaponry beneath her skin-tight dress.

Gael spun, searching for Lola. She only knew because she was looking for him too. Their eyes locked and she nodded, confirming she was okay.

After the initial panic, shrill giggles sounded. "That was one hell of a kiss!" someone cried to more laughter.

"It's probably just a power surge," Walt said. He picked up a candelabra, looking like a character in an old-school horror movie. "I'll see if anything else is affected."

In the silence and the flickering darkness, the mood shifted from party games to something wilder. Tension crackled beneath the surface of the crowd, a sense of something unspoken and potent waiting to be unleashed. Whispers fluttered through the crowd, delicate and poisonous, much of it directed at Reiko and Nix. The incense mingled with the tang of sweat in the air into something darker, heightening the jittery electricity that surrounded them.

Lola's pulse raced as she tried to calm down, though every one of her senses told her to be on guard. Something Otherworldly hovered around them.

"I think it was a ghost," a girl said. The whispered words

caught on the edges of conversations until everyone was repeating them.

"You guys are, like, so gullible," Violet said. "It's one of the Seabourne's little jokes they like to play. I can't believe you fell for that."

"No, this house is haunted," a boy said. He was standing near the food, where most of the boys had gravitated again. "My dad told me he's seen it. A woman all in white."

A girl, one of Cassidy's giggling friends, stepped to the centre of the floor. Lola didn't have any classes with her but knew her name was Ember. Her long black hair was tucked under an elaborate beaded headband, and she wore a burgundy kimono. Loose sleeves swirled around her dramatically as she held her hands up.

"I know about this stuff," she proclaimed, dark eyes burning in the candlelight. "My stepmom's a psychic." She lowered her voice now that she had everyone's attention. "There is some serious dark energy in this room. I think a spirit is close. We might be able to contact it."

"What, with the crystal ball?" someone called.

Ember scowled. "I'm serious. Let's have a séance. It's the perfect place for it." She gave a dramatic sweeping gesture over the long table set with the tools of the occult. She ran her fingers over the tarot cards, then knocked sharply on the table, causing several people to start. "If we want to know who's here," she said, her whispery voice barely audible, "all we have to do is ask."

TWENTY-ONE

Nervousness and curiosity rippled through the room like an electric current, the gathered crowd caught between intrigue and unease. Some partygoers flocked to the table at once, claiming seats, while others lingered at the edges. The candlelight flickered over the embroidered cloth, casting shifting shadows that seemed almost alive—and eager.

Nix broke away from Reiko's embrace, hurrying to sit stiffly at the table. Her copper hair caught the light as she fixed her gaze downward, her fingers running over the intricate stitched patterns.

Left behind, Reiko watched her, tension in every line of her body. Her knife had disappeared, replaced by the camera that clicked as she snapped photo after photo. Lola half-expected her to back away from the séance, but instead, the demon hunter took a seat directly across from Nix, her eyes riveted to the girl in a tuxedo. Nix didn't seem to notice.

Ember's imperious voice cut through the murmurs. "Everyone needs to join for this to work." Her words carried a challenge, her amber eyes sweeping the room. The last of the stragglers squished in, chairs creaking as they sat hesitantly, leaving only Lola hovering near the windows.

Violet sighed dramatically. "Are you against *all* fun? You heard the girl. Either sit down or get out and stop sucking the energy from the party."

Lola froze. Memories of another summoning gone horribly clawed at her mind. It had started an awful lot like this: A careless circle of thrill-seekers had called forth something far worse than a spirit. She could still hear the gurgled screams of those who had prayed to contact the spirits of their departed loved ones. Jacquotte had laughed until she cried.

Lola let her eyes fall shut. So had she. This *was* what she'd used to consider fun.

Cassidy giggled then. The girl perched on Gael's lap, whispering in his ear, flushed from alcohol and the excitement. Her sidelong gaze made Lola sure she was whispering about her. Even worse, Gael smiled.

Taking a steadying breath, Lola forced herself to the table, glaring at Violet. It seemed unlikely that Ember, or her fraudster stepmom, would have the power to conjure a demon. Even so, it felt like it would be a betrayal to walk away from a helpless group of drunk teenagers who had no idea what they might be getting into.

She slid into the seat beside Nix, nudging her with an elbow. Nix stirred but didn't look up, her head drooping. Perhaps it was only the champagne.

"Everyone take the person's hand next to you to complete the circle." Ember's voice lowered, taking on a theatrical flair. "We must be as one in our intent."

Skeptical groans mingled with nervous giggles, but everyone obeyed, linking hands atop the table. Nix's palm was clammy, and the girl on Lola's other side gripped tightly, eyes glued to Ember.

"Close your eyes." Ember's voice dropped to a dramatic whisper.

"This is bullshit," someone whispered, earning a sharp "Shh!" from Sam.

"I saw a documentary on it," she said. "It's, like, totally real."

They had no idea how real. Lola watched over them like a worried mother hen.

Ember let out a groaning chant to more giggles. Once those had died down, Ember intoned her plea. "Oh, spirits, we call on you to make your presence known. Be with us, spirits. Join us in peace and lend us your wisdom."

Her words echoed as the room was plunged into unnatural silence. Pressure built until Lola thought her ears would pop.

A sudden spark of electricity shot from Nix's palm into hers, sharp and cold like a needle of ice.

Around the table, everyone's eyes snapped open, with cries of pain or shock. The candles lining the tables flared, their flames stretching up to the ceiling, casting warped shadows that surrounded them.

Lola had had enough of this. She tried to break the circle, to let go of Nix, but their hands seemed to be glued together. She tried to speak, but the pressure held her back.

"You are with us, spirits!" Ember's voice trembled. "We wish to hear your story! Come to us and make yourself known."

A gasp rippled through the room as a faint light appeared in the far corner, a whirl of pale white that hovered and flickered like a will-o'-the-wisp. It hovered, coalescing into the shape of a woman, her eyes burning blackly from her face. She held a phantom candle aloft, crimson streaking from her hands and dripping to the floor.

An overwhelming scent of earth and rot permeated the room, suffocating. People gagged, choking on it, but no one could cover their faces to shield themselves. They were frozen spectators to the show.

The figure glided to the table's centre, passing through several people in her unearthly movements. Her mouth slowly opened, impossibly wide, revealing a gaping black void beyond. Her face hinged open as if consuming itself in a soundless scream.

The blackness expanded and her form broke apart into a thousand glowing particles, swirling in a storm of light and shadow before vanishing.

Ember's scream shattered the spell. Hands broke apart as chairs scraped and tumbled, people scrambling to get away from the table. Chaos erupted in the room.

The lights came back on, and the music started up, the heavy beat of the rock music pounding discordantly. Someone turned it down as the guests at the party stared at each other, eyes wide with disbelief.

"Your faces!" Ethan's laugh rang out, doubling him over. "That was epic!"

Violet smirked, her expression cutting. "Did nobody notice that Walt left right before the séance? Obviously to set the whole thing up. Right, Ember?"

Ember looked like she might throw up. As everyone turned on her, she stepped back and shook her head wildly. "I didn't do that, I swear!"

Violet spun on her heel like a detective uncovering a mystery. "You guys. We just got pranked so bad."

Someone started to giggle, then someone else. It caught on like wildfire, euphoria and relief spreading through the crowd. But Lola's focus was elsewhere. Nix had slumped forward, her face hitting the table with a dull thud.

"Nix!" Lola grabbed her, panic tightening her voice. "What's wrong?" She tugged at her shoulders; her tiny friend seemed to weigh a thousand pounds.

Reiko appeared at her side, crouching opposite Lola. "Is she okay?"

Lola glared. "What's it to you?"

Reiko laid a hand on Nix's arm, giving her a gentle shake. "A massive explosion of Otherworldly energy just went off like a bomb, and it's concentrated around Nix."

"How do you know?" Lola's heart squeezed. Nix should have never come here tonight.

"The readings are off the charts." Surreptitiously, Reiko took out her bizarre compass, the needle spinning wildly.

"I don't understand what this means," Lola said, bewildered by the array of knobs on the device.

"Something came through from the Otherworld. This wasn't just a prank." Her mouth was set in a grim line.

Nix stirred, groaning as she raised her head. A red mark on her forehead showed where her face had hit the surface. "What happened?" she asked, her voice hoarse, as her eyelids fluttered open. She found herself face-to-face with Reiko.

Lola expected Nix to jerk away, but instead, she gave a puzzled frown.

"What are you doing here?" Nix asked.

Reiko took one of Nix's hands gently. "I'm here for the party, don't you remember? You fainted and hit your head."

Nix glanced warily around the crowd, then snatched her hands out of Reiko's grasp. The hunter sat back on her heels, a flicker of hurt running across her face.

The doors to the games room opened to a smiling Walt. "I got the power back on," he said.

He was met with an uproarious cheer. Everyone jostled him, cheerfully telling him he'd scared the crap out of them.

"Epic, man!"

"I've never seen anything like it!"

Walt endured the ribbing with an uneasy smile but quickly made for Lola and Nix. "What the hell happened? I went downstairs to see that only the power to the parlour had gone out. I just had to flip the switch in the fuse box to turn it back on."

"Walt, we all saw an apparition of a bleeding white woman. Everyone thinks it was a prank."

Walt's face paled. "There are no projectors in here."

"That's what I'm trying to tell you," Reiko said. "This was bona fide."

Walt frowned at her. "Why are you here?"

"I'm trying to help you, you idiots. There's paranormal activity in this house."

The three of them stared at Reiko.

"Obviously," Nix said. "Thanks for catching us up."

"There's a ghost in the servant's quarters," Lola explained.

Reiko frowned. "Are you sure? I have definite readings of demons inside this house."

"Trust me on this one. It's a ghost."

Nix's face had lost all colour. "I don't want to be here anymore." She tried to get up but seemed barely able to support herself on shaky legs.

"Right," Lola said, getting an arm around her. "Let's get you home."

Walt went to prop up Nix's other side, but she spun on him. "Don't you touch me," she said, her teeth bared in an animal scowl.

"Sorry." Walt jumped back, his hands up. "I just wanted to help."

"You've done enough," Nix practically spat at him, eyes burning.

"Fine." Walt's mouth turned down and his shoulders slumped as he backed away, then turned towards the stereo equipment.

Violet was listening to their conversation, her gaze following Walt. Behind her, out of her line of vision, Ethan stared at her, his eyes full of rage.

Gael joined them, brows furrowed. "What's going on?"

"Nix isn't feeling well," Lola said. The girl was nearly asleep on Lola's shoulder, but she gave a sleepy wave to Gael. "I'm going to take her home."

"Should I come with you?"

Lola pondered. She could probably handle getting Nix downstairs, and a line of taxis waited down the road to take guests home in the later hours. "I think you should stay here," she said and lowered her voice. "Ethan looks like he has it out for Walt, and I think he needs someone watching his back." She paused, wanting to say a million things to him but not finding the right words. "Be safe."

He nodded, complicated emotion swirling in his warm brown eyes. "You too."

Lola began to move the stumbling Nix away from the séance table. Most people thought she was drunk and laughed, holding their drinks up in salute.

As they passed the bar table, Lola noticed something that made her skin crawl. Every one of the hundreds of flowers that had been set on the table had wilted, shrivelled in on themselves into husks. She glanced around the room.

All the flowers were dead, and nobody else seemed to notice.

Twenty-Two

"Nix!" Lola called out as she passed her in the hallway.

Nix kept walking, her pace steady, eyes fixed ahead as if Lola didn't exist.

Frowning, Lola quickened her steps, falling into stride behind her. It was Monday, and they hadn't spoken since the disastrous Harvest Ball.

"How are you doing?" Lola tried to keep her voice light despite her worry.

Nix turned her head, taking Lola in, but her expression remained flat. "I'm fine."

"But you haven't..." Lola faltered. Nix had ignored all her texts over the weekend. When she went to the lighthouse, Nix's mother simply said she was asleep—that she'd slept through most of the day. "I was just worried after everything that happened."

"I just slipped," Nix said, her hand brushing the swollen bump on her forehead. "It's embarrassing, and I'd rather not go over it. Besides, I feel totally fine today."

Lola narrowed her eyes, inspecting her friend. Nix did look okay; her cheeks were in high colour and her blue eyes were sparkling. "Well, I'm glad you've recovered. Things got scary at the Seabourne Estate."

Nix's face twisted into a smirk. "I can't believe everyone fell for that trick Walt played."

Lola blinked. "Nix, it wasn't a trick. There was actually a ghost in the room."

Nix laughed scornfully. "You don't actually believe that, do you? It was so clearly a prank. I think your panic attack the other day has gotten to you."

"No, Nix, it was all real." Lola's voice dropped, urgent. "The Seabourne Estate is haunted. Recovered vampire here, with new visions of supernatural things, remember? I think I get to call it when I see the Otherworld."

Nix blinked, and her focus sharpened on Lola as though just seeing her for the first time. "Right. I mean, okay, it just doesn't seem like it should be such a big deal."

Stung, Lola fumbled with her bag to cover her reaction, and she stopped in front of her locker. "Wait, I wanted to show you something."

"Wanted to show us what?" Gael's voice interrupted, and he leaned against the lockers, joining them with an easy grin. His energy seemed as bright as ever. "Hey, pint, how you feeling?" He put an arm around Nix, who gave him a shove—a return to normalcy, at least for her.

Lola gave him a small smile, but it faded when she caught a glimpse of Cassidy hovering behind him. Of course, she was the reason Gael was in such good spirits. Biting back a wave of bitterness, Lola busied herself with her bag again.

"So? What is it?" Gael asked.

"It's kinda something I can't share with everyone," Lola said pointedly.

Gael caught on quickly and turned to Cassidy. "I'll catch up with you, okay?"

Cassidy's face flashed with outrage, but she flounced off, leaving them alone. Lola tried not to feel vindicated—but failed. Gael might have moved on from her, but he still cared about his friends. And their Otherworldly secrets.

She pulled out the stack of yellowed letters.

"I finished translating the papers."

"The ones from the Belowstairs?" Gael's eyes lit up. "When everything went, you know." Gael wiggled his fingers in mock spooky gesture.

"Exactly." Lola's lips quirked. "The letters were from Irene Seabourne, Walt's ancestor, sent to Alice."

"The one who stole the jewelry?" Gael asked. Nix was silent, her eyes burning into the papers.

"Maybe not," Lola said. "It's clear Alice treasured these letters. They were wrapped in silk, tucked away in a secret place. And I think Irene was in love with Alice."

"Secret love notes?" Gael's grin widened. "This gets better and better."

Nix's voice was tight. "How could you possibly know that?"

"She gave her gifts, like books, that were precious at the time. And they arranged secret meetings. It feels...intimate."

Gael leaned in. "Forbidden love affair? How steamy."

"What's steamy?" Walt appeared, joining them.

"Nothing from this century," Lola said. "How was the fallout from the party, Walt?"

"It was fine. No more horrifying incidents."

"Unless you forgot about when Cayan took his pants off and started doing the worm on the floor." Gael started laughing.

"That was horrifying, you're right." Walt caught sight of the yellowed papers in Lola's hands. "Working on the Belowstairs mystery?"

"We think Irene Seabourne was in love with her maid," Lola said.

Walt raised an eyebrow. "How nonconformist. I bet the family loved that."

"I can't tell if Alice reciprocated the feelings or not."

"Why not?" Nix finally looked at Lola, her look intense.

"I haven't finished her entire diary, but mostly it talks about how she was jealous of Irene."

"So that points to Alice stealing the jewels and running off," Gael said.

"God, why can't you all just leave it alone?" Nix said, her voice snapping like a whip. "I don't want to hear about any of this."

"I think there's more to it," Lola said. "If Irene loved her, maybe she gave her the jewels so she could start a new life."

"But why not run away together?" Walt asked. "Irene had the means, though it would be unconventional."

"Forget unconventional; a lesbian relationship in that era was illegal. They would run into all sorts of problems and would never be able to live out in the open. Irene might be cut off from her family's fortune if she did anything like that, so maybe she just tried to give Alice her best shot."

"But, if that were true, why wouldn't Irene have said something? Why let the girl she loved have her name dragged through the mud?"

"What would you know of it, Seabourne?" Nix scowled at Walt, who faltered under the ferocity of her look. "Like your family has ever been noble? Maybe Irene was happy to let someone else take the blame." Her face darkened in anger.

Not just anger, Lola realized. Nix wasn't annoyed with Walt. Her face twisted in fury; she looked like she wanted to kill him.

Walt backed away in alarm. "I didn't mean anything by it."

"No. People like you never do." Nix's voice was low and harsh. "You take and you judge and you destroy and you never look back."

The fluorescent lights lining the ceiling buzzed and flickered. A strange tension filled the air, crackling like static, and students milling in the hallways glanced up in alarm.

Lola froze. A sound she knew too well reached her ears—scratching, faint but insistent, like nails against metal. She whipped around. "Does anyone hear that?"

"Hear what?" Gael asked.

The scratching grew louder, joined by muffled sobbing. Lola's heart raced. "It's coming from the locker." The world telescoped in around her as though she was the one trapped. Behind the locker, behind the brick wall, desperate to be released. She was drawing a crowd but didn't care. Pressure built up inside her skull. "Let her out!"

"Lola, wait," Walt said, grabbing her arm. "Maybe it should be left alone."

"You would think something like that," Nix said, her voice venomous. "Get out of the way." She shoved Walt aside and wrenched the locker open. They all peered inside. Lola held her breath.

Inside was nothing but some discarded snack wrappers and an old fleece jacket. A mirror hung crookedly to the door.

"It's empty." Gael gave her hand a squeeze, and Lola looked down. Somehow, she had grabbed his hand in her panic. She didn't remember doing that.

She released Gael's hand with a gasp. "Sorry, I have no idea what just happened."

"Was it a vision?"

"Maybe? I felt like I was trapped, like I was in the alcove."

"You mean the locker."

"Yes. No. I mean..." Lola thrust her hands into her hair and tugged, looking into the un-Otherworldly locker. "I don't know what I mean."

"Your nose, Lola," Walt said. "You're bleeding again."

"*Merde.*" This time, at least, Lola was prepared and grabbed a tissue of her own to dab at her nose. She angled the locker door to better see her nosebleed. As the reflection caught Nix's face standing behind her, she froze.

Nix was scowling, a look of hatred on her face. And her eyes... they weren't blue anymore. They were brown.

"Nix?" Lola's voice wavered.

Nix blinked, her eyes blue again. "What?"

"Um..." Lola grabbed her hand. "Come with me."

"What are you doing?" Nix protested, but Lola didn't stop until they were in the bathroom.

"Something strange is going on and we need to figure it out."

"You're the only strange thing around here," Nix muttered as Lola checked under all the stall doors to ensure they were alone. "Are you completely stunned?"

"Nix, something is wrong. Why were you attacking Walt?"

"I wasn't attacking him." Nix rolled her eyes. "He's just so condescending. He has everything he could ever want because of who his father is and his money. I hate..." Her voice had built up until she was nearly shouting, but she cut herself off. "I hate people like that. Everything is so easy for them."

Lola watched Nix's face intently. "You were going to say that you hated *him*, weren't you? That you hated Walt."

"What? No, I don't hate Walt." Nix hesitated over the words.

Lola sighed and turned to the mirror, grimacing at the blood still streaking her face. Nix stared at her intently in the mirror. "Who is Walt to you?" Lola asked suddenly.

"My enemy," Nix responded without thinking, and the lights above them flickered. That's when Lola saw a flash of it; under the flickering lights, Nix's reflection changed. Her eyes darkened to brown and her cheeks thinned. It was like looking at a picture of her with deliberate differences.

The signs of a spectral hitchhiker.

Nix had been possessed by the Seabourne ghost.

"Alice?" Lola asked in a low whisper. Nix took a step back, then another, eyes widening.

"Wait—"

As Lola called out, Nix spun and fled from the washroom. Lola dashed after her to see her figure fleeing down the hallway, her copper curls trailing out behind her. She was about to run after her when a hand caught her wrist, pulling her backwards.

"What the hell is going on?"

TWENTY-THREE

Lola spun around, surprised to find Reiko gripping her arm, her face fierce. The dark slashes of Reiko's eyebrows pulled together in a way that made Lola glad she wasn't a vampire anymore. Demon strength or not, she wouldn't want to face this girl in a fight.

"Only the worst possible scenario," Lola muttered, shaking Reiko off. "Nix is possessed by a ghost."

Reiko's expression faltered, shock flickering across her face. "Are you sure?"

Lola rubbed her hands over her face. "Getting more sure by the minute," she snapped. "I've seen this before, and trust me, it doesn't end well. So, what exactly are you doing here? Are you here to help or hurt her again?"

Reiko dropped her gaze to the ground, her voice softer. "I never meant to hurt her."

"Well, you did. So, I'll ask again—why are you here? You're a demon hunter with some secret society backing you, right? Surprise me. Show me something helpful."

Reiko stood in silence, long enough for Lola to consider walking away. But then, Reiko raised her hand slightly as if calming Lola or maybe herself. "Okay. Maybe...we call a cease-fire. Share what we know. Together, we might figure something out."

Lola crossed her arms, tension stiffening her shoulders, but after a moment, she nodded. "I'm listening."

"I have some images from the night of the séance," Reiko said, pulling her camera from her bag. "It might help us understand what's happening."

Lola cocked an eyebrow. "Not exactly Polaroids, I'm guessing?"

Reiko gave her an arch look but handled the device with care. "It's a hybrid of digital technology and pressurized magic. It captures traces of Otherworldly activity." She brought up a few photos on the screen.

Despite herself, Lola leaned in, intrigued. "I thought your other gadget already detected Otherworldly stuff."

Reiko sighed. "It detects the presence and type of activity. This camera shows us what's invisible to mortal senses."

Lola's gaze flicked to the faintly glowing mark on Reiko's collar. "Like your brand?"

Reiko's face went still. "Like that, yes."

"You didn't bother covering it up the other night."

"Mortals can't see it." Reiko shot back, her narrowed look meeting Lola's unflinching stare.

"Bet your camera could, though."

Reiko ignored the jab. "I wasn't exactly taking selfies."

Lola tilted her head, weighing Reiko's words. Her instincts screamed fight-or-flight, but she stayed put. "And did you take pictures of me?"

"Of course," Reiko replied coolly. "If you're not connected to the Otherworld, I'll eat this camera."

"So, you're a spy for your bosses?"

Reiko exhaled sharply. "I'm trying to help. Are you ever going to trust me?"

Lola leaned in. "I don't know what you or your Order wants. And until I do, there won't be any trust between us."

They locked eyes, the tension thickening between them until Reiko's gaze faltered, and she looked away first.

"Fine," Reiko muttered, scrolling through her photos. "Here's one of Nix from that night." She showed a photo of Nix laughing with another girl. "Everything seems normal." She flicked through more photos—mostly of Nix at the party.

Lola raised an eyebrow. "A lot of pictures of Nix. Thought she was a demon?"

Reiko flushed, her cheeks blotchy red. "No. Not at first. I mean, I didn't think...that's not the point." She flipped ahead. "This was taken right after the séance."

The photo showed kids fleeing the table, faces frozen in terror. In the centre, Nix lay slumped, her head on the table, with Lola leaning over her, trying to wake her. Above Nix's head was a swirl of white mist, eerily bright.

Lola squinted at the screen. "It looks like... a shape."

Reiko nodded. "I enhanced the image." She showed the next frame, where the white form sharpened. It wasn't just mist—it was a face, faint but unmistakable.

Lola's heart dropped. The mist was sharper now, its features unmistakably human—a face eerily similar to Nix's. "*Merde.*"

"Oh my gosh, are those party photos?" a sickeningly sweet voice interrupted.

Cassidy bounced up beside Reiko, giving Lola a cold look before grabbing the camera. "Any cute ones of me?"

Her posse crowded behind her. Violet hung at the back, uncharacteristically quiet.

Reiko tensed but didn't move to stop her. Attacking a student would blow her cover, after all. "Be careful with that" was all she said.

"These are so blurry," Cassidy said, wrinkling her nose. "You need a better app." She scrolled through the pictures, and the girls behind her giggled. "This one's adorable! Look at us!"

Lola gritted her teeth as Cassidy showed a picture of herself and Gael dancing. Her patience wore thin, and she fought the urge to snatch the camera back.

"Oh my God, is that Walt and Violet?" one of the girls exclaimed.

Everyone crowded in. Reiko had caught a tender moment between Walt and Violet, their kiss illuminated by the candlelight. Walt cradled her face, and Violet's eyes burned with intensity. The photo captured a perfect moment—but Lola's stomach churned.

"Seriously, Vi, I don't even know how you kissed that freak," Sam said.

Cassidy tilted her head. "That kiss was totally iconic, though." She waved at someone. "Gael! Come see this!"

Lola's breath caught as Gael approached, followed by Walt and Nix. Gael's look flickered over the crowd as though trying to find an escape, while Walt's gaze locked on Violet's.

"Hey, can I send this photo to myself?" Cassidy pressed several buttons, and the camera began to whirl and blink.

"No, don't do that!" Reiko snatched it out of the girl's hands.

Cassidy stared at her like she'd grown two heads. "Oh my God, like fine. I wasn't doing anything."

"What are you doing with *her*?" Nix demanded, pointing at Reiko.

"Nix, it's not what you think—Reiko can help."

"Oh, she can?" Nix's voice dripped with venom. She snatched the camera from Reiko's hands. "Photos of people kissing. How very invasive."

The camera began to glow white, emitting strange pops and clicks.

"What is this?" Nix's eyes widened.

Reiko grabbed the camera, pressing buttons frantically. "It's malfunctioning."

With a final flash of light, the viewfinder went dark.

"Did it just... die?" Lola asked.

"I don't know," Reiko said, worry flashing in her eyes. "That wasn't supposed to happen."

Before Lola could respond, her phone buzzed. Then, one by one, everyone's phones began to ring or vibrate.

Lola glanced at her phone, stunned. Reiko seemed to have somehow sent out the photo of Walt and Violet—but Reiko's horrified expression told her it wasn't intentional. The lights above them flickered again.

"I didn't do it," Reiko whispered. "This camera can't send photos."

Gasps and murmurs spread as students glanced at their phones, and all eyes turned to Walt and Violet. They'd moved towards each other, almost as if they didn't know it was happening.

Nix's expression twisted with fury. "Get away from him!" she screamed, pointing at Violet. But her voice sounded strange, like someone—or something—was speaking through her. She turned an accusing finger on Walt. "Why can't you just leave people alone?" Her voice raised into an unholy screech.

The sound erupted through the school, building into a deafening, unearthly wail.

The sound pressed against Lola's skull, unbearable, until—it released with a silent boom.

Every lightbulb above them exploded.

TWENTY-FOUR

People screamed, throwing their hands up for protection. Lola was pressed against the lockers, Gael protecting her with his body as shattered glass whistled through the air.

When it was over, Lola brushed her hair back from her face, slowly looking up at Gael's worried face hovering above hers.

"You okay?" he whispered.

She nodded, hesitant. "You?"

"Just a few scratches."

With a trembling hand, Lola turned him to see that his arm had been sliced by some flying glass, blood welling in the cut. Her fingers tightened on him. "Gael!"

Up and down the hallway, students gasped and cried, inspecting their wounds as blood dripped from their arms and faces. Teachers darted into the hallways, yelling out panicked directions.

Cassidy was brushing glass out of her ponytail, glaring murder at Lola.

And in the middle of the carnage, Nix stood untouched, her expression blank but her eyes burning darkly at Walt and Violet.

Walt had thrown his arms out to protect Violet when the glass exploded and was now bleeding in several places.

"What the hell is this?" Ethan stormed down the hallway, his gaze riveted to Violet; a trickle of blood ran down his cheek, his phone brandished in his hand.

Violet retreated instinctively towards Walt. Her confidence seemed as shattered as the glass on the floor; she cringed away from Ethan as he stopped only inches from her face.

"What is this?" He shoved his phone under her nose. The image of her and Walt glared on the screen. "What are you doing with this loser?"

"Ethan, he was just protecting me from the glass." Violet's voice was strained, the words tumbling out. "And that kiss was part of a game. You were there."

"This doesn't look like a game, you bitch." His words cut like a dagger, low and mean.

Lola stiffened at the sharp edge of his tone; one she knew all too well—an undertone of violence there. Beau would speak to her like that, make everything her fault, make her cringe and apologize for his moods, his temper, and all his imperfections.

"And it doesn't look like you're playing now." Ethan's hand shot out to grab Violet's arm, but Walt stepped forward, shoving him back.

"Back off," Walt said, his voice steady despite the storm brewing between them.

Lola could barely breathe. Reserved, unassuming Walt, going toe-to-toe with Ethan? His eyes blazed as he met Ethan's furious gaze.

"Freak." Ethan shoved Walt back, his lips curling. "You think you're one of us? Nobody's ever liked you; nobody ever will."

"At least I don't have to hurt people to feel important." Walt's voice was low and even.

Ethan's fists curled. Without warning, he lashed out, his fist slamming into Walt's face. The force of the blow sent Walt into the lockers with a sickening crack.

"You mean like that?" Ethan loomed over Walt, triumph gleaming in his eyes before spitting on the ground.

"What the hell is wrong with you?" Lola shoved her way forward, planting herself between Ethan and Walt, as the others stared on in shock. Ethan's fist clenched as though he wanted to punch her, too, but she stood her ground until low murmurs began to sound from the crowd gathering around them.

Ethan sneered. "Whatever. You aren't even worth my time."

Grabbing Violet's wrist, he jerked her towards him. She seemed in shock, slipping on the broken glass as she tried to pry herself away from his grip. Her dishevelled blonde hair framed her tear-streaked face as she glanced back at Walt before disappearing down the hallway in Ethan's grasp.

"Hey, man, are you okay?" Gael crouched beside Walt.

"I..." Walt blinked, his focus slipping. He pressed a hand to his temple, looking nauseous.

"Wow, he really got you." Gael examined the swelling around Walt's eye. "You need ice—and probably a nurse."

"I'm fine." But his muttered assurances and attempts to brush Gael off were unconvincing, as his face went ashen when he stood.

"Sure you are, buddy." Gael exchanged a glance with Lola. "I'll take him to the nurse, but he'll be okay. You good?" He nodded to Nix as he turned to go.

The girl still stood transfixed, her expression unreadable.

"He'll never be okay." Her voice suddenly cut through the tense air, hoarse and chilling. Her eyes burned dark as though lit from within by some unnatural force as she pointed at Walt's receding form. "He'll always be haunted by what he did."

"Nix?" Reiko asked, reaching out to gently take Nix's arm. "What's wrong?"

Nix spun at her voice. Her eyes were blue but clouded with confusion as she met Reiko's gaze. "We can't! This is wrong, don't you see? They'll never understand!" Her words spilled out in a rush before she pulled out of Reiko's hold and bolted, her boots skidding on the glass.

Reiko stared after her in stunned silence.

"Shit, I messed up," she said.

"Do you mean with Nix, or the camera, or coming to the island?" Lola wasn't in the mood to comfort the demon hunter.

Reiko's pale face betrayed her guilt—likely all three.

"Can the camera be fixed?" Lola pressed.

"Screw the camera," Reiko said. "Can Nix be fixed?"

Lola studied her. "What is she to you?"

Reiko stiffened, her expression pained. "She can't be anything to me," she said. "Members of the Order—we don't get involved. Especially not with people under investigation."

"You're investigating Nix?" Lola's hands clenched. "For what?"

Reiko's look was pained. "She's possessed by a ghost; you admitted it."

"That's not her fault. She has nothing to do with the Otherworld."

"You have no idea how much I wished that was true, Lola. You have no idea." Reiko let out a broken laugh. "But she's always read as Other. Always."

TWENTY-FIVE

Lola's breath caught in her throat. "You must be joking." No way Nix was Other; she'd stake her mortal life on it.

"That's what my readings tell me." Reiko sagged against the wall, her shoulders hunched.

Lola stared at her, the silence thick between them. Finally, she huffed out a breath of disbelief. "I need to find Nix."

"Will you tell me if you do?"

Lola gave her a long stare of appraisal. "We'll see" was all she said before walking away. Very unlikely. Reiko was as untrustworthy as the Order she represented. If they believed Nix was Other, then the entire Order of Hanta Cythraul was working with broken tools.

But Nix *was* possessed by a ghost—probably Alice McCullough's. The shattered glass crunching under her feet was proof enough. A possession of this strength was almost unheard of, especially one so far from the spirit's place of death. Blood ties, maybe?

It was unusual for a spirit to be able to possess a body outside its place of haunting, especially with the kind of power the Seabourne ghost just displayed. Lola shivered. Typical possessions were passive. The spirit was called a *hitchhiker*: It resided in the host body and rarely made its presence known.

But Alice wasn't hitching; she was *hijacking*. She was taking over. If she stayed within Nix's body long enough, she could overpower her completely, leaving Nix's spirit trapped inside without any will of her own.

Most forsaken spirits that didn't pass over immediately after death were focused on a single goal. But what was Alice after? What did she need Nix for?

She tried to text Nix, her fingers clumsy with urgency, then spotted Walt slouching down the hall towards her, an ice pack pressed to his swollen face. Waving to catch his attention, she stepped carefully over broken glass to meet him.

"How are you holding up?" Lola winced at his bruises.

"Surviving." Walt's attempt at a smile twisted into a grimace. "No concussion, so that's a win. Never been punched in the face before. Feels...educational."

Lola could remember so many instances of that pain, the explosion behind the skull on impact. When she was a vampire, her body would repair itself quickly, though the pain was always there. "Not fun, right? Although I'm surprised this is a first for you."

Walt let out a bark of laughter. "Am I that punchable?"

Lola laughed. "No, not like that. But I remember the way you dove at Ethan in Lost Souls back in the spring. You're brave like that when it comes to protecting your friends. It could get you into trouble one day."

Walt's gaze softened like he was filing the words away.

"So," she said, nudging his arm. "What's up with you and Violet? Seeing as she's the reason you look like this?"

"No idea. Violet is selfish and mean; she's tormented me for years. She never once pretended to be fake nice to my face like the others." He frowned. "I always appreciated the honesty."

Lola tilted her head. "And she's super hot."

His face reddened. "I had...noticed that. She's dating someone else, though."

Lola shrugged. "She and Ethan barely tolerate each other. They possess each other more than anything. It's a spell that will end someday, maybe sooner than later."

His face shifted. "You think?"

"Honestly, I don't know anything." She shook her head. "Never mind. Have you seen Nix?"

Walt shook his head. "Not yet, but we've got math club right now. She might show."

"I'm coming with you," Lola said, already moving.

As they walked, Walt frowned. "What's up with her, anyways? She's been weird. To me, especially."

"Don't take it personally. I think she's possessed by the Seabourne ghost, who might have it out for your family."

"What?" Walt slipped on glass and nearly sprawled out on the floor. Lola grasped his arm to keep him steady.

"I know it sounds crazy."

"No, it actually explains a lot." Walt got his feet under him. "How do you know?"

"I saw another face in her reflection." Lola was quiet for a moment. "I think it's her ancestor, Alice McCullough. Remember how Nix found the diary in that very hidden place? I think Alice targeted her since she first went into the Belowstairs."

"What are we going to do?"

Lola pressed her lips together. "First, we find her."

She barely noticed Matt approaching down the hallway when he called out, his tone sharp. "Ms. Monteux, wrong direction. Journalism room's that way."

"Right. Journalism." Lola slowed to a stop. She'd forgotten, with everything going on. "The thing is..."

"I don't care what your thing is," he said. "This shouldn't be something you ditch because you have other places you want to be.

Or because the school exploded. This is when we lean in and get creative."

"I understand that. It's just that—"

Matt shook his head. "You seemed engaged and you have plenty of talent, but if your heart isn't in this, you're off the paper."

Lola's heart squeezed; she had enjoyed working on the *Tribute*, but finding Nix was more important.

Walt caught her arm. "Go. I'll look for Nix. We'll meet up after."

"Right." Lola nodded. "Don't tell her everything, though. We can't scare her off."

Matt nodded as Lola came into the classroom. "I'll go over your project first, okay? If you still feel like you have to duck out afterwards, I'll look the other way."

"*Merci.*" In her anxiety, Lola slipped into French.

"*Bienvenue,*" Matt said with a strong Anglo accent, earning a smile from her. She hurried over to place herself next to Gael.

He leaned in, brows furrowed. "Everything okay?"

She shook her head. "Have you heard from Nix?"

"No. Why? What's wrong?" Gael asked. Before she could answer, Matt began outlining the upcoming issue, leaving Gael to study her with a worried look creasing his face. On his other side, Cassidy watched the two of them with narrowed eyes, but Lola couldn't be bothered to care about her today.

She twirled her pen in her hand, more agitated the longer she had to wait. A school-wide haunting wasn't normal, not when the site of the original haunting was Seabourne Estate. Hauntings didn't just get up and move—unless powerful forces were at work. She bounced her knee, desperate to get moving, to search for Nix.

Her phone vibrated, and she checked it out of Matt's eyeline.

A message from Walt: *Nix didn't make it to math this after-noon.* He was searching the school for her now.

Lola's eyes stung with tears of frustration as she tried to convince herself this delay wasn't going to cost her anything.

Like her friend.

Gael tried to get her attention. *Nix?* he mouthed. She nodded, then glanced up. Matt had finally finished handing out new assignments, and he started towards her to go over her project.

"Right, I have a story idea based on a diary found of a sixteen-year-old maid from 1921." She displayed the diary as well as the notes she'd taken from it.

Matt raised an eyebrow. "I'm loving the use of primary sources, but it's hardly riveting stuff."

"It might not be current affairs, but I thought it would be an interesting piece to show how a person our age lived a hundred years ago on Duchesne. Like a compare-and-contrast slice of life thing."

"You sound more like a historian than a reporter."

Lola met his skeptical gaze. "So many mysteries lay unsolved in our past. You never know when a real-time story will develop out of ancient history."

Matt tilted his head. "Okay, I'm convinced. I'd like to see where you go with this. Get some interesting graphs and visuals and I'm sold." He quirked a smile. "Although I should have you do a write-up about the Seabourne Harvest Ball. I heard it was quite something." He moved on to the next student.

"It was definitely something." Lola rose to leave, jamming her papers into her bag.

Footsteps followed behind her. Gael had grabbed his papers and hurried out of the classroom after her.

"Lola, wait! Whatever you're doing, I'm in."

She paused to wait for him, a curious blend of hope and worry stirring in her chest.

Then, a flurry of voice sounded from the classroom, and Cassidy trotted out. "Babe, where you going?" She approached him with a sultry walk.

"Oh, I have to go do this thing." Gael rubbed the back of his head, his cheeks flushing.

Cassidy put her hands on his shoulders and leaned in to give him a kiss full on the lips, her mouth curving into a smirk. "Well, don't forget about Lost Souls tonight. Everybody's going to be there." She spun and returned to the classroom, where she was met by giggling shrieks. Clearly, she'd had an audience.

Gael just stood there with his mouth open, staring at Lola as if he had no idea what to do or say. Feeling as though she'd been belted in the stomach, Lola turned, her hands grasping her bag until her knuckles whitened, and started down the hall.

She heard the crunching of the glass as he ran after her. "Lola, listen, about that—"

"None of my business." It took every ounce of her willpower to look straight ahead, to not let her heart wring out the tears that wanted to fall. "What matters is that Nix is missing. Something bad is going on; something that has to do with what happened at the séance, and we have to find her before things get worse. So, are you coming?" she gritted out. "Or do you want to take off to Lost Souls, where *everybody's* going to be?" She couldn't help the mocking tone in her voice.

"I want to find Nix." His voice was low. "She's my friend, Lola. That's never changed."

Lola let out a steadying breath. Her back might be up about Gael and Cassidy's kiss, but they were on the same side. "Good. Because we're going to need all the help we can get."

They exited the school to find Walt pacing outside the front entrance. His face was even more swollen now, his eye barely able to open.

"I've looked everywhere in the school," he said when he saw them. "Nobody's seen her since the fireworks." He nodded to the school.

"So where would Nix go?" Lola asked Gael, who knew her

best. "If something was wrong, does she have a place where she might look for comfort?"

"A few," Gael responded. "But I don't understand why this is such a big deal, though."

"At the séance the other night, Nix was possessed by the ghost of her ancestor."

"Wait, what?" Gael froze mid-step.

"The floating figure we saw? We called it to us. She's connected to Nix by blood, and she entered her body."

Gael's mouth sagged open. "Is that...normal?"

Mounting anxiety built in Lola's chest like a volcano ready to blow. "Definitely not. A ghost can inhabit a body for a short amount of time, to sometimes deliver a message or something. Those spirits are called hitchhikers, but their power fades when they are away from their essence—usually where their death happens. Every so often, though, a spirit has the power to take over a body entirely. It's considered a hijacker, where the host's spirit is pushed to the side entirely, even cast out."

"Like, Nix, what makes her *her* could be gone?"

Lola met Gael's eyes, opened wide with horror, all anger forgotten. "It's rare. I don't know how this could happen. But I'm pretty sure the weird things that happened at school were energy surges coming from Alice. I saw her face in the mirror, like an overlap on Nix's face. She's inside of her."

"So, what do we do?" Walt asked.

"We need to find Nix. Check the lighthouse, I guess?"

"I can do that," Gael said. "I'm over there all the time; it won't be weird if I stop by."

"Walt, maybe you can see if she's at her mom's shop or if her mom's seen her?"

Walt nodded, his jaw tight and his fists jammed into his pockets.

"And I'm going to check the wharf," Lola said.

"Why there?" Walt asked.

"If Alice is trying to live out her dream of travelling the world, her first instinct might be to get off the island. We should see if she's on the ferries or if anyone saw her leave."

Gael's face blanched. "The spirit might kidnap her right off the island?"

"Maybe." Lola let out a shaky sigh. "We have to stop her before she tries. If she gets to the mainland, she could go anywhere."

"Alice or Nix?"

Lola shrugged. "I'm not sure who is more in control. Either way, she's probably very confused. Meet back at the Pain Perdu by sunset if we haven't found anything. Hopefully, she's just at home."

Lola took off for the ferries at a run. Gael and Walt started out in different directions. If all went well, one of them would text her soon and they could figure out what to do with Nix.

Lola's gaze scanned the glittering expanse of the Atlantic Ocean. If things didn't go well, who knows where her friend would disappear to?

Her frantic search of the ferry building and the surrounding boardwalk turned up nothing. Everyone who lived on the island knew Nix, the lighthouse keeper's daughter, and nobody had seen her. The ferry master swore he'd have known if she'd snuck onto the 4:15 to Halifax, and she wasn't there.

Gael and Walt's increasingly frantic texts revealed the same thing: Nobody had seen Nix. But where could she have gone if she was still on the island?

Crushing guilt seemed to cave in her shoulders. Lola had kept on diving deeper into Alice's history; she was the one who forced this out into the open. Maybe if she'd just been able to let the past go, Nix would still be safe.

Lola trudged back to the Pain Perdu, her mind flicking over the possibilities. More and more, Lola's mind drifted towards the last place that made sense.

TWENTY-SIX

"Faye!" Lola burst into the warm, fragrant café. She spotted the baker behind the counter and hurried over, ignoring the rich aroma of coffee. "Have you seen Nix?"

Faye glanced up from the cash register, her brow creasing. "What happened? Everybody's been asking about her." She nodded to the corner table, where Walt and Gael looked up at her, both nursing half-empty cups of coffee.

"She ran off from school—she was upset. We can't find her," Lola said, the words tumbling out.

Faye hummed as she thought. "Maybe she just needs a minute to herself. We all do sometimes, even that firecracker. I'm sure she'll be back at the lighthouse before dinner."

Lola clenched her jaw. "If you hear anything, *anything at all*, text me."

"Of course." Faye's stance changed as she registered Lola's concern. "I'll ask around."

Lola sank into a chair next to Walt, her voice dropping to a whisper. "We need to search your house, Walt. It's the only place that makes sense. Nix has to be there."

Walt grimaced, lifting his phone. "I just got a text from my mom. All the power at the house has gone out, and nobody can figure out why. She sent the staff home and has taken a suite at a hotel on Main Street." His voice dropped to not be overheard. "Seabourne Estate's a dead zone now."

"Or a zone for the dead," Lola said as her stomach dropped at the news. "I'll bet you anything Nix, or rather Alice, is there." She chewed on her thumbnail. "Nix would never have gone there. It means that Alice is becoming more powerful. She's taking over. Whatever is going to happen, it'll happen there."

"What are we waiting for? Let's go!" Gael threw some bills on the table, and the three of them rose together. Nobody spoke, though Walt kept on cracking his knuckles while Gael stared at the path with an intensity that should have scorched the earth.

The sun was slipping below the horizon as they made their way up the winding path towards Seabourne Estate. The trees hunched over the path, ghostly mist drifting between their trunks. Tangled branches formed a gnarled arch overhead.

Lola pressed forward, increasing their pace until they were all but sprinting, her thoughts racing with every step.

When the mansion came into view, its silhouette loomed against the dying light. The iron gates stood ajar, swaying gently in the autumn wind. The three of them stopped short.

The decorations from the Harvest Ball littered the path leading to the looming front porch, tattered and in disarray. Pumpkins were smashed, and leaves were torn apart as though a tornado had swept through.

"Did I miss something?" Lola asked. "Was there a mass riot at the ball, Walt?"

He looked at the destruction in dismay. "It didn't look like this in the morning. Everything was normal."

"And the place is empty?"

"Someone's home." Gael pointed to the darkened windows. A faint, flickering light moved within.

"Could it be your dad, Walt?" Lola asked.

He shook his head, his eyes glued to the light moving away from the window. "He left town yesterday. That's not him."

"Then I think we just found Nix," Lola said, swallowing hard. She didn't add *"or what's inside of her."*

The front door creaked open as if on cue, and the three of them stepped into the oppressive stillness of the house. The air was heavy, suffocating, and the scent of rot clung to every breath.

"Okay, first point goes to the terrifying mansion," Gael said. He squared his shoulders and walked across the front hall, Lola following him closely. Walt brought up the rear, leaving the door open behind him.

The house had the eerie quiet of a place devoid of life: no buzzing of electronics or humming of appliances, just stifling silence. When Walt's foot creaked on a floorboard, Lola jumped, taking in a shaky breath.

The remnants of the party were even more spoiled inside. Once-vibrant vines were wilted and black, and the air reeked of decay. A collapsed pumpkin oozed onto the floorboards near the stairs.

"It didn't take long for her to take over," Lola whispered, then cleared her throat. "Nix!"

Her call bounced off the ceiling, and they all waited with bated breath for a response. Lola's skin buzzed with tension, and the three of them huddled together, skin brushing skin as if to find comfort from the contact.

"If she won't come to us, we'll have to find her," Lola said.

"Where do we start?" Gael asked.

Walt's voice was hoarse. "Where she was possessed?"

They all looked upstairs towards the games room. In unspoken agreement, they moved together as though separating would spell disaster. The heat from Gael's body was a comfort to Lola. Walt was trembling, as anxious as she was.

The games room seemed untouched: the crystal ball and tarot cards spread out over the table as though mocking them for thinking they could play with the occult and not pay the price. There was always a price to play with darkness; most didn't discover the truth until it was far too late to take it back.

A light flickered and held—Lola spun in surprise to see Walt lighting a candle left from the party décor. The flame sparkled in the crystal ball as she went to stand behind the chair where Nix had been during the séance.

"We saw Alice's spirit come into the room over there." Lola pointed. "Then she disappeared at the centre of the table, right in front of Nix. She must have been drawn to her as her bloodline, allowing her not just the ability to enter into her but to remain." Lola slapped her hands against the chair back, wishing desperately she could take it all back. "Nix!" she called, then changed tactic. "Alice! I know you're here. Show yourself!"

They waited in the ensuing silence as Lola's angry yell faded. Nothing happened. Lola turned to the boys on the other side of the table when the smell hit them. A stench so vile it filled her nose, choking her, an oily coating down her throat. She gagged, hands flying to her face as she stumbled back.

Walt and Gael were suffering equally; they scrambled from the room, slamming the door behind them. Still, the smell clung to their skin, a reminder that Alice was there—watching.

Gael grimaced. "What was that?"

"The smell of death," Lola said. She'd come across corpses left out to rot in the elements. She'd seen open mass graves after atrocities, bodies abandoned like sacks of meat. "Concentrated death."

"That was...bracing," Walt said.

"Where to now?" Gael asked.

Walt still held the candle, and shadows bounced over their faces as they exchanged a long look.

"The Belowstairs," Lola whispered.

"Right." Gael cleared his throat. "Can I just say that I really don't want to go down there?"

"We have to." Walt's voice cracked, echoing in the emptiness of his home. "For Nix."

The word *Nix* seemed to hiss around them, echoing down the hall. "Let's go," Lola said, though her hand shook as much as her voice as she took the banister and descended to the study.

The dark Victorian room seemed even more grave under the influence of the haunting. The candlelight picked up elements on the shelves Lola hadn't noticed before: a polished animal skull tucked behind some old leather volumes, a fox's glass eye glinting dully as they passed. The crystal decanters glowed amber in the light, though Lola now imagined them full of poison.

Before she could hesitate, she pulled at *Treasure Island*. Gulping, she grabbed onto both Gael's and Walt's arms as the secret passageway creaked open with a booming groan. Cobwebs lit by the ghostly light drifted on air currents as they stepped into the space.

The Belowstairs stretched before them like the maw of a beast, dark and unwelcoming. They continued into the mansion's underbelly in tense silence. The fact that nothing jumped out at them only ratcheted up Lola's tension.

She stopped at the mirror, where the alcove was hidden. She ran her fingers over the walls, searching for the door she swore had been there. But the surface was smooth, unyielding.

"It's so strange," she said as Walt and Gael watched her. "When I was alone, there was a door here. It was so obvious I couldn't believe I'd missed it."

"But there isn't a door," Gael pointed out.

"Yes, thank you. I can see that." Lola's voice was clipped. "But there *was*. She's playing with us."

Walt waved the candle in front of them for their attention. "Let's just keep going."

In uneasy agreement, Lola and Gael followed him to the kitchen. Holding her breath as she entered the space, Lola wasn't sure if she was disappointed to see it empty.

"Where is she?" she said. "I was sure she'd be down here."

"We definitely saw a light in the window," Walt said. "She must be somewhere."

Lola let out a sigh. "Let's go back upstairs, then."

Her disappointment deflated her fear somewhat, and Lola marched through the doorway. Only as she entered the corridor a crushing sense of nausea overwhelmed her, and she doubled over.

Walt and Gael were doing the same thing, bracing themselves on their knees. When the feeling passed, Lola straightened, only to find herself inside the kitchen again. Disorientation crashed down on her, causing her heart to drum inside her ears.

"I thought..." She turned down the hallway and walked back again, towards the entrance to the Belowstairs. But before she'd gone a few paces, the world spun, and she ended up back at the threshold of the servant's kitchen.

She grabbed Walt's and Gael's arms, tugging them away from the kitchen. As the world spun again, evil laughter began to sound, surrounding them. It was a girl's laugh, cold and cruel.

"She's trapped us," Lola whispered. Walt's face was ashen, and Gael's eyes were open so wide she could see the whites around them. She had to find a way to break out of the spirit's influence.

Lola braced herself on the countertop, trying to still her heaving stomach. The kitchen was empty but for some old games and ancient salt and pepper shakers.

Her eyes opened wide. Salt! It repelled evil spirits. She grabbed the tarnished saltshaker.

Dashing to the door of the kitchen, she started to shake out the salt as she moved forward. "Follow me," she urged, pulling Walt and Gael behind her.

As the white grains of salt spilled out, she was able to move forward. The cruel laughter continued around them while glacial wind rushed down the hallway like an arctic storm. Every step took the same effort as if they were cresting a mountaintop.

Finally, they made it to the mirror. But when Lola glanced at her reflection this time, she found herself looking at Nix's face. She was banging against the mirror, yelling for help.

"Nix!" Lola screamed, grabbing the mirror on either side.

Nix's blue eyes turned to her as though she could see her, wide with horror.

Lola! her mouth shaped as though screaming her name.

Tears welled up in Lola's eyes as she beat her hands against the wall. She didn't know how to get to her. "Nix! I'm coming for you. Hold on!"

The mirror faded to black, and a voice simmering with hatred sounded from behind the wall. "You can't have her; she's mine."

"Like hell she is," Lola growled.

She braced her hands against the wall and closed her eyes. Ignoring the sounds around her, Walt and Gael's shouts and the laughter and the wind that rushed by, she descended deep inside herself. She sought to find the connection that had given her the power to break out of the alcove when it had been her that was trapped.

The singing force of the earth started to wash over her, warming her, filling her with power.

But a wailing like a freight train descended on them, and the wind came back with the force of a hurricane. They were shoved away from the mirror, and Lola's concentration was broken as they were forced back down the hallway. They tumbled into the kitchen and the door slammed shut.

The wind stopped, leaving them panting. Fury grew inside Lola as she thought of Nix's terror-stricken face in the mirror. She jerked open the kitchen door, only to find a brick wall blocking her.

She pounded against it, but it was solid.

"Still think it's only in my head now?" she screamed at Walt.

"You were right, okay!" He pressed his hand to the brick as though unable to believe it was real.

"Calm down!" Gael shouted. "How do we get out of here? We're trapped."

Walt backed away from the door, eyes wide in disbelief. "Not trapped," he said. "There's a cellar door. Over here." He pointed to the metal log rack where the woodpile used to be stored.

Gael pulled at the heavy iron, the rack screeching over the stone floors. "There's an old door here," he said. "With a padlock. I don't see a key..." The crunch of wood sounded as he smashed his shoulder against the wood, then he let out a grunt of pain.

Unsteadily, Walt grabbed the rusty axe in the abandoned kindling. He swung; the mouldering wood splintered under the dull blade until the padlock could be pulled right off.

The door swung outwards, letting in the cool salty breeze of an Atlantic evening.

The three of them tumbled out into the night air, falling into the dirt. Next to them, the wall of the ballroom terrace jutted out towards the cliffside. Lola could hear the crashing of waves far beneath them.

She rolled over, inspecting Walt and Gael. Both were panting but in one piece. They sat up slowly and, as one, looked to the cellar door.

A brick wall stood in its place. The mortar had been done haphazardly, slopping over the edges, but it was as solid as cement.

Gael stared at the wall, his face sagging in horror. "She's trapped inside."

Walt's expression was stony as he took in the wall. "The house is finally starting to show how it feels inside."

"I don't know how to deal with a possession like this," Lola said. "We need to talk to an expert."

"We can't just leave her in there!" Gael's face flashed between furious and desperate.

Lola had to swallow down the urge to cry at the thought of leaving Nix inside the Seabourne Estate. "I don't think it will hurt her. The spirit of Alice is using Nix's body. She won't harm it."

"So that's just fine, then? We'll leave her alone in there?"

"It's not fine!" Lola bit out the words, responding to the hostility in Gael's voice. "But I don't know how to fix this! Unless you have any big ideas, we need to figure out another way!"

Gael stared at her, his jaw working, his anger focused entirely on her. But then it was spent, and he slumped. "I don't know either."

"Who could possibly be an expert on this?" Walt said.

"Marissa has better resources than us—we'll talk to her first thing tomorrow. We need the help of a witch."

TWENTY-SEVEN

Lola didn't sleep that night. Every time exhaustion crashed over her, the image of Nix's face in the mirror resurfaced —pleading, desperate. Adrenaline jolted her awake again and again.

Eventually, she gave up. Rolling out of bed, she blinked wearily and reached for Alice's diary. Though she'd finished the translation, she preferred to read the original. The looping scrawl felt intimate, as though Alice would reveal her secrets if only Lola could read between the lines.

"Who were you, Alice?" She fingered the powdery pages of the diary. "Were you a thief or a lover? Why did you never leave Seabourne Estate, no matter how badly you wanted to?"

The cramped, almost overlapping text reflected Alice's urgency when she grew excited. The girl had been intelligent and sharp, and her keen observations reminded Lola so much of Nix that sometimes it pinched her heart. They were like shared souls. Only Alice wasn't interested in sharing; she wanted to take over.

Cold air flowed into the room as Lola opened her window, scrubbing at her face to shake off the dregs of fatigue. She stared into the night sky, just starting to lighten to a misty grey. The hoot of an owl in the oak forest reminded her of nights spent on the hunt, grounding her.

The reflection in the mirror had shown her Nix's spirit, trapped inside her own body, taken by another. Alice's presence was too strong to ignore. Resolving to set things right, Lola dressed before dawn and made her way downstairs to the café.

The smell of fresh bread greeted her as Faye pulled the first loaves from the oven. But Faye's grim expression caused Lola's stomach to sink.

"No sign of her?" she asked.

Faye shook her head. "Nix didn't come home last night."

Lola ran her hands over her face, unsurprised but disheartened. She'd hoped Alice's spirit might have faded to the background at some point, letting Nix regain control. The fact that she didn't spelled a world of trouble for Nix; the spirit was strong, and they would have to fight to get her back.

Letting out a long breath, Lola slid onto a stool at the counter. "So, what's happening?"

"I've been on the phone with Theo." At Lola's questioning look, Faye gave a flicker of a smile. "That's Sergeant Greyson. He's organizing a search party. Now you say she was upset yesterday? Why was that?"

How to explain? Stalling, Lola poured herself a cup of coffee and fiddled with the handle. "The lights all exploded at the school. Everybody was upset, and she ran off right after that. She didn't say why." She hesitated, debating whether to share what she truly knew. But there was no point in sending the police to Seabourne Estate. What could they do against a ghost?

Faye's mouth pressed into a grim line. "Her mother's frantic. Nix never runs off like this. She's as responsible as they come."

"I know." Lola's voice came out a whisper. She was the one who led Nix into this situation. If only she'd left the diary alone, stopped pushing to explore hidden passages and hidden histories, none of this would have happened and Nix would be fine.

But Lola couldn't take it back. So now she had to move forward and do whatever it took to get Nix back. "I'm going to find the guys and keep searching," she said.

Faye pushed a croissant towards her before she left. "I'll join in when I can. Theo's setting up the search headquarters here so people can refuel if they need to."

"That's kind of you."

Faye's eyes were haunted. "It's the least I can do for a lost child," she said.

Lola squeezed Faye's shoulder before stepping out into the crisp morning air. Her phone showed no updates from Walt or Gael. They'd crashed at the Main Street Hotel late last night in the suite Mayor Seabourne had taken. She decided to let them rest— she didn't need them for her next stop.

She hurried up the front steps of the library, hoping Marissa was awake. Halfway up, a voice called out.

"Lola!"

She stumbled as Reiko sprinted towards her. But the demon hunter only stopped at the foot of the stairs, eyeing Lola warily.

"What do you want?" Lola asked, taking in Reiko's dishevelled appearance. Her dark hair stuck out in every direction and deep shadows lined her eyes. It softened her usual sharpness, making her seem vulnerable.

"I heard," she said, her voice husky. "About Nix, I mean. This has to do with the other night, doesn't it?"

"What's it to you?" Lola's tone was cold as she turned away.

"Stop." Reiko jogged in front of her, hands raised. "Listen, I know I wasn't the best to her when we first met."

"You think? You *knew* what your friendship meant to her, and you used that to your advantage. Nix has been hurt enough; I won't allow you to do it again."

Reiko eyed her darkly as though to argue, but her shoulders dropped after a moment. "I get that. I don't have to get close to her, but I want to help."

"Help?" Lola raised an eyebrow, skeptical.

"Yes." Reiko hesitated, then added, "I have resources at my disposal; I know things. Let's just assume we're on the same side in this one." She let out a huff. "I am a junior agent of the Order of Hanta Cythraul, for goodness sake. Let me use that!"

Lola considered her, tugging on a stray curl. For all she didn't trust Reiko further than she could throw her, she did believe she wanted the best for Nix. And she wasn't wrong that having the resources of the Order at her disposal might be helpful. *"Junior* agent?"

Reiko reddened. "I wasn't supposed to say that." She kicked at the ground. "But yes. I have to complete a mission solo before I become a full agent."

"And what happened this summer didn't count? With the carnival?"

"That wasn't the mission." Reiko looked away. "I can't talk about it."

Lola crossed her arms. "I'm not really interested in working with someone who keeps all her secrets hidden."

"Like you don't?"

Still, Lola didn't move, and Reiko broke first. "Fine. The mission was to investigate what caused the surge of energy that blasted out from the island in the spring. And I haven't figured it out yet. I'm sure you know *nothing* about that."

Reiko's pointed look glanced off Lola. She wasn't going to share her secrets with the demon hunter, no matter how helpful she was prepared to be.

"I'm sure I don't," she said and turned back to the library.

"Wait, that's it?" Reiko cried behind her.

"I'm busy," Lola called over her shoulder. "You want to be a part of this, keep up."

Reiko's footsteps pounded behind her, and she was at Lola's side a second later, glaring. "What are you doing here?"

"Some of us don't have fancy Orders to feed us information, so we have to do it the old-fashioned way."

"Please, this is a community library. What's it going to show us?"

Lola gave a grim smile as the door opened to the haunted space. "By now, you've probably figured out Duchesne isn't like other islands. You're not the only one to have noticed. Others have stockpiled their own resources. Like a massive collection of info on the occult."

Reiko's gaze showed nothing but scorn, but Lola didn't have the time or patience to convince her.

"Marissa!" she called. To her surprise when entering, though, Marissa wasn't alone. She heard her, chatting with a deeper male voice.

Then, Marissa *giggled*. Lola stopped in surprise; the librarian was not a giggler.

At the front desk, Marissa stood with Matt Vernon, their heads together as they pored over a book.

"Marissa?" Lola asked.

"Ms. Monteux," Matt said, eyebrow raised as they both looked up. "What brings you here so early? The library's not even open."

Lola stared at him for a moment. She could ask him the same question. Opting to disarm, though, she gave a girlish laugh. "Why do you think we're here?" she said. "Time for an epic study sesh."

"Before school?"

"No time like the present! There's some research stuff I wanted to talk to Marissa about." She gave the librarian her sweetest smile, opening her eyes wide to try to convey to Marissa how important this was.

"We're actually busy right now, Lola." Marissa's head tilted to Matt, and she gave a pointed look.

Lola's smile hardened. "This is the kind of thing that can't wait."

A boom sounded from the floor above them, and while Matt

and Reiko flinched as though under fire, neither Lola nor Marissa broke their staring contest. "I think you'll want to check out what just happened up there," Lola said.

Matt watched them like a tennis match for a moment, eyes twinkling like he didn't understand what was going on but found it amusing. He pulled the book they had been looking at towards him. "Well, Marissa, looks like my time here is done. Thanks for the help you've given me; you're a preeminent historian."

Marissa blushed at his wink. "See you later." Her wave to Matt was flirtatious, but as soon as he left, she turned a poisonous gaze on Lola. "Why are you here? I'm closed for another hour!"

Lola shrugged. "The door was open. Besides, what was *Matt Vernon* doing here first thing in the morning?" Her hand flew to her lips as she had a thought. "Unless he spent the night?"

Marissa's cheeks turned crimson. "No! He just said he needed info on some of the island's history and he needed to check it before work." Marissa finally seemed to notice Reiko, who was inspecting the library. "Who is that? Why do you keep on bringing people here?"

"It's a public library," Lola hissed back. "And that thing I was worried about at the Seabourne Estate? It's gotten worse. Like, exorcist worse."

"Are you sure?" Marissa drew back, eyes wide.

Reiko approached. "What are you doing, bringing a civilian in?"

"A civilian?" Marissa's face frosted over. "Who are *you*?"

"This is Reiko, who promises to keep her mouth shut if she wants to be involved." Lola levelled a glare at her. "Marissa is well aware of the Otherworld and is an expert in the occult."

A scathing snort came from Reiko, but when both Lola and Marissa turned on her, she crossed her arms and shrugged. "Sorry. Continue."

After a glare at Reiko, Marissa refocused on the issue. "When you say exorcist, you mean—"

"I mean, Nix has been possessed," Lola said, noticing how Reiko flinched as if in pain.

"Nix. The angry little redhead? Are you sure it's a possession?"

"Positive. We also know the spirit is her ancestor, Alice McCullough."

To her credit, Marissa took all this information stoically, jotting tidy notes on a legal pad. "And you know this how?"

As quickly as possible, Lola explained everything that had happened over the past few days at the estate, ending with the brick walls that had appeared. As she spoke, Marissa paced the library, picking up books as they fell to the ground.

Eyes wide, Reiko started following her, surreptitiously pulling her device out of her pocket.

"There's a huge level of Otherworldly power in this building," she said. "It's concentrated around you."

At the sight of the device, Marissa gasped. "You're with the Order!"

Reiko whipped the device behind her back like a guilty child. "No, I'm not."

"Yes, you are."

Reiko narrowed her eyes at Lola. "How does she know about the Order?"

"Show me." Marissa held out her hand like an annoyed school-teacher until finally, Reiko placed the device in her palm.

Marissa's eyes flickered over the readings as though they meant something to her. "Interesting. How does it work?"

"It's calibrated to the user," Reiko said. "I need to offer a sacrifice for it to work for me. The more powerful the user, the more powerful the device."

"Sacrifice?" Lola asked.

"It works by pricking a finger. The blood orients the machine to you." With a glare, Reiko snatched the device back.

Marissa grabbed her pad and began scribbling away as even more books fell.

Reiko frowned. "You're an energy source. What *are* you?"

"That's rude," Marissa said without looking up.

Reiko fiddled with a knob and read the device again. "You're a witch," she said finally, her lip twitching in a faint sneer. Her hand itched as though to grab her knives, hidden somewhere on her body.

Marissa finally looked up, arms folded over her chest as if it didn't matter to her in the least. Only her whitened knuckles showed how tightly she clenched her fists. "What of it?"

"Does the Order not like witches?" Lola asked. "Because you're going to have to change your position if that's a problem."

Reiko eyed them both. "Witches who are registered and practice only the prescribed levels of white magic are tolerated," she said. "No witches are registered on this island, so I'm going to guess you're an illegal."

"I'm going to have to ask you to take that back." Lola stepped in front of Marissa, and her skin prickled as she faced the demon hunter.

Reiko's intolerance didn't bode well, not for her presence on the island, nor the fact that Marissa's father was in the Order. "Marissa is a good person and a good witch, and she doesn't have to obey any kind of bossy rules from your stupid secret society."

Marissa's face paled as Reiko continued to glare at her. Lola needed to get everyone back on track.

"What matters is Nix," she said, giving Reiko's shoulder a shove. "Did you mean it when you said you wanted to help, or do you just want to be a bigot?"

Colour rose in Reiko's cheeks, and she glanced away. "I want to help."

"Then sit still and listen. Marissa, what do you think we're dealing with here?"

Marissa finally pulled her gaze from the demon hunter. She shook her head as if to rid herself of what had just happened, then frowned at Lola. "You were right. When it comes to possession, there's only one way to get rid of the spirit." She held out the book that had fallen at her feet and Lola took it.

The cover blared a bright red and white title: *Exorcism and You: Dealing with Your Demons.*

"But I don't have this kind of power," Marissa said. "People who attempt exorcisms without enough magical strength, without the proper anchors, are eaten alive."

Lola opened the book to a printed sketch of a ghastly figure ripping itself out of a man's chest. Everyone in the portrait was screaming.

"I know," Lola said quietly.

"I've never seen an exorcism in real life," Reiko said, peeking over Lola's shoulder at the picture.

"Well, buckle up." Marissa set her jaw. "If we're going to do this, we're going to need to bring in the big guns." She had a new steely glint in her eyes.

"Is this going to happen to Nix?" Reiko's face was ashen, staring at the horrific engraving.

"Nothing is going to happen to Nix," Lola said. "I'm calling Gael and Walt, and we'll figure this out."

"Tell them to meet us at McInnes' Tea Shoppe." Marissa gathered books into a pile, stuffing papers and jars into a leather bag.

Dismay filled Lola like a rolling fog, and she hesitated before making the call. The last time she'd seen McInnes, she'd spoken of a price that must be paid, and Nix had warned her against hearing her fate. That it would destroy her hope.

But if it meant helping Nix, Lola would have her fortune told. She needed to face her destiny on this island once and for all.

"Chin up, Lola," Marissa said, noticing her reluctance. "I know she's a bit odd, but she came to me not too long ago...after what happened this summer. She's been my mentor since then. And we need help from the most powerful witch on the island."

"Also unregistered," Reiko muttered.

"Seriously with that?" Lola threw up her hands in exasperation. "You can either follow the stupid rules of your Order, or you can help Nix, but apparently you can't do both. Make a choice now, Reiko, but then you have to stick with it. I'm more than happy to cut you out completely."

For a moment, Reiko looked murderous, her grey eyes darkening like stormy skies, but finally, she nodded. "Fine, I'm in."

"Good. Because we are going to get Nix back if it's the last thing I do, and anyone who gets in my way is going to regret it."

TWENTY-EIGHT

L ola followed Marissa to McInnes' Tea Shoppe, her steps heavy as though she were mounting the scaffolding to a guillotine.

Her dread was irrational but undeniable. Ever since reclaiming her soul, something had been shifting inside her, like a fault line ready to rupture. She couldn't explain why the thought of hearing her fortune from the witch made her tremble, but she was certain she wouldn't be allowed to escape her judgment.

Whatever happened now, she wasn't going to be left unchanged.

The logical part of Lola's brain insisted the woman was just a dusty old fortune teller. But the part of Lola that had lived and breathed the Otherworld for nearly a century knew better. McInnes didn't hand out fortunes like some county fair fake—she dealt in the real thing: prophecies.

Since Lola had first seen the witch, she'd sensed magic radiating from her. Even the uninitiated could feel the raw power. It was the kind of presence that demanded belief, like the way Nix inherently trusted every word McInnes spoke to be true. Lola couldn't dismiss her as a charlatan.

Deep in her bones, she knew she held the answer to the question that had haunted her since she'd become human.

Why had she been given her soul back? And what if the answer changed everything? Because she knew more than most, there was always a price.

And who could measure the price of a soul?

When they reached the corner of Wharf Street and Main, the Victorian mansion loomed before them, its towering shadow creeping across the cobblestones. Lola paused at the wrap-around porch, which spilled over with potted plants. The house had a feeling of a fairy-tale home, complete with a witch who waited inside.

"Lola!"

She turned to see Walt and Gael sprinting down the road, rumpled as if they just rolled out of bed. Gael was fumbling to tuck in his shirt, and Walt clutched a piece of toast in his hand as though he had grabbed it from the hotel buffet.

Gael's golden-brown eyes locked on hers. "Any word?" he asked, his voice rough with worry.

She shook her head, unable to speak. Tears stung her eyes. With anyone else, she could be the strong one, the girl who would make things happen. But in the light of Gael's open concern, knowing how important this was to him as well, she saw her own fears reflected back. She wanted so badly to step into his arms.

A gust of wind swept around her, icy and sharp, tugging her towards him. She resisted, wrapping her arms around herself against the chill. "She hasn't come home. We think she's still at Seabourne Estate. But we have a plan—"

"Sort of," Marissa interjected, her voice tight.

Gael finally noticed the others on the porch. Walt was glaring at Reiko, who ignored him. Marissa's eyes were flicking between Lola and Gael with a speculative gleam.

Gael extended his hand to Marissa. "We haven't met. I'm Gael."

"Marissa," she said, her voice cautious as she accepted his handshake. Outside the shelter of her library fortress, she seemed fragile, exposed. Lola appreciated how much Marissa was willing to push herself out of her comfort zone to help them out.

"Gael, Marissa is a friend and a witch. She's going to help us figure out how to get the spirit out of Nix." She nodded to the mansion. "But we're going to need more power to do this."

"And what's the HC doing here?" Walt jerked his chin at Reiko.

"She's not a friend," Lola said flatly. "But she seems annoyingly set on getting involved."

"The HC?" Reiko tilted her head at Walt.

"For Hanta Cythraul. Way easier to say."

The flash of outrage on Reiko's face was almost enough to make Lola laugh, but the moment passed quickly. She grabbed Walt's arm and ushered everyone to the front door. "We're wasting daylight. Let's get this over with."

The grand mahogany doors swung open on their own, stained-glass panels catching the light that sparkled over witchy runes and symbols.

She took a shaky breath. Inside, the mansion was breathtaking. Sunlight streamed through the domed skylight, casting golden rays on polished wood floors. Greenery spilled from every corner, climbing over railings and draping from chandeliers. The air was fragrant with lavender and rosemary, soft and welcoming—an unsettling contrast to the tension thrumming in her chest.

A cool, whispery voice floated towards them. "Come to the back."

They exchanged glances before following the sound down a narrow corridor that opened into an Otherworldly greenhouse.

Crystals studded the glass walls, scattering rainbows of light over ferns, orchids and towering palms. Vines draped from wrought-iron arches, creating a labyrinth of growing things.

Leather-bound tomes lined walls of shelves, interspersed with bottles filled with richly-hued liquids.

Lola nearly ran into Gael when he stumbled to a halt. "I've heard about this place," he said, his voice lowered. "I've never seen anything like it before."

In the centre of it all, McInnes waited for them, her silvery dress billowing to the floor. Her lineless face gave nothing away, but her pale blue eyes seemed to look through them like all their secrets were being laid bare.

Marissa approached and gave an awkward bob. She was trembling. "Blessed be, *Hellerune*. Thank you for seeing us on such short notice."

McInnes's eyes lit up. "Blessed be, Sister. And I've asked you to refer to me as Maude."

"Yes, *Hellerune*." Marissa nodded and took a step back.

McInnes gave a rueful smile. "I see you are one for the rules, Sister. Still, I am content you came to see me. How may I offer assistance?"

"A girl has been taken by a spirit who will not let her go. I suspect...I believe an exorcism is required, but I have not the knowledge in such matters."

The older witch placed a thin hand on the pile of books weighing Marissa down. "Yet you are the collector of knowledge, are you not? I believe you seek something else from me."

McInnes turned and regarded each of them in turn, her gaze seeming to pierce soul-deep. She ended on Lola.

"An unusual group," she said, her voice low and measured. "But your strength lies in the unity of your purpose. You want your friend back, but you already know what must be done. What you seek is power."

"Yes, *Hellerune*. We do not have the power to see this through."

"But you do. I will help you see. First, though, I must speak to the novice." Her graceful hand lifted and pointed to Lola.

"I'm the novice?" Lola asked. It seemed odd to have existed for so long and to find herself as a novice, though to what she wasn't sure. Was she a novice human? A novice to her powers?

"But we all want to help Nix!" Gael burst out, his cheeks in high colour. "We're all a part of this, even the ones who aren't magic."

McInnes inspected him for a long moment, causing his face to flush even more.

"I couldn't agree more," she finally said. "But for this group to proceed, the novice must understand the part she is to play. It is imperative, and without her understanding, this will go precisely nowhere."

Her gaze met Lola's and seemed to be asking her many things. *Are you ready for your destiny? Will you accept the consequences of everything you set in motion when you took back your soul and your life?*

Lola's breath caught. This was her last chance to back out.

Even if she wanted to live a life of ignorance, though, she couldn't let Nix down. She wasn't ready for this, but she nodded all the same.

"Come." McInnes's tone left no room for argument. She disappeared into the lush greenery, leaving Lola to follow.

TWENTY-NINE

Behind a trellis of flowering vines was a private space with two armchairs, the faded leather piled with bright-coloured cushions. Candlelight danced across a gnarled wood table, casting flickering shadows that curled like claws around the room. The air was heavy with the scent of earth and living things.

McInnes sat, laying her hands deliberately on the armrests, and gestured for Lola to take the other seat.

The chair was soft and squashy, inviting her to sink into it, but Lola could only perch at the edge. She trembled, wound tight like a bowstring about to snap, her instincts screaming that this conversation would cost her something she wasn't ready to give.

"Blessed be, novice," McInnes said.

"Blessed be." The words were strange on Lola's lips. "I didn't realize I was a novice."

McInnes's stare was long and measured. "You have great understanding of the darkness that lies beneath us, don't you? And yet, as a souled creature, you are brand new."

Lola's breath was shaky. She'd come to accept that there was little McInnes didn't see of the truth of this island. "My soul isn't that young," she said, her voice hoarse. It felt strange to discuss this with someone who understood what she had done: where she had gone.

The memory of the moment when her light was returned to her was like a dream. For decades, her soul had waited for her, while a looming emptiness threatened to hollow her chest as a vampire.

"It is young and untried. Come, have a cup with me." A tea set had appeared on the table. Lola blinked, certain the pot and cups hadn't been there before.

McInnes served, pouring out not tea but dark coffee. "My nerves will suffer for this," she said with a gracious smile. "But I know it's your preference." She handed the bone china cup to Lola, who inhaled the rich perfume like oxygen.

The offering felt like a gift, and she bowed her head like Marissa had. "Thank you, *Hellerune*." She repeated the term the librarian had used, unsure what it meant.

McInnes raised a silver eyebrow as though she'd read Lola's mind. "It means seer. It's not entirely accurate, but it's a generous way of granting respect."

"I don't wish to be rude, but can we get going? I'm really worried about my friend."

"Yes, to the point." McInnes cleared her throat. "There was a recent flare of magic on the island."

"You mean Saturday night? A séance was performed, allowing a spirit to slip its bonds and possess Nix. My friend, I mean. It was misguided, but I didn't believe anyone in that group had actual power."

McInnes shook her head. "Earlier than that. About a week ago, powers long dormant on this island were used. Do you know anything about that?"

"I'm not sure..." Lola tried to match McInnes's calm gaze, even as her heart banged in her chest. "Something did happen, but I can't explain it. I was bricked up in the walls by the spirit of Seabourne Estate. It was dark and suffocating, and I panicked."

"You don't enjoy being trapped?"

Lola's hands were clammy, her palms slipping across her knees. "Who in their right mind likes being trapped?"

McInnes gave a knowing smile, her voice soft but sharp as a knife's edge. "You'd be surprised. Many of us cling to the prisons we build around ourselves. True freedom? It's rare, Lola. Most run from it, terrified." Her gaze met Lola's under heavy-set lids, her eyes glinting in the candlelight. "What does freedom mean to you?"

"To explore the world with nothing holding me back," Lola said, but the words rang hollow.

"We all have limits set upon us." McInnes's voice interrupted her thoughts like the slash of a knife. "We are limited by our circumstances, by our relationships, by our very bodies. We are limited by our responsibilities."

"I don't want any of that," Lola said with a thrum of disquiet. "Two more years on this island, establish my human identity, then the world is free for me to take."

"Is that what you truly want? Freedom, at the cost of everything else?"

Memories surfaced in Lola's mind: Walt when he let loose and actually smiled at a joke, Faye's singing drifting from the back of the bakery, Nix's carefree laugh as they lay on the beach. Gael, when he looked at her like he wanted to devour her.

She crushed the images like glass shards in her mind. Freedom to travel the world was what she wanted. It had to be. Wasn't that the point?

"Yes." Impatience coursed through her veins. Lola wasn't here for a metaphysical conversation; she wanted to save Nix. "What does that have to do with anything?"

"Everything."

From out of nowhere, a set of cards appeared in McInnes's hands, and she shuffled them with practiced ease.

"Show off," Lola grumbled.

McInnes laughed, a startling low rumble in her chest. "Apologies. Most of my clients appreciate the spectacle. You are clearly more discerning. Let's peer into the future together."

Lola sat rigid as the cards, black with gilded trim, flashed through the witch's hands. "I'd rather hear how to save Nix."

"What if I won't tell you until you've seen what your fate holds?"

"Then I would call you cruel."

McInnes nodded. "Fate can be cruel, but you are aware of this. I cannot, in good faith, tell you what you need to know until you've heard what you have no desire to learn. It's all connected, you see. You can't have one without the other." She laid the deck of cards on the table. "I will show you three cards that determine your fate. These cannot be changed; there is no way to avoid it. Cut the deck if you dare to help your friend."

Lola made as if to take the cards, then snatched her hand back as though burned. "What's the price?"

"You will see."

With a steadying breath, Lola closed her eyes and reached for the cards, thinking of Nix. Worn and leathery, the cards were surprisingly warm in her hands, and she cut the deck in two.

With a trembling hand, McInnes reached for the cards. A brief flicker of emotion marred her smooth face; was it pain? Or remorse? Lola couldn't tell, but it seemed the witch's abilities took a toll on her as well.

McInnes didn't look at the cards as she flipped the first one over. "The Eight of Swords. Entrapment Kent."

Lola studied the card, her breath catching as she took in the picture etched in gold on black, the rendering both beautiful and disturbing: A woman, bound and gagged at the edge of the ocean, surrounded by a prison of swords driven into the sand.

"Entrapment," Lola murmured. "Is it Nix who's trapped by the spirit? Or Alice herself, trapped for a century in the Seabourne Estate?" She frowned. "Or is it me who's trapped?"

McInnes's jaw tightened as she laid out the next card. "The Knight of Swords," she said, her voice an iron-like rasp as though the words burned in her throat. A gilded knight drove a winged horse forward, sword unsheathed, his face furled in rage. "It brings violence and danger."

Lola wanted to leave the reading then. But she had to see this through if McInnes would help her get Nix back, so she clenched her fists. "And the last?"

The witch's hand trembled, and there was a flicker of hesitation before she flipped it over with a gasp.

A skeleton, bearing a scythe in its bony hands, grinned up at Lola—a grim, mocking reminder of her past—and it hit like a punch to the gut.

Lola finished her own reading. "Death." Of course. Had she ever really escaped it?

"Behold what you have brought to Duchesne Island." McInnes's voice rose as she swept her hand over the three damning cards, her voice a croak. Sweat rolled down the sides of her face.

Heart hammering Lola studied her guilt cast in fortune cards. "I never meant to."

The witch's crystal gaze pinned her in place. "Never meant to, or didn't care? You came to Duchesne seeking freedom and treasure, two of the most selfish desires."

"Freedom isn't selfish," Lola said, though her words seemed empty.

"To live without ties to others, to rules, to society, to responsibility. For the world to be at your disposal, to do as you please." McInnes's mocking words lashed over her. "The definition of self-indulgence. You came here to take, consequences be damned."

"I didn't know..." Lola stopped then.

She didn't have any excuses. McInnes was right; her actions

had been entirely selfish, coming to the island. "I wanted to save myself, yes. I didn't know I would become human. I didn't know I would..." *Fall in love with a group of humans so flawed and so perfect.*

A tear spilled over her cheek, and she wiped at it with her palm. "I should go, then. If I bring calamity, I need to leave."

McInnes's long finger, bony as the hand of death itself, pointed to the bound woman. "What will be has already been set in motion." Her finger hovered, then landed on the Knight of Swords. "You can't hide from her forever."

Her voice was a hiss, as though coming from very far away, over rivers and deserts and oceans to damn Lola. "Look."

The image twisted on itself gradually, so Lola blinked before she could understand what it had morphed into her. No longer a man but a beautiful, vengeful woman bearing Jacquotte's face, watching her craftily from the corner of her eye.

A stab of panic thrummed through Lola, making her fingertips burn. Her creator was watching her, following her. She'd catch her eventually.

How childish she had been to think she could outrun her fate.

"I could read you a new fortune, one that follows you if you were to flee, vastly different than if you were to stay." McInnes's eyes were clouded over as though she spoke through the mists of time. "It would include everything you ever wanted. Treasure, yes, adventure. Freedom to do as you wish for the rest of your unnaturally given life. But—" Her finger fell on the grinning maw of the Death card. "Nothing will change what has already been decided for Duchesne Island."

"If she comes here..." Lola began, quavering.

"*When* she comes here, my dear."

"When she comes here, then." It hurt to say the words. "She'll go after them one by one. She won't stop until everything I've cared for has been destroyed. How can I stop this?"

McInnes held up her finger to hush Lola. In the strained

silence, she reached for the card at the top of the deck. She hissed as though it burned her fingers, but the witch gritted her teeth, laying it in front of Lola.

The gilt figure etched on the card was bound at the feet and hung upside down from the boughs of a tree. An oak tree, Lola noticed, just like the Tree of Life.

"The Hanged Man," McInnes whispered. "There must be a sacrifice."

The words sliced through Lola's chest. "Who will be the sacrifice? I won't let it be Nix."

The witch shook her head slowly, ponderously, as though she'd aged a great deal over the last minutes. "If you stay..." she gasped. "If you stay, you will find the power to help them. But the cost, my dear." She croaked and sat up straight. "The cost is great. There is always a price to pay."

Lola's eyes were riveted to the card. She looked at the card, the figure hanging from the tree, and saw herself. Bound, stuck, forever part of this island. Deep inside, she knew this would be the answer she didn't want to hear. Her vision blurred. "Tell me."

McInnes nodded and tapped the card. The oak leaves surrounding the hanging figure ruffled in a mystical breeze. "Here, on Duchesne, you can find the power to protect them. But, once you have connected with this force, once you have willingly accepted it, you may never leave."

The looming plants seemed to crowd in around Lola, their branches reaching out to imprison her as her breath caught in her chest. Never leave? She'd fought so hard for this life, had gone to the edge of the world and back again, only to find she must give up any hope of living it the way she'd dreamed.

No visits to Paris with Nix, no great adventures across continents. She'd seen so much, but never in the daylight. The soul she'd battled for would live and die on Duchesne Island.

She choked back tears. "I would be trapped here, forever." She looked to the bound woman again, on the shore of the ocean, never to cross it again. "Duchesne would be my prison. My sentence for what I've done."

"Duchesne would be your life. Your existence is so intricately tied to this island. What lies beneath our feet is power, and you can tap into that force. Every time you reach for that power, the ties that bind you to the island will strengthen. But so will you. You will live out the years you have been blessed with here."

"On a rock."

"In a home." McInnes's voice had regained its sharpness. "We all exist within one type of prison or another. Yours will be clearly delineated."

"What happens if I leave?"

"Your spirit will be too tied to the island; it cannot leave." McInnes's fingertips hovered over the Death card. "You would no longer exist."

"I'd die?"

"Body and soul would be separated once more. Only this time, your soul would be annihilated." Lola choked at the witch's harsh tone, but McInnes didn't back off. "You need to understand the consequences. You live and die here, or you cease to exist. That is what you would be accepting."

Lola stared at the cards, her damned future, her gaze falling on Jacquotte's sneering face. Could she leave the island behind now, knowing it would mean leaving those she cared for unprotected? They would suffer if she abandoned them. She could live out her years as she had foreseen them, travelling across the world in sunlight, but without the friends she'd come to see as family.

"If I accept..." she said, tapping the Hanged Man card. "If I choose this path, can I get Nix back?" She lifted her chin and faced McInnes, pleading with the fortune teller to give her some good news.

The witch stared at the cards for a long time. "This I cannot foresee. There is enough power, but it is the might of your will that matters. All I can tell you is that you will have a chance."

Nix's face swam into focus, pale and afraid. Lola sighed, and straightened her back. "A chance is more than nothing."

"Spoken like a true warrior." A light returned to McInnes's eyes, and to Lola, it seemed to hold an element of respect.

"If it will save Nix, then it's not a choice, not really." Lola let out a long breath. She didn't have time to contemplate what she was giving up. "I accept. What do I have to do?"

"Go save your friend," McInnes said, something resembling affection softening her stern face. "The answers will come to you as you need them."

THIRTY

"Please don't tell them," Lola said. "I don't want them to know yet."

The witch's expression was unreadable, but she nodded. "They will only know your secrets when you are ready to share."

She rose, movements smooth and deliberate, and they rejoined the others. Gael's gaze found Lola immediately, scanning her as if checking for cracks.

McInnes faced them like a commanding officer before uneasy troops. "You have everything you need to complete the required rituals."

"Wait," Marissa said, her face as pale as china as she clutched a book to her chest. "This magic is so new to me. What if I can't do it?"

McInnes raised an eyebrow. "And I've told you, you have everything you need. What happens first?" Her voice was commanding, a teacher demanding an answer from her student.

Marissa hesitated, then rifled through her books. "First, we need to find Nix."

"We know where she is," Walt said. "Holed up in the walls of

Seabourne Estate." He cleared his throat when McInnes turned her glittering eyes on him. "Sorry, didn't mean to interrupt."

McInnes's lip twitched. "This is a team effort, my empiricist. Tell us what you know."

"We've already faced her there; she's said she wants to keep Nix's body. It's where we assumed she died. Alice disappeared in 1921, but her body was never found."

McInnes nodded her approval. "We must make several assumptions here. That Alice was murdered, that her soul remains, that she seeks revenge. That ghosts exist at all. How does that make you feel?"

Walt fidgeted, trying to avoid her gaze, but finally, he sighed. "It's impossible, that's how I feel. About all of this. Vampires and ghosts and werewolves and witches? If this is real, what else have I been blind to?" Walt's gaze fell on Lola. "And yet I've seen the impossible. I'm not losing my mind, am I?" His voice was almost pleading.

"Not yet, and not necessarily. You must come to have faith in what you are experiencing. Not all the world is calculable; you must accept some powers go far deeper than the human mind is capable of understanding. Bend your mind so it will not break. Can you do so?"

Walt hesitated, then nodded.

"The spirit is in the walls of the estate, which gives us a focal point," McInnes said.

"But she's bricked up the Belowstairs," Gael said.

"If you can't get to her, then get her to come to you." McInnes gave a significant look at Marissa.

"A summoning," Marissa said, brightening. "I've read about that." She dumped her books on the table, rummaging through them.

"There is a swifter way," McInnes said, warmth in her voice as she watched her apprentice. "The power that runs through you is attracted to words. They call to you. Try calling back."

Marissa chewed her lip and stepped back from the pile of books, glaring as though they could catch fire from her gaze. Her hands thrust forward. "A summoning," she whispered over and over until it was only her lips shaping the sound.

A stirring of wind through the conservatory whistled past, and one of the books flopped open with a solid thump. The pages flickered past at lightning speed before stopping abruptly, settling like leaves falling in autumn.

Reiko's eyes were huge. "I've never seen anything like that before.

"Fascinating." Walt stepped forward, reading the page. "A summoning spell."

"You're progressing quickly," McInnes said, approval shining through her steely gaze. "But the summoning is only the beginning."

Magic had brought a flush to Marissa's cheek and her eyes sparkled, their normally dull grey more like the dark green of the ocean after a storm. "The spirit's angry, and she's dangerous. I don't have enough power to stop her."

"You have great power, my dear. And you will not be alone." McInnes nodded to Lola. "Lola at your side should be enough."

The others turned to Lola, and it felt like the ground had crumbled beneath her feet. She didn't want them to know how she had damned the island, how she must pay to make amends and bring Nix back.

"What kind of power? The visions you've been having?" Gael seemed to want to take a step towards her but held himself back.

"It's a part of it, I think," Lola said haltingly, looking to McInnes, who nodded in confirmation.

"The visions are a guide, nothing more. They can give you direction when you don't know where to go."

As much as she hated the intrusive, painful visions, Lola had to admit they could come in handy. She clenched her fists and faced her friends. "It's new, but I can access power. I did once before when I was trapped in the walls." She'd felt a connection to the Tree of Life then and, for a moment, imagined herself being hung among those ancient branches. "It has something to do with how I came back. I think I brought some of that power inside of me."

"Are you a witch now?" Marissa asked. "I've never heard of someone *becoming* a witch. I thought you were born to it. Then again, I've never heard of a vampire becoming human, either."

"Wait, you were a vampire?" Reiko rounded on Lola, who brushed her aside.

"Now's not the time, Order girl. One fight at a time, okay?"

"Not a witch," McInnes said. "Though not dissimilar. A witch's power comes from living things drawn from the earth. Lola's power comes from the place beyond that."

Reiko continued to side-eye Lola, but they didn't have time to work it out right now. "Let's assume we have the power," Lola said. "What do we need next?"

Marissa's hands spread over the books, pages falling open, and she read as quickly as she could. "The spirit must be brought to the place of transformation."

"Transformation?" Lola said. "Which transformation? From living to dying? Or from spirit to possession?"

"Both happened at Seabourne Estate," Gael said.

Marissa nodded, muttering under her breath as she read. "We'll need a circle of salt and some candles, standard stuff I have. But we'll also need a blade of pure silver and *acqua santa*. Holy water."

McInnes pursed her lips. "I have a blade of silver you may use," she said. "But I do not have holy water. I've often wondered how effective Christian priests truly are with their blessings."

"I wonder." Lola tugged at her hair absently as she thought it through. "What if *acqua santa* could mean something different, something powerful that exists only on this island?"

"The Elixir of Life," Gael said, picking up on what she meant.

"But the Well of Souls is closed," Walt said. "We can't get any more."

Reiko's head swung back and forth, extremely interested in their conversation, and Lola regretted allowing the demon hunter inside this group.

"But we have everything we need," Lola said, bringing up her hand to stare at her palm. "The Elixir of Life runs in my veins."

Walt's look was that of the skeptic. "You ingested the water. Technically most would have been discharged from the body by now."

His scientific tone made Lola smile. "Think less technically, Walt. You're thinking of the Elixir like a drug, but it's magic, and magic permeates deeper than flesh, lingering in our essence. To be touched by life-giving magic will linger in your blood, perhaps forever."

"Why blood?" Walt asked.

"Because it's always blood," Lola said. The words sat heavy on her tongue, the memories as a vampire rising up in her chest, thousands of lives spilled in blood, sacrificed for her survival. Ironic that she would spill hers willingly now. "That is where life lies within us."

"Then my blood would work as well," Gael said, brow furrowed.

"And mine," Walt added.

"Your magical theory is sound," McInnes said. "A creative solution. As I said, you have all you need. But you need to make haste."

"Wait," Reiko said, scowling at the group. "I want to help too. I might not be magic or whatever you all are, but I'm strong. I know about rituals, and I can fight if need be."

"We don't need you," Walt said immediately. "I don't even know why you're here."

"I'm here because of Nix," Reiko said, bringing her hands up and letting them fall helplessly. "I don't want her to be hurt. I..." She seemed to have nothing to add.

Walt looked scornful, but Lola held up a hand. "We might need a fighter," she said.

"I'll fight for Nix," Gael said, the protest evident in his voice.

"I know you will. But Reiko's been trained to fight the forces of darkness. I suspect she's a good person to have at your back."

"If she does have our backs," Gael said. "Or is she more likely to stab us?"

Reiko's eyes were dark grey, conflicted. "No, I'll fight for you. For Nix."

"I'm looking forward to seeing what you can bring forward together." McInnes strode to the side of her fortune-telling grove, to a trunk painted with esoteric symbols, and reverently lifted a package bound in silk. She unbound it, bringing forth a blade engraved with runes down both sides.

She held it out in two hands to Marissa. "Take this, Sister, with my blessing."

A faint crack of thunder rolled across the sky as McInnes handed the silver dagger to Marissa. Lola glanced out the windows of the conservatory towards the horizon, where dark clouds loomed like a shadow waiting to pounce.

The others had formed a circle around the witch, who spun, satisfaction gleaming in her eyes. "The change I've foreseen is already happening. As you act together, your strength grows. *So mote it be!*" McInnes shouted.

A ripple of power passed through Lola. She clearly wasn't the only one, as Reiko's body spasmed, and Walt stared at his hands in wonder.

"Did I just engage in witchcraft?" he asked, uncurling his fingers as though he still felt the current of magic.

"I gave direction to the bond between you, your goal to help the lost soul," McInnes said. "It will bind you together and allow you to pool your power when necessary."

Reiko's nostrils flared as if she would breathe out fire, her face tight and rigid. "How dare you infect me with your spells!"

Her nails dug into her arms as she held herself. "You had no right."

McInnes's gaze puzzled over the demon hunter. "All of your power comes from witches' rites; you brand our symbols into your skin. Why do you cringe in the face of it?"

A snarl like a wounded animal rose in Reiko's throat. "Your magic is dirty," she spat, though her voice wavered. "The Order protects us from this. From people like you."

"I see," McInnes said, impassive. "The spell I cast will last no longer than sundown and will fade entirely. Whether you choose to use it or not is entirely in your hands. But the time will come, young one, when you must decide what matters to you most. Now." She clapped her hands. "You have until the end of the day to perform the exorcism—after that, the magical bonds strengthening you will shatter. Go forth with my blessing."

Soured by Reiko's outburst, the group filed through the Victorian mansion.

Walt glared at the hunter. "We don't need her. What's she even going to do—punch a ghost? She can leave."

Faced with following them or being left behind with McInnes, Reiko reluctantly took up the rear. McInnes watched them, her expression opaque.

It wasn't until they were out in the Atlantic air that Marissa stopped and turned to Reiko, holding the silver dagger in her hand.

"You call our magic dirty, but you take it anyways—steal it like it's yours to own." Her voice trembled, but she didn't back down. "I may be new to this, but I see the truth: The Order's power is built on fear, not strength. And I won't let you talk down to me or my people again."

And Marissa turned and marched away, hunched over by the weight of her heavy books, leaving Reiko stricken by the dressing down from the frail librarian.

Lola ran after Marissa.

"Why are you doing this?" she asked her. "Nix is our friend. And Reiko, well, she seems to have her own reasons." She nodded back to the demon hunter who followed behind them, kicking the occasional rock. "But why are you willing to risk your life for a girl you met once?"

"I want to help Nix! She seemed nice. Well, a bit aggressive, actually." Marissa sighed. "But it's not just that. I also need to understand my power. How can I know what I'm capable of if I don't push myself?" Marissa gave her a quick look, her cheeks flaring. "And being with you has been a little bit like having a friend."

Lola swallowed hard and put an arm around Marissa's shoulders. "I'm kinda new to friendship too," she said. "I'd be honoured to be your friend."

"Hate to break up the love fest," Reiko said from behind, her eyes guarded. "But that storm brewing to the east isn't natural."

The roiling clouds off the coast were massing closer, pulsing with purple lightning. A crack of thunder split the air, so loud it rattled through Lola's bones.

THIRTY-ONE

"We need to get inside, now!" Gael's yell was nearly swallowed by the wind as it roared towards them. The group braced themselves against its violence, sprinting up the rocky path that led to the cliffside. Overhead, the silhouette of the Seabourne mansion loomed, black against the flickering skies as though watching their approach.

Lola's gaze strayed to the Atlantic again and again. No longer blue but a snarling expanse of white-lashed waves, foaming as though the sea itself was furious. If she saw this through to the end —if she did what it would take to bring Nix back—it would mean she would never again set sail across those waves to new horizons. The thought struck her like a blow to her chest. This would be her view from this day until she died. Doomed to live out her life on a rock, cut off from the world. Trapped.

She tore her eyes away as they climbed. *No more thinking about the past or an impossible future,* she reminded herself firmly. *Concentrate on the here and now—and keeping Nix in it.*

Below them, Port Despardoux sprawled out like a colourful quilt, a stark contrast to the wild weather above. The pastel homes with their chimneys puffed smoke, seemingly untouched by the storm. The lights were on at the Pain Perdu, its golden light spilling out over the cobblestones, while down the coast, the lighthouse flashed bravely in the storm, the eternal sentinel against darkness.

That lighthouse was Nix's home. Nix's legacy.

Gusts of wind carried muffled calls to them, one word over and over: "Nix! Nix!"

Along the winding streets, faint clusters of lights bobbed like fireflies—lanterns carried by search parties. The people of Duchesne were looking for their lost daughter.

Lola concentrated on putting one step in front of the other up the rocky path. She wouldn't let them down; she was going to find her friend and bring her back.

Rain hit them in icy sheets as they neared the mansion, the air tasting of salt and metal. Lightning split the sky in an explosion of purple-white, illuminating the iron gates and the yawning mouth of the manor as spectral shadows were cast along the ground.

The boom of thunder hit as they made the last dash onto the covered porch.

Soaking, they paused in the shelter outside of the stinging rain, gasping for breath. Seabourne Estate was darker and more foreboding than ever, its windows as black as empty eye sockets. The dread clawing inside Lola mounted until she could choke on it.

"Okay, let's take on a ghost," she forced herself to say, her voice trembling more than she would have liked.

As they approached, the door swung inwards. They cringed back as though expecting an attack, but the house met them only with cold stillness.

Lola stuck her head inside. The air was both clammy and stifling, as though it had sat empty and shut up for years. Shivers wracked through her. "Definitely still haunted," she said. "Let's go."

They stepped inside, and Seabourne Estate swallowed them whole.

The blackness of the mansion seemed alive, devouring the faint beams of their flashlights. A clinging smell of rot lingered in the air—mouldering leaves, wet earth, and something deeper, older. Lola forced herself to step carefully, avoiding the decomposing carcass of a pumpkin. Her breath puffed white in the frigid gloom.

"Do you feel that?" Gael whispered. "It's colder in here than outside."

The others clustered closer, their collective silence thick with tension. Then, a flicker of light caught Lola's eye, a soft glow bleeding into the hallway ahead.

Candlelight.

Her stomach dropped. *Alice!*

The flickering became brighter, and she tensed, wishing she had some kind of weapon, though what would work against a spirit? Besides, she couldn't hurt Alice as long as she was inside Nix.

They pressed together into a clump, even Reiko, nobody even breathing as the flicker grew brighter. The light came around the corner, revealing a white face lit from below by a trembling flame. A glint of metal caught Lola's eye; the figure held something in the other hand.

Someone shrieked and the light sputtered out.

"Walt?" A voice wavered in the dark, fragile and sharp as glass. "What are you doing here? You frightened me—I dropped my candle."

Lola's flashlight beam found the figure: Mayor Seabourne.

The woman winced, holding up her hand to block the glare. "Enough!" she commanded, her voice cold and icy again. The beams fell, allowing her to find her fallen candle, and with a flare of a match, she re-lit it.

The mayor looked smaller than usual, a black puff coat engulfing her frame, one hand cradling the candle, the other shoved deep in her pocket. Lola thought of the glimpse of metal she'd seen and became very certain that Mayor Seabourne held a gun in her hand.

"Mom?" Walt whispered. "What are you doing here? I thought you were at the hotel."

The mayor's bitter laugh echoed off the walls. The tang of gin floated in the air. "Yes, well. That would be more comfortable, wouldn't it? But someone has to clean up his messes."

Lola glanced around the shadowed room, debris littering the once-grand hallway. Her instincts prickled; the mansion was disastrously filthy, and yet she got the sense the mayor didn't mean a physical mess.

"Is Dad here?" Walt asked carefully.

"No," his mom said, her eyes like ice chips in the dim light. "Once again, your father has vanished, leaving me to deal with the fallout."

"What fallout, Mom? What's going on?"

Mayor Seabourne turned misty-eyed for a moment, her face almost soft as she took in her son. "Darling, it would be best if you weren't here tonight. It's not safe."

"What isn't safe?" Walt pressed, but the mayor's gaze hardened.

"You need to leave," she snapped, suddenly sharp again. "All of you. Go back to the hotel. Please, Walt, go. You shouldn't be here."

"We're looking for Nix, Mom. She's gone missing."

"Nix? The little lighthouse girl? I can assure you she's not here. There isn't a single living thing here besides me."

She might be right at that, but Lola couldn't allow the mayor to throw them out of the house. "Mayor Seabourne," she said, "the search parties are passing close to here. We said we'd search the estate grounds, and we came in out of the rain. If it's not us that looks for her here, then another group will be along soon."

The mayor's head jerked up. "No one should be here tonight."

"No," Walt said, catching on. "We'll let everyone know it's all clear. I'm just going to grab something in the study that she might have left, okay? We won't bother you again."

"It's not the bother, darling. It's that it's not safe."

"What isn't safe, Mom?"

She reached out to cup his face. "Life, I suppose. I'm sorry for all of it, darling. I suspect you deserved better."

Walt's hand went to his cheek his mother had stroked while Mayor Seabourne swallowed hard and seemed to regather herself. "You go along now and finish up here."

"You should leave, too, Mom."

"In time, darling." She nodded a few times, then wandered towards the ballroom. Her hand slipped out of her pocket, and Lola caught the edge of a snub-nosed pistol.

What on earth was the mayor protecting the house from? She doubted she was on guard against ghosts. She believed something else would happen tonight.

Lola tried to think back: Walt's father's abuse, his fury to find them in the Belowstairs, the fact that the hidden corridor had been swept clean, obviously being used again.

Did it have something to do with the man who had scared him so badly at the Harvest Ball? What else was going on at Seabourne Estate?

She hesitated, wondering if they should follow the mayor's advice and get out while they could.

But nothing could stop them from saving Nix. Lola glanced at the others, their faces pale in the flashlight beams, and jerked her head. "Let's get to the study."

They were shaking with cold as they entered the room. Walt braced himself against the fireplace, his face in shadows as he stood very still.

"Are you okay?" Lola asked.

His smile was ghostly in the darkness. "Of course, what could possibly be the matter?" He grabbed a lighter sitting on the mantel and bent down to set the flame to kindling, the fireplace still prepared for a fire.

Within a minute, the dry logs had roared to life, crackling and sending off hisses of heat.

"Is that wise?" Reiko asked. "Someone might notice. Who knows who's in the house tonight?" Her hunting blade had appeared in her hand again, and Lola was suddenly glad to have Reiko with them.

"What difference could it make?" Walt said, his voice gone flat. "We might as well not die of hypothermia before then."

Lola couldn't argue that the heat was delicious against her icy skin, and they clustered around the fireplace, absorbing as much warmth as they could.

"Walt, man." Gael's voice was quiet. "What's going on with your family?"

Once again, that bitter, brittle smile. "I don't know everything. The answer would likely get us arrested or killed." He shrugged. "It doesn't matter now. The only thing that matters is getting Nix back."

"Then what are we waiting for?" Gael said, and the others straightened, shaking out chilled hands and rummaging through bags.

"Are you sure this is the best place to summon Alice?" Marissa asked.

"We should be in the Belowstairs," Walt replied. He went to the *Treasure Island* book. On a grinding screech, though, the bookshelf refused to open.

Reiko's device was out, clicking as she waved it around the room. "There's a confluence of Otherworldly activity," she explained, stopping in front of the hidden passage. "It's strongest right here."

Marissa glanced back at the exit before dropping her bag where Reiko pointed. A few books wiggled on the shelves as she passed, like friendly dogs wanting to say hi.

"We'll set up here and hope Alice comes to us," she said as she unloaded books and supplies. "Lola, have you ever seen a spirit circle before?"

"Yes," Lola said, ignoring Reiko's searching gaze. "I can start setting up." She gathered materials from Marissa's bag, even as dark dread pulsed through her. She had seen things, yes, but nothing she'd like to see repeated here. Would Nix survive the ritual?

Would any of them?

Thirty-Two

"Make a thick circle of salt—enough to contain her—but keep an edge open for now," Marissa instructed Lola, her voice steady despite the unease crackling in the air. "It would help if we had something of Alice's. It'll anchor the summoning, show her where to go."

"I have her diary."

Marissa's head snapped up, her eyes widening behind enormous glasses. "Perfect."

"What can I do?" Gael asked, his voice tight with anticipation.

"Candles, five of them, set around the outside perimeter of the salt circle." Marissa handed him a bundle. "They're infused with rosemary. It'll cleanse the space."

Walt stood by the fire, watching placidly, while Reiko prowled the room like a restless predator.

When everything was in place, Marissa positioned herself opposite the secret passage, shaking out her hands as though expelling nerves.

"Gather around the circle." Her voice came out hoarse. She muttered the spell under her breath, her lips moving quickly—memorizing, focusing. Then at last, she joined the group, the dagger gleaming in one hand. "Space yourselves evenly. We're summoning the spirit of Alice McCullough. Once she's inside the circle, Lola, you close it with salt. It'll hold her in place while we perform the exorcism."

A hush fell. Marissa drew a slow, shaky breath as though bracing herself for impact. Then she straightened her shoulders.

"Alice McCullough, we call you by name! Show thyself and join our circle!"

The words rang through the heavy silence. The room felt as though it had shrunk, like something unseen pressed in on all sides. A surge of energy washed over them; thick, electric, alive.

A sharp rapping at the door shattered the moment. Marissa choked on a gasp.

"Is it working already?" Walt asked in a whisper.

"I...I don't think so." Marissa's glasses flashed as she turned towards the sound.

"It's probably my mom. Her timing is priceless." As the door swung open, Walt went to stop it, his voice etched with annoyance. "Mom, we just need...oh, it's you. Why are you here?"

A figure swept past him, swathed in a long black coat and smelling of rainstorms. The beam of an electric lantern cut through the gloom.

"What the hell is going on?"

"Violet?" Lola's breath caught as she recognized the girl's long blonde hair, rumpled and damp from the storm. Violet's cheeks were flushed, her eyes locked on Walt with something between fury and hurt.

"Violet, what are you doing here?" Walt asked, taking a step towards her. He looked at her as though she was the ghost, like he couldn't believe she was standing there. Then he shook his head, remembering. "Listen, this isn't a good time. The power is out, and..." He waved his hand vaguely at the salt and candles, though there was no easy way to explain it.

She shook her head. "I needed to talk to you about what

happened. And I came here today, and I know it's all dark, but the door opened for me, and I thought maybe it was another game. I heard a voice calling out..." She trailed off as though just registering there were others in the room with them. "Right. Not a good time."

"What do you mean, another game?"

She spoke low, as though just for Walt, though her hiss carried. "You *kissed* me like that the other night. In front of everyone." Her words tumbled out fast as though she'd been saving them up.

Walt's face darkened. "It *was* a game, Vi. I didn't mean to embarrass you."

Her eyes flared. "That's not what I meant. I just wanted to know if it had meant..." She raised her hand as though she wanted to touch him but then let it fall. She glanced around at the circle of people staring at her, and her cheeks flushed magenta pink. She gasped out, "I'm sorry," and turned to leave.

"Violet, wait!" Walt took a step towards her but then hesitated, his hands clenched.

They stared at each other for a beat before she sniffed and smoothed out her coat. "Right. I'm interrupting...this." Her gaze fell on the circle of salt and the flickering candles. She froze, frowning. "Whatever this is?"

"Oh, this?" Lola forced a laugh that felt stiff in her throat. "Just...something we're doing for fun. Getting together in candlelight. And stuff." She elbowed Gael, who chimed in with a false laugh.

"Right. Totally normal candle stuff."

Violet stared at them like they'd lost their minds. "Totally normal...candle stuff." She turned to Walt. "This looks like occult stuff. Like what happened at the ball."

"No, it's nothing like that!" Lola said, a little too brightly.

"It kinda has to do with that," Walt said, even as Reiko hissed at him in anger.

"More games?" Violet said to Walt.

"It was never a game, Vi." Walt's look was intense, and Lola didn't think he was talking about the séance.

"For crying out loud!" Reiko stormed up to Violet. "Can somebody get the civilian out of here? She's going to mess up everything. And then Nix—" She cut herself off sharply as though shocked by her outburst.

Violet squared her shoulders, her purple-toned eyes glittering in the firelight. She didn't say a word, but the tilt of her head screamed, *Make me.*

"We don't have time for this," Lola said, worried Reiko might do exactly that. Panic was starting to settle in her chest; what if they missed their chance to get Nix? "The only thing that matters is getting Nix back."

"What happened to Nix? I heard she was missing."

"She's not missing, but she's..." Walt stopped, flustered. "Violet, maybe you should—"

"Something's happening!" Marissa's voice rang out in alarm.

The candles erupted, their flames roaring upward nearly to the ceiling.

"Quick, get into position!" Marissa shouted. "She's coming!"

They scrambled into place. Without hesitation, Violet joined the circle, planting herself beside Walt.

"What happens if we don't contain her?" Gael asked, his voice taut. Lola stood next to him, ready with salt in shaking hands.

Marissa's face was grim. "Then all hell breaks loose." She lifted her face upwards, calling into the echoing spaces of the house. "Alice McCullough! We call you by name! Show thyself and join our circle!"

"Who's Alice McCullough?" Violet asked out of the side of her mouth.

Reiko shushed her, her glare promising violence if she spoke again, and Violet set her mouth. A tense silence built as the candles burned, emitting incandescence and heat like miniature bonfires.

Sweat rolled down Lola's back under her damp sweater, which steamed in the heat.

"This isn't working," Marissa said. "She's fighting me."

"What can we do?" Lola asked, fearing the answer would spell her end, doomed to remain on the island forever.

"There is one thing the book says," Marissa said. "Something to add urgency to the spell. It's called divine gunpowder, but I haven't been able to figure out what it is."

"You need a powder that's a stimulant to bump up the spell?" Walt asked, his eyes peering into Marissa as though testing the depths of the water.

"Something like that. Throwing the powder into the flames provides a boost."

"Hang on; I have something." Walt left the circle and strode to the desk. He felt his way underneath the drawer and a false bottom popped out. Inside were dozens of bags of white powder. Lola gasped; thousands of dollars' worth of cocaine was hidden in the desk. That must be how Walt's father made his money, and it explained his scary business associates.

"Walt!" Violet's eyes were huge.

His mouth was a grim line. "Now you all know the family secrets. Classy, isn't it? The Seabournes never stopped their smuggling ways." He brought a baggie over to the circle. "What do you think?"

After a moment's hesitation, Marissa gave a shaky nod. "I think...yes. It could probably work."

"Maybe my father is good for something after all." Walt opened the baggie and threw the fine white powder over the searing candles.

The powder caught fire mid-air and went up in an explosion of purple light and heat. As one, the group turned their faces away from the flare, as the smoke cycled upwards into a fiery tornado before dissipating.

"Alice McCullough, we call you by name," Marissa said, her

voice hoarse as the spell took its toll on her. "Show thyself and join our circle."

The scratching sounded around them, behind every wall, like a nest of rats trying to claw their way out. The scratching swelled, an infestation within the very bones of the house, as though the walls would crack open and spill their contents. Alice was very close.

The scream began as though a long way away, echoing as though from down a mile-long tunnel. It rose to a howling shriek that reverberated around them, full of desperation and sorrow. Lola wanted to press her hands to her ears, but she held the salt and couldn't let go.

The room grew colder, a deep, marrow-sapping chill.

"Hold steady," Marissa's whisper was an agonized rasp; sweat poured down her face. "It's working; she's coming."

Sobbing filled the air now, suffused with despair, a weak, defeated sound. "Please, please, please..." A girl's voice repeated the murmur as she cried.

"Please *what*?" Violet's eyes were wide with dismay. "Can we help her?"

"We're going to try." Marissa's entire body was shaking. Her face was wet with tears or sweat—Lola couldn't be sure which—dripping off her chin and jaw. "Alice McCullough, show thyself!"

Her voice went deep on an influx of power, echoing around them. After that was a stifling silence.

The bookcase moved as if alive, groaning with a resistance that made Lola's breath catch. As the door opened, the gaping blackness beyond seemed to hum with a life of its own.

THIRTY-THREE

A rush of fetid air washed over the group in the study, bringing with it the eye-stinging scent of decay. The candles burned higher, prison bars of flame.

A figure materialized in the darkness, walking towards them in stilted steps, like a marionette being moved on strings. Jerkily, she came into focus, although Lola had trouble distinguishing her features. She glowed with purple light; the Otherworld surrounded her.

It was Nix, but not, still wearing the T-shirt and jeans from the day before and covered with filth. Her copper hair hung in knotted loops, and her cheeks seemed sunken, pressing against the skull beneath. Her eyes burned with shimmery light.

She carried a candle, red wax dripping down her hands.

"Alice McCullough, we call you," Marissa said. Lola repeated the plea, and beside her, Gael took up the chant. The rest of the group began to repeat it together in low tones that bounced off the walls. The name Alice McCullough whispered around them as though someone else was speaking as well.

Fighting them every step of the way, Nix's body was brought forth out of the passageway and into the circle. Lola nearly reached out for the girl, then grabbed her hands back, clenching them into fists, knuckles white.

Nix entered the circle of flame and salt. Lola's belly tensed; if she didn't get this right, they could be trapped inside the study with a murderous ghost. As soon as Nix's sneakers stumbled past the salt line, Lola crouched and completed the circle, ensuring there were no gaps.

Now Alice McCullough couldn't escape.

Lola straightened and gasped to find Nix standing only inches away from her, her face transformed into a terrifying scowl, eyes burning with a vengeful madness.

"Oh God," Violet said, pointing to Nix's hands. It wasn't candlewax that dripped freely down her wrists but thick drops of scarlet blood flowing from her fingertips where the nails had been ripped off.

"Nix," Lola whispered. The ghost snarled but moved on around the circle, facing each of them as though memorizing their faces for later. She came to rest in front of Walt.

Her lips curled back to show her teeth, and she lunged for him, bloody fingers outstretched.

And she came to a halt as though hitting a wall, an inch away from him. Walt held his place, barely wincing as Nix lunged. "Nix," he said softly, his face creased in pain. The girl growled—an animal sound.

Beads of sweat stood out on Marissa's brow. "The spirit of Alice McCullough has been summoned and cannot leave the circle so long as it remains unbroken." Her voice held firm, but her hands betrayed her, trembling as they clutched the dagger. "We must establish contact with the spirit and ask her to leave Nix's body and this house."

"You make it sound simple," Gael said.

"I didn't mean to," Marissa replied in a flat voice. "Most lingering spirits will fight to the death to remain, not wishing to face their end. They are attached to this plane for one reason or another and will not easily relinquish their hold on it. Unless we can convince her to go, we'll have to force Alice McCullough into her afterlife. It takes serious magic and risks opening doorways to other planes."

"Like, to the Otherworld?" Gael asked.

"What *is* the Otherworld?" Violet's voice shook and she was as pale as Nix. Walt reached out to take her hand and she grasped him like a lifeline.

"Maybe now's not the best time for an explanation," he said.

Violet gave a curt nod, her eyes sharpening. "Right. If we're going to do an exorcism, then we should, like, do it."

Marissa raised McInnes's ceremonial blade, and in the candlelight, the runes glinted with purple fire. "The silver will help channel the spirit from this plane to the next, and the holy water is offered to purify the soul. Or, in this case, the holy blood."

Violet startled. "Blood?"

Walt shook his head and gave her hand a squeeze. "Don't worry, we don't need yours."

She gave him a look as though she'd never really seen him before.

Marissa lofted the dagger. "Hold out your palm," she said to Lola. Her voice remained steady, but her hand jerked. "I don't want to hurt you," she whispered.

Lola held her gaze. "I'm doing this for my friend," she said. "Set aside your uncertainty and claim your power."

Marissa took a steadying breath and scored a shallow cut across Lola's palm. The wound slashed Lola's lifeline in two with a searing sting, and she folded her hand as dark blood welled up. She turned to Gael, who watched her with his golden gaze.

"You okay?" he asked.

Her smile was shaky. "Well worth it."

Gael and Walt both held out their hands and with surer strokes, Marissa cut them as well. Lola held her fist out, letting the crimson drops splash inside the circle. The boys did so as well.

Where the blood hit the wooden floor, it sizzled as though scorched.

Nix's head flew back as she cried out, and her hands went to her chest as though she'd been stabbed.

"You're hurting her!" Violet cried.

"She doesn't want to go," Marissa yelled, tears running down her face. "I can feel her anger, her sorrow. There's too much horror here."

"Do me as well," Reiko said. She held out her left palm, the one not holding a knife. Her gaze hadn't left Nix, now pacing the edge of the circle as though searching for a way to escape.

"You don't have Elixir in your blood," Lola said.

"I don't care." Reiko raised her chin, her tone harsh. "I have power in my blood, whether it's stolen or not. If it can be used to save Nix, then it's worth it. Please." Her voice faltered.

Marissa's head tilted as though considering Reiko in a new light. "I don't think it would hurt," she said. "Magic is about intention as much as anything. At the end of the day, it's only blood."

"It could mess up the spell," Walt said, watching Reiko uncertainly.

"If you won't, I will." In a sudden movement, Reiko took her own hunting knife and cut her palm deeply, the blood splattering to the floor.

Nix stopped still as a statue then.

They all froze. Slowly, as though moving underwater, the possessed girl turned to face Reiko and began to glow.

"That got her attention," Violet muttered.

Nix's features blurred and reformed, her skin mottling as bones pushed against it from beneath. Her eyes darkened and her face twisted into somebody else. And she was thin, so thin, like a starving famine victim. A bone jutted out from her collarbone. Lola swallowed back her cry.

"Alice McCullough," Marissa said, her voice deeper with the

influx of power that filled the room as she spoke. "We ask you to return our friend. It is time for you to go home. It is time for you to pass on." The words echoed off the walls, the command repeating itself over and over.

Alice stared at Reiko. "Irene. You forgot me." Her voice was scratchy, as though unused for a very long time, with a different cadence than Nix's.

Reiko's breath hitched as Alice's words washed over her. Her bloody hand pressed to her chest. "I never forgot you. I've been trying to bring you back."

"After what your father did..." Alice let out a sighing breath and flickered for a moment, appearing as a skeleton standing in front of them.

Reiko didn't break eye contact with Alice, playing along. "What did my father do?"

"You must have known! He found us, in our place. Our place..." Once more, the sighing sorrow. "I would wait for you there. I loved it, our secret haven away from the world, tucked away from everyone who would look at us the wrong way. So very few people ever thought to peek in there, so we could stay, stealing minutes or even hours." Alice reached out as though to touch Reiko. A soft smile played over her face.

"She's connecting with you, Reiko," Lola said. "Keep on talking."

"I loved meeting you there." Longing played over Reiko's face.

"Me too," Alice whispered and closed her eyes. But when she opened them, her brow furrowed and she screamed. It pierced the air like an eagle's screech, causing Lola to flinch back. "But when he found us, your father, he was furious. Like a demon." She twitched as though tormented by pinching hands. "He tore you away from me, out of my arms, and hit you. I couldn't handle it. I couldn't see him hurt you. I grabbed his arm, and he turned on me, striking me with such force." Her voice garbled. "I fell back and don't remember the rest."

"He must have killed her in a rage," Gael said. "The original Mr. Seabourne murdered her and claimed she was a thief to cover it up."

"The Seabourne family walls up their secrets." Alice's voice lowered to a malevolent hiss as she turned on Walt, who resembled her murderer far too much for comfort. "You take what you want from people, don't you, and leave us to suffer when you're done."

"I...I'm sorry for what happened to you." Walt swallowed hard as he faced Alice McCullough's fury. "You didn't deserve to die that way."

"If only I had." Her voice was a harsh rasp, and she let out a maniacal laugh.

"How can I make this up to you?" Walt asked.

"Let me out." Alice's voice hissed around them. "Let me free."

"We're going to free you, Alice." Marissa took up her book in one hand and the bloody knife in the other, a priestess in tweed. "With all the power of creation and beyond, we ask this soul to depart from this plane and find peace in the next. We beseech thee; take flight from this earthly prison and make haste to the rewards beyond!"

Alice crouched in the centre of the circle like a trapped animal and hissed. "Let me out! Let me out! Let me out!"

"It's not working," Gael said, horror plain on his face as Alice cringed on the ground.

"Lola," Marissa said. "I don't have the power to finish this. I need your help."

The dread that had been hovering inside Lola's chest dissipated as the time came to act. She didn't want to be trapped on Duchesne Island for the rest of her life, but she wouldn't allow Nix to remain in such a state. The decision, finally, was easy.

She closed her eyes and reached within herself, thinking back to when she had felt the power stir beneath her feet to release her from the wall. A slow building of energy unfurled deep in the earth in response; she could feel it reaching out for her.

For you, Nix, she thought, and with her mind's eye, reached for the power and drew it inside of her, like a plant drawing up from its roots.

The energy grew, looping around her like vines, twisting around her ankles, her wrists, her neck and holding her in place, suffocating with the power. And still, she called to it, demanding it fill her up.

A quiet warmth wrapped around her hand; Gael had taken it, palm to palm. She focused on this warmth only and pushed back the power that sought to overwhelm her. Her heart rate slowed, and she drew in a deep, replenishing breath.

With tremendous effort, she lifted her hand and squeezed; fresh blood splattered over the floor.

"I understand what is required of me," she said. Her words were a murmur, meant to be heard by unseen forces. She pictured the Tree of Life swaying in the wind and spoke to it. "I accept your offering. You have your sacrifice; my life is yours."

The power flooded through her unimpeded, and she gasped. It was intoxicating, both agony and ecstasy, as it filled her. It whispered promises of strength and permanence yet demanded pieces of her she would never regain. A green light glowed from within.

"Alice McCullough," she said to the spirit, who stared at her through wide, hateful eyes. "We ask you to return our friend. It is time for you to pass on."

The power thrummed through her. Despite everything she was giving away, she gloried in it. For a moment, she imagined her old life, stalking through the woods with the power of ancient forces in her veins, entering the hunt and knowing she would win. She had missed that feeling.

Alice stood there, though, and glowed with her own purple light. Her face was tight with horror, her mouth open in a scream of suffering. It went on and on, and she clawed at the invisible walls holding her captive inside the prison of candles and salt. "Let me out! Let me out!"

"Why isn't it working?" Marissa asked, frantic. "We want to let her out!"

It struck Lola like a thunderclap, her thoughts racing back to the renovations done on Seabourne Estate. The sloppily mortared brick wall. The scratching had never been a threat—it was a plea.

Slow horror trickled through her. "She's still trapped. She's been there all along." Lola's voice was barely a whisper, but it cut through the room like a knife.

Gael's gaze darted around the circle, his golden eyes sharp with fear. "Where?"

The scratching grew louder, more frantic now. Lola's chest tightened as the realization sank in. "She's in the wall," Lola said. "Her tomb. Mr. Seabourne must have stuffed Alice's body into the alcove and bricked it over. But she wasn't dead. Not yet. He buried her alive."

"Oh God," Violet whispered.

Alice sobbed and the scratching sounded all around them. Understanding of the girl's suffering seemed to flood the group, each of them looking nauseated or pitying in turn.

A surge of magic rose in Lola again, soothing and peaceful. It spoke of retribution and healing. "We need to trust Alice. She was a victim in all this. We shouldn't force her into the next life. We need to be at her side, guiding her."

"You've suffered alone long enough," Reiko said, her voice trembling with conviction. "If you'll trust me, I'll walk with you. You won't face it alone." She held out her hand to Alice, across the salt circle.

Alice's bony hand hovered just above Reiko's, her expression torn between hope and suspicion. The group held their breath as the darkness seemed to lean in, waiting for what would come next.

THIRTY-FOUR

"Hold on to me," Reiko said, her voice steady but soft, her grey eyes searching Alice's face. The spirit's light flickered within Nix's body. "Show me the way."

Haltingly, Alice's trembling hand met Reiko's. Their blood-slick palms met over the salt, and Alice gasped, the contact sending ripples of light over her form.

"I miss you," she whispered, her voice a fragile thread.

"I miss you too." Reiko's voice cracked, and she leaned in, pressing a gentle kiss to Alice's cheek as light and fleeting as smoke. The spirit let out a shuddering breath.

"But it's wrong," Alice said, her voice broken. "We knew it was wrong."

"No." Reiko's tone sharpened. "It was never wrong. The only ones in the wrong were the ones who hurt you. Who tried to make you less than you are." Her fingers tightened around Alice's. With a deliberate move, Reiko brushed her toe across the salt grains, disturbing the circle and leaving a gap.

The air crackled with energy as the salt scattered. Lola braced herself for an onslaught, but Reiko's grip on Alice didn't falter. "Show me," she repeated. "Let me set you free."

Alice's luminous eyes searched Reiko's, filled with ancient grief. Finally, she nodded and shuffled forward, past the salt circle and into the looming passageway to the Belowstairs.

Marissa clutched her book and dagger, her face taut with apprehension. Lola stooped to grab a candle, and the others followed suit. They filed into the darkness, a candlelit procession led by the dead.

Violet brought up the rear, her face a pale, wavering mask. When she passed the threshold into the passageway, the door slammed behind them with a resonant, final crunch.

"How do we get out?" Violet's voice, edged with panic, cut through the stillness.

"There's a lever—" Walt stepped forward, paling as the lever crumbled in his grip. He stared at the dust on his palm, his face pale.

"I'm guessing that's not good," Violet said. Her tone was dry, but her knuckles whitened as she gripped her candle.

Lola's jaw tightened and she forced steel into her voice. "We have to keep on moving. We came here for a reason."

The others nodded in agreement and pressed on.

In silence, they descended the stairwell, each creaking step echoing in the suffocating darkness. At the bottom, they found themselves in the Belowstairs corridor. Down the hallway, Alice came to a halt in front of the faded gilded mirror, which loomed like a malevolent sentinel.

The group clustered in front of the mirror. "I am here," Alice said. Her reflection flickered, a distorted picture of anguish. "It was so dark, and I was so very alone."

She cast her ghostly candle to the side, the flame sputtering out, and pounded her fists against the glass. Cracks spiderwebbed across the surface and the mirror trembled in its ornate frame. "It wasn't fair!" she cried, her voice rising to a wail. "I wanted to leave, but this is where I stayed!"

Her fists shattered the glass, shards raining down on her. Blood smeared her hands as a jagged crack split the mirror in two.

Gael stepped forward, his jaw clenched. "Let me." He gripped the frame and heaved it from the wall. With a grunt, he set it down, the remaining shards clinking like broken teeth on the ground.

The empty expanse of the wall was revealed; weeping mould had spread along the wallpaper, forming the image of a glowering skull.

Alice beat at the wall until the wallpaper cracked and floated to the ground like dead leaves. Behind it was a brick wall, the mortar sloppily applied and dripping over the clay.

"This is where she is," Lola said, her voice barely audible. "Seabourne bricked her in. She woke up entombed."

A collective shiver of horror ran through the group as they stared at the bricks, the weight of Alice's fate pressing heavily on them.

Alice threw herself into Reiko's arms, sobbing. Reiko held her close, stroking her hair.

"How do we get in?" Reiko asked, her voice low.

"I don't know." Lola ran her hands over the bricks. "There's no way in or out; Seabourne made sure of it."

"But you got out before," Gael said. "Do what you did that time."

Lola drew in a breath. What was done was already done; she would use the power of the island. She set her candle on the ground, where its reflected light fractured across the shattered mirror shards. "Everyone, stand back. Last time it was...messy."

The others retreated, their faces tight with apprehension. Taking a breath, Lola pressed her palms to the bricks; the sorrow and terror held behind these walls had steeped into the material itself. The icy cold seeped into her bones.

Beneath everything, she could feel the energy—the pulsing, ancient power of the island. This time, she didn't have to search for it. It rose eagerly to meet her, flowing through her like an unstoppable current. From underneath, where the roots curled in the ground, she felt it. It was interconnected, a network of energy, and she belonged to it.

The power built behind her sternum, her breath hitching as it swelled, filling her until she thought she would burst.

In her mind's eye, she gathered the energy and drove it into the bricks. A blinding green light erupted from her hands into the offending wall, illuminating the hallway. The bricks trembled and groaned, cracks spreading outward like veins.

With a deafening boom, part of the wall crumbled, leaving a dark void beyond.

Lola stepped forward, clawing at the remaining bricks. They crumbled beneath her touch like ashes. One by one, the others joined her, hands tearing at the wall until the opening was large enough to enter.

Reiko held a still-sobbing Alice, shielding her from the sight of the alcove to protect her from what was inside.

Lola took up her candle and eased into the confined space, her pulse quickening. It smelled heavily of mustiness and rot, a sweet underlying smell of things decaying. She'd been trapped behind this wall, banging to get out.

So had Alice. How long had she lasted before wasting away?

Inside the remaining parts of the wall, scratches were visible in the brick, an etching of Alice's desperate struggle. Darkened smears of blood stained the clay, where she had scraped off her fingernails.

Gael shuffled in beside her, holding his candle high to light the whole alcove. "There," he said, his voice a low murmur.

At the back, huddled on the bench, was a skeleton, legs tucked up and hunched over itself.

"Oh, Alice," Lola breathed. "There you are."

The clothes and hair were still discernable, though her flesh had long ago rotted away. Clutched in her skeletal hand was a tattered piece of paper; similar to the letters Irene would exchange with her. Lola wondered what this precious page revealed, the one Alice died holding.

"Reiko," Lola said. "Bring Alice in."

"No!" Alice howled, scrabbling to get away, but Reiko held her gently, stroking her back.

"It's time, Alice," she said with far more tenderness than Lola could imagine from the demon hunter. "I'll be with you. You must face this one last time, and then you can go."

"I don't want to go in there."

It broke Lola's heart to see Alice crumpled in terror, a weeping mess.

"We won't let you be trapped anymore," Lola said, holding out her hand. "It's time for you to be free."

"Free?" Alice sniffed and hiccupped. Shuddering, she held out a trembling hand, taking Lola's. With Reiko helping her over the lip of the demolished brick wall, Alice entered her tomb one last time. Nix's body seemed frailer than it ever had been, as though she was becoming a skeleton of herself. Alice needed to release her hold on the girl before it was too late.

A flood of healing magic, gentle and green, rose up from the ground and seeped into Lola. "Alice McCullough," she said quietly. She found herself smiling at the peaceful power growing inside of her, like the first growth of spring. "We ask you to return our friend. It is time for you to go home."

A soft green light rose from the ground, wrapping around Alice like a gentle embrace. "Home," she murmured, and her spirit form shimmered, separating from Nix's body.

The light grew in strength until the whole alcove lit up. Then, as suddenly as it had come, it faded. For a moment, all was still. Then Nix's body slumped in Reiko's arms.

"So, is that it?" Gael said after a beat. "Is it over?"

Walt stared at the skeleton, rubbing at his skin. "I'm disgusted to be a Seabourne."

Violet took his hands to stop him from scratching up his arms. "You didn't do this."

"But this is my legacy."

"Irene Seabourne sounded like she was good," Violet said.

"Was she? Did she know her father had killed the woman she loved? Did she ever do anything to try to clear her name?"

Lola was only half listening to the conversation as the power continued to build inside her. The peaceful sense she'd had just moments before morphed into unease.

"Something's wrong," she said, stumbling back. "I don't think it worked the way it was supposed to."

They all looked to Nix, trembling in Reiko's arms. The girl's eyes snapped open with a gasp. Her eyes were brown, not blue; Alice hadn't gone anywhere.

The spirit met Lola's gaze, terror tightening her thin face.

"He's here," she whispered.

THIRTY-FIVE

A crash reverberated down the hallway, sharp and jarring in the oppressive silence. It came from the direction of the servants' kitchen.

"Who could that be?" Lola's whisper was taut with unease. She glanced at Walt. "Was there anyone left in your house? Other than your mom?"

"No one," he replied, his tone flat but his eyes sharp as they scanned the dim corridor. "And it couldn't be my mom. We would have seen her pass us. Besides, she never comes down here."

The flickering candlelight cast shifting shadows, but beyond their glow, the hallway was an abyss. Lola squinted into the darkness, straining to make out any forms, but the light blinded more than it revealed.

"Get rid of the light," she hissed, a primal urgency clawing its way to the surface. Without waiting for agreement, she blew out her candle. One by one, the others followed, snuffing out their flames until they were submerged in shadows.

As their vision adjusted, faint flickering lights became visible— emanating from the kitchen ahead.

"Should we check it out?" Gael asked.

"That's a terrible idea." Marissa's face was nothing more than a sliver of pale light, but her voice was tight with fear.

Lola straightened. "I don't know what's going on, Marissa, but we're trapped inside the passageway with a skeleton, and the exorcism didn't work. I think the only way to go is forward. Silently."

After a moment's hesitation, Marissa nodded with a ruffle of movement. Lola took the lead, her hands brushing the wall as she moved cautiously down the passageway. Warmth at her side told her Gael followed close, his presence a reassuring pressure. Despite her brave words, her legs trembled with every step.

Alice clung to Reiko, a pale luminescence lighting her like an aura. The failed exorcism seemed to have made her stronger. Or perhaps it was something darker that kept her bound.

The thought sent a cold shiver through Lola. What if Nix was gone forever?

Ahead, the light grew brighter, shadows twisting and stretching as the group reached the kitchen doorway. Lola peeked around the edge to take in the scene playing out in front of her.

The kitchen was lit by a kerosene lantern placed on the table, its oily stench mingling with the faint tang of sea air. Smoke curled lazily beneath the low ceiling.

Mr. Seabourne, unrecognizable from the polished businessman Lola had seen before, paced in front of the cold fireplace. His hair stood on end, dishevelled and revealing thinning patches. His face was red and puffy, his expression harried. Though he still wore tailored clothes, the jacket was gone, the sleeves of his rumpled shirt rolled up. His pants were soaked to the knees, the briny seawater clinging to him.

"D-dad?" Walt stepped into the kitchen, his voice cracking with disbelief.

Mr. Seabourne froze mid-step, his bloodshot eyes locking onto his son. Like a storm gathering, his surprise darkened into simmering fury. "Walt," he spat, advancing on his son with slow, deliberate steps. "What the hell are you doing here? I told you this place was off-limits. And you show up now, of all times?"

"Dad, listen—" Walt began, but his father cut him off, his voice dropping to a low, menacing growl.

"No, you listen, you disobedient little—" He broke off, face contorting. "What did you do? Who did you bring?" Mr. Seabourne's glower faded to something like horror when he finally realized Walt wasn't alone. The rest of the group filed into the room, standing at the edge of the ring of light cast by the lantern.

Alice cringed and hid behind Reiko, her pale glow dimming.

"They're my friends," Walt said, his voice steadier now.

"Your friends," Mr. Seabourne repeated, his tone dripping with contempt. He glanced at the others and gave a strained laugh. "How could you be so stupid?" Mr. Seabourne whispered. "Bringing people down here? Might as well spill all our secrets. You could not possibly have picked a worse time you complete... utter..." He spoke through clenched teeth. "Do you have any idea what you've done? Bringing people down here—do you want to get us all killed?"

His eyes were wild and rolling around in his face, and Lola wondered if he had taken too much of his own drug supply. She moved in front of Walt, who watched his father with an impassive gaze. Violet came to his side, putting an arm around his waist.

"Mr. Seabourne." Marissa stepped forward, her tone firm despite the danger. "Something very serious is going on and you need to listen to us. We've found human remains in your house. The police need to be called." She straightened her glasses and glared, disapproval frosting off her as she appeared every inch the righteous librarian.

Mr. Seabourne stared at her, eyes widening, then let out a deranged laugh, more of a high-pitch giggle, entirely disconnected from reality.

"Human remains?" Seabourne's wild eyes flicked to Marissa, then back to Walt. "You brought them down here to dig up skeletons?" His voice cracked. "You idiot!"

The kerosene lamp flickered as he raked his hands through his hair. "They'll be here any minute," he muttered, more to himself than anyone else. "If anything goes wrong—if they think I've double-crossed them..."

Lola's heart stuttered. Who was coming? Who had created such fear in a man like Mr. Seabourne? Obviously, he made his fortune smuggling drugs through his property. But now he seemed out of control and panicked. Had he overstretched himself, and did it have anything to do with the man who'd come into the ballroom? The one that carried a shimmer of Otherworld with him.

Was Mr. Seabourne making deals with demons?

"Who's coming?" Violet asked, her voice strained and forced. "We need to call the police."

For once, Lola wanted nothing more than to see Sergeant Greyson scowling at her. But when she took out her phone, it was blank and powerless.

"It's a dead zone," she whispered. "We can't call anyone."

Seabourne ignored her, turning abruptly and bolting the kitchen door with a sharp click. "Nobody's calling anyone," he said, turning to face them, a pistol gleaming in his hand.

"Mr. Seabourne, what are you doing?" Marissa demanded, taking a step back.

"You have no idea what you've stumbled into." His eyes darted between them. "No one's leaving. Not tonight."

Lola's blood ran cold. Whoever, or whatever, was coming had pushed him beyond reason.

"Get against the wall," Mr. Seabourne ordered, his voice rising to a shout. "Now!"

Nobody moved, frozen in place. Walt's father lunged forward, slamming the gun into Gael's chest.

"Do it!" he bellowed.

Gael staggered but didn't flinch. "Mr. Seabourne, you don't have to do this," he said, his voice calm but firm.

"Shut up!" he screamed. "Christ Almighty, on tonight of all nights. I need to think." He was rubbing his head again, his pistol waving alarmingly close to them.

A long, mournful groan sounded behind the fireplace. The sound was deep and guttural like the earth itself was crying out.

Mr. Seabourne lost his bluster, his face draining of colour. "They're here."

"Who's here?" Violet asked again, her voice barely audible.

It seemed to spur Mr. Seabourne. "Back!" he screamed at them. "All of you, against that wall. Turn around, hands on your heads so I can see them."

Nobody moved. The only sound was Alice's pitiful whimpering.

Mr. Seabourne shoved the muzzle of the pistol against Gael's cheek. Lola gasped as Gael stumbled backwards.

"Against the wall," Mr. Seabourne said through gritted teeth.

Shuddering, they shuffled back, reluctantly turning their backs. The raving man pressed the gun to Gael's head, and Lola held her breath, so afraid for him she was frozen. One wrong move, one psychotic outbreak from Mr. Seabourne, and he would be gone.

Then the man backed off, and Gael turned his face to Lola.

"What do we do?" he mouthed.

Her eyes flicked over the group. She believed without a doubt Mr. Seabourne would shoot them if he felt compelled; he seemed to have lost all grasp on his own sanity. But they weren't without weapons. Marissa had her dagger tucked into the pocket of her sweater. And Reiko's hunting knife must be close at hand; it always was.

Lola tried to catch Reiko's eye, but the demon hunter was

distracted by Alice, who cringed against the wall. Her hands came up and made to scratch against it; Reiko grabbed the bloody fingertips and held them away, keeping her from further damage.

Mr. Seabourne had moved to the fireplace. "Goddammit, the little idiots. This will have to be dealt with."

He let out a sigh, heavy with resignation, and Lola's blood went cold. It sounded like Mr. Seabourne had made up his mind about something.

"*Merde*," she whispered.

Mr. Seabourne pressed at a brick in the back corner of the hearth. The fireplace made a heavy *thunk* and the back wall swung outwards, revealing a dark, yawning tunnel beyond.

The air that rushed out was damp and cold, smelling of the sea. Seabourne Estate, so full of secrets and passageways, connected to the tunnel network that riddled the island. This would likely lead to the cliffs on this side of Duchesne Island. The Seabournes had never stopped their smuggling ways, evolving with the times but keeping up the family business of drug trafficking.

"All of you," Mr. Seabourne said, gesturing with the gun. "In the tunnel. Now."

"Dad, don't do this," Walt pleaded, stepping forward.

"You could've ruined everything."

Walt's head snapped back as his father cracked him across the face with the gun.

Violet lunged for Walt with a cry, but his father hauled her back, the barrel of the gun shoved against her temple.

"Get in the tunnel," he said, his voice low and menacing. "Or I blow her head off."

For a moment, nobody moved. Then, slowly, they began to file towards the open passage. Seabourne's laughter followed them, high-pitched and unhinged. "If tonight goes south, I'm dead anyways, so I have nothing to lose."

Lola glanced at Reiko, her mind racing. They couldn't let him control the situation any longer. Maybe they could make a break for it. Whatever lay at the end of the tunnel, it couldn't be worse than what Seabourne was planning.

But the groaning sound came again, louder this time. And deep down, Lola feared she was wrong.

THIRTY-SIX

Walt clutched his face, blood flowing freely from his temple, and cast an anguished look at Violet. Staggering towards the tunnel entrance, he tripped as he passed the woodpile but kept moving. The others followed in a tense, terrified line.

The tunnel was crudely carved out of the soft limestone. Lola ran her hand over the rough surface; the jagged walls were streaked with dampness. The air reeked of mineral decay, and the chill of the earth seeped into her skin.

Mr. Seabourne shoved Violet roughly ahead of him. She tripped, landing hard on hands and knees with a sharp cry.

"Violet!" Walt was at her side in an instant, hauling her to her feet. The look she gave him was a mix of defiance and fear. They turned to face their captor, Violet's fingers reaching out for Walt's.

Mr. Seabourne paused at the threshold of the tunnel, turning to shoot the hinge of the hidden door. The gunshot cracked like thunder. Lola winced against the burst of sparks created. She blinked the bright spots from her vision, and when she looked again, the stone door had swung shut, trapping them inside. The only light came from the dim glow of the kerosene lantern, filling the space with bitter fumes.

"There we are." Mr. Seabourne's voice carried an edge of unhinged glee. "Nice and comfy. I hope you're proud of yourself, Walt."

Walt said nothing, blood trickling down the side of his face.

"You just *had* to ruin everything, like always." Mr. Seabourne began pacing erratically. "It had to be tonight, right, when you... what was it? Found human remains? Of course you did. Always sticking your nose where it doesn't belong."

"You're insane!" Lola burst forward despite Gael's warning hand on her arm. "How can this be worth it? We don't care about the drugs. Whatever deal you're trying to make, it can't possibly justify—"

"Drugs?" Mr. Seabourne's wild gaze snapped to her, and for a moment, his expression was so incredulous it bordered on amusement. "You think this is about drugs? You have no clue what I'm dealing in—the things that come out of the dark..."

His words trailed off as a sound carried up the tunnel—a chittering noise that wasn't human. It grew louder and Mr. Seabourne's expression twisted in genuine fear.

"What have you gotten yourself into?" Lola's voice wavered, her hand tightening around Gael's.

"I am dealing in forces you couldn't possibly understand. I am dealing in *magic*." For a moment, his eyes seemed to glow with the fervent zeal of a convert. "It's all real, and I'm tapped into a whole new world of power. My old businesses are nothing compared to what I could possibly gain now."

"No, Mr. Seabourne, listen to me." Lola had seen humans when they brushed too close to the Otherworld, who thought they might make it to the other side unscathed. "Whatever is coming up here, it's not going to be good for any of us, including you. We have to get out of here."

"Nobody's going anywhere," Mr. Seabourne said, his voice cold. "Now you know too much."

"We don't know anything at all other than you're a raging psychopath," Violet yelled. "Let us go; this will be the end of this. We won't say anything about your tunnel."

"Mr. Seabourne, think this through," Gael said. "There's no way you can hide the disappearance of seven kids on this island. They'll come for you."

"Anything can be hidden on this island. Nobody will know where to look; nobody will ever find you. A tragic turn of events for a group of children who went wandering where they shouldn't."

The air in the tunnel felt heavier, pressing against them as he raised the pistol again, this time aiming it directly at Walt.

"No!" Violet stepped in front of Walt, her arms outstretched.

Mr. Seabourne's face contorted with rage. His finger twitched towards the trigger.

And Reiko lunged.

In a blur of motion, she moved between Mr. Seabourne and Violet, her hunting knife flashing as she aimed for his arm. The blade sliced into his forearm just as he fired.

The gunshot rang out, deafening in the enclosed space. Reiko staggered back, her hand clutching her upper arm as blood seeped through her fingers.

Alice let out a wail of anguish. Was she remembering what it was to die at the hand of a Seabourne? She reached out for Reiko, whose face was twisted in pain.

"I'm fine," Reiko said, her voice snarling over the words as she panted.

The chittering grew louder, and a shrill whistle sounded from further down the tunnel, followed by the murmur of accented voices speaking in a language Lola didn't recognize. Mr. Seabourne's eyes darted wildly towards the noise, his fear deepening into panic.

"Goddammit, they're early," Mr. Seabourne barked. "Get back against the wall."

Alice screamed then, a piercing Otherworldly call that sent shivers down Lola's spine.

"Shut up!" Mr. Seabourne turned the gun on Alice, his hand trembling.

"No!" Lola screamed, hurling herself forward. She collided with Mr. Seabourne as the gun fired again, the bullet ricocheting off the tunnel wall with a sharp ping.

Angry shouts erupted from further down the passageway, accompanied by the sound of rushing feet. The chittering reached a fever pitch.

"No, no, no!" Mr. Seabourne howled. He lashed out wildly, throwing Violet to the ground as he swung the gun in every direction. Walt surged forward, his fist connecting with his father's jaw. The force sent Mr. Seabourne reeling, but he managed to fire again down the passageway.

A rumble followed as rocks and debris rained down from the tunnel ceiling. Lola and Gael both looked up in terror. They had been through a cave-in at the Well of Souls, and nobody wanted to repeat that.

Alice screamed again, the shrill sound increasing in volume until it enveloped them.

"Shut up. Shut up." Mr. Seabourne still had the gun in his hand. Gael made a run at him.

In a flash, Lola could see what would happen before it happened. Blindly, the madman would fire. Gael, his path taking him directly into the course of the gunfire, would see the shot but be unable to stop his course before it was too late. His chest would explode.

The pain in her head from the vision spiked like an ice pick behind her eye socket, but Lola was moving before she had time to work it all out.

Throwing herself at Mr. Seabourne, she grabbed his gun hand.

Her other hand stretched down towards the earth. There wasn't time to think; instead, she grabbed all the energy she could from the ground and siphoned it up through herself.

She thrust the energy into Mr. Seabourne, and his forearm snapped upwards, broken neatly in two. The gun fell uselessly to the ground, and he let out a garbled groan.

"Go!" Lola screamed to the others. But as Mr. Seabourne fell to his knees in shock, he blindly grabbed and hooked Lola's ankle, pulling it out from under her.

She slammed into the ground, smashing her face on the rock floor. Stunned, she couldn't force Walt's dad off as he crawled to her, his one good hand reaching for her throat.

He squeezed. She clawed at his grip, gasping for air as her vision blurred. Choking, Lola's body spasmed against the lack of air, but Mr. Seabourne's body weighed her down. She couldn't move, couldn't breathe.

Gael struggled to pull him off her, yanking at his throat and hair, but Mr. Seabourne had the strength of a madman: someone who had nothing left to lose.

Her strength was flagging. She tried to funnel more power from the earth, but she was blacking out and it felt like the thread that connected her was slipping out of her numb fingers.

Not like this, she thought, as the pain faded, leaving behind a drowsiness. Her eyes locked on Gael's as she tried to say something to him, but her voice was gone.

THIRTY-SEVEN

A bony hand clamped over Lola's, its grip surprisingly strong. Lola grasped it, a lifeline to the world. Where palm met palm, a spark of energy sizzled. From the corner of her eye, she saw Alice kneeling beside her, her skeletal face framed by tattered hair.

Her glowing eyes burned with an unrelenting fury as she stared at Mr. Seabourne, her gaze promising destruction. He didn't even notice her, consumed by his madness and bloodlust as he choked the life from Lola.

Lola's vision blurred, her thoughts disintegrating into static. But the spark of power from Alice jolted something awake inside of her; a thread she could grasp. The earth below hummed, like a pulse waiting for her to connect.

With a silent plea, she reached for it.

Alice poured her supernatural energy into Lola, a current that burned hot and sharp. Grounded now, Lola found the strength to draw deeply from the island's magic. It surged upwards like a geyser, wild and untamed, pooling in her chest.

Lola gathered every ounce of power at her disposal and shoved it into Mr. Seabourne.

A thundering crack split the air, and a blinding flash lit the tunnel.

Mr. Seabourne screamed, flung back as though struck by lightning. He clawed at his face, his shrieks echoing like a wounded animal. "You bitch!" he spat, trying to rise, but Walt was already there.

He let out a guttural cry as he charged forward, brandishing something metallic in his hands, swinging it in a wide arc. It struck his father's head with a sickening crack. The older man's skull snapped violently to the side, and for one moment, he stood swaying.

Then he collapsed like a felled tree, his body crumpling against the stone wall of the tunnel.

Walt's weapon, now dangling in his hands, glinted in the flame, and she caught a glimpse of the corroded blade of an axe. The axe that had sat in the woodpile. Walt must have grabbed it when they were being herded into the secret tunnel; a desperate gamble to find a way to overcome his father.

Lola's breath caught in her throat. "Walt?" she whispered, barely able to form the word. "Are you—"

Walt stood frozen over his father, his chest rising and falling in shallow gasps. In the flickering lamplight, Lola saw tears streaking down his face, carving clean lines through the grime.

She stepped towards him, her hand gently resting on his shoulder. He flinched away, his body stiff, hands trembling violently.

"Walt," she said softly. "You did what you had to do. He would have killed us."

For a moment, he said nothing. Then, through clenched teeth, he murmured, "Yes, well..."

His gaze dropped to the crumpled body sprawled on the filthy floor, limbs twisted at odd angles. There was no dignity left in the man now, only a husk of violence and abuse, finally silenced.

"Is he...?" Gael's voice was barely audible, as though the word itself was too heavy to speak. None of them moved at first. No one wanted to be the one to touch him, to confirm the truth.

Lola knelt finally, her knees scraping the stone. Her fingers hovered for a moment before pressing against the side of Mr. Seabourne's throat. The skin was already cooling and there was no pulse to find.

"I think so," she said. Her voice cracked.

Walt let out a breath that was almost a sob and began to collapse backwards, the adrenaline draining from his limbs. But Violet was there, quick and steady, catching him in her arms. She held him close, her cheek brushing against his as she whispered into his ear.

"You saved me," she said. Her voice, though soft, was fierce with conviction. "Do you hear me, Walt? You saved us all. You're a hero."

Walt finally released the axe, letting it clatter to the floor. His laugh was bitter, raw, as he looked away from his father's crumpled form. "It's over," he said. His tone suggested he wasn't convinced.

"It ends a cycle," Alice's voice rasped, brittle as autumn leaves. She rose unsteadily, a wraith in the dim light. Her glowing eyes were sunken in the hollows of her skull, and Lola tried to hold back a sob. Would there be anything left of Nix, even if they could get her back? "The Seabourne legacy of abuse and power and greed ends here."

Reiko stepped into the light, clutching her arm, where blood dripped steadily from her gunshot wound. She gave little regard to Mr. Seabourne's body, eyes on the skeletal girl in front of her. "Alice," she said, her voice thick with pain. "It's time for you to go."

Alice's burning gaze flicked to her, then to Mr. Seabourne. "Justice has been served. The sons pay for the sins of the fathers, and they pay in blood." She extended a hand to Reiko.

Hesitating only a moment, Reiko took it, and Alice's gaze softened. "Follow your heart," she murmured. "It's the only way to survive in this world. It will guide you to the very end." Her glowing eyes turned to Lola. "I am ready now."

Lola's throat tightened. They had none of the proper tools here; would they be able to complete the exorcism? Still, the power that connected her to the island pounded through her, and if ever she was going to be able to deliver a soul from this world to the next, it would be now.

"We need to make a circle," she said, her voice hoarse. "Hold hands, and whatever happens—*don't let go.*"

Gael was the first to grasp her hand, steadying her. She looked into his eyes and saw unwavering trust. If anyone would keep her grounded, it would be him. On her other side, Marissa linked hands, her face pale but determined.

"You got this," Marissa said softly.

Lola nodded as Marissa's power flowed into her and mingled between them. The others joined, hands trembling but steadfast, with Alice at the centre. When the circle was completed, a spark of energy snapped through them. Incandescent light surrounded Alice. The group gasped as the power surged through their joined hands.

Lola closed her eyes, reaching for the power rooted deep within the island.

"Alice McCullough," she said with kindness. She focused on the bright spirit she'd met in Alice's journal, the inquisitive spirit, the one with big ideas and a desire to see more of the world. "Your suffering is at an end. It is time for you to move on to the next life. We ask that you safely return our friend to us. We release you from this world, with our blessing. Go home."

As she spoke, Lola glowed with the greenish light she'd come to identify as the source of power on the island; rising all the way up from the Well of Souls, it tangled inside of her. Then she noticed the others in the circle were glowing as well; they were sharing in the power she was channelling. They gasped, and she saw a delighted smile on Violet's face. Reiko's eyes were stretched wide.

The air stirred and shifted, and ghostly lights shimmered in the air around them. "Alice McCullough, it's time for you to go home," she said.

Marissa took up the refrain, and soon, the rest of them were chanting the words.

Darkness swirled behind their circle of light as though they were cocooned in a cave of their own energy. The light surrounding Alice intensified, her silhouette outlined in translucent radiance. The aura lifted up, detaching from Nix's body like a shadow peeling away.

"Alice," Lola gasped, her voice cracking. "You have to let her go."

Alice's ghostly form nodded, her expression one of relief tinged with sorrow. "I never meant to hurt her." Her ethereal whisper sounded of longing and forgotten dreams. "Take care of her; her soul is precious."

"You're free now," Lola said as Alice hovered above them.

"Freedom." Ecstasy played over Alice's face, and her eyes glowed with new energy. "Yes, no bonds shackle me here anymore. Perhaps I will have an adventure."

The particles of light that made up her form scattered, filling the darkness like stars across the night sky.

The beauty of it was breathtaking, but Lola's relief was short-lived.

The air shifted as the encroaching darkness pressed in around them, alive with malevolence. Their circle had opened a passageway into another plane of existence; in doing so, it left a door open for others to get in. Shapes with gleaming eyes and jagged teeth loomed, clawing at the boundary. They wanted in, and she needed to close the gate to the Otherworld before they entered inside.

"Don't let go," Lola said, gritting her teeth as an icy wind whipped against her. The darkness pressed and pinched along her body, trying to find a weak spot.

"Lola, you have to close the door!" Marissa's voice cut through the windstorm.

"I'm trying," Lola said through gritted teeth, the effort nearly breaking her. The darkness pressed harder, its pleas clawing at her mind. The circle faltered, their light flickering.

Panic surged, but she drew deeply on the magic of the island, channelling it through the group. The power dispersed through each of them, building to a brilliant glow of green, each of them outlined in light.

She focused all that energy into a final push, thrusting the power into the centre of the circle, demanding that it close.

With a sonic boom, the connection was severed, and they were all thrown backwards. The spinning darkness disappeared.

Nix's body collapsed like a puppet with its strings cut. "Nix!" Reiko cried, rushing forward.

Nausea rose inside Lola, but she forced herself to her knees, crawling towards Nix. She had to make sure it had worked.

"*Lola?*" Nix stirred, struggling to right herself. Only her voice wasn't Nix's; it wasn't Alice's either. It was older, rich with wisdom and pain.

Nix's eyes opened, glowing bright white.

Fear tumbled inside Lola: what had they brought back?

"*Lola, je n'ai qu'un moment,*" the figure said. "*Ma fille, ma chère fille bien-aimée; méfies-toi du démon au visage d'amant.*"

"What?" Lola's voice cracked, desperation clawing at her.

The glow in Nix's eyes dimmed as the voice faded to a whisper. "*Je t'aimerai pour toujours...*" The words echoed deep inside Lola as the light faded from Nix.

"Wait!" Lola cried, shaking her. Tears streamed down her face as she whispered, "Who are you?"

But there was no answer. Only silence.

Thirty-Eight

Nix's eyes were blue as the Atlantic once again. "Lola?" she croaked.

Stunned, Lola could only nod. The spirit that delivered her a message from beyond was gone, leaving behind Nix, safe at last.

"Oh, Nix." Relief surged through Lola as she pulled her friend in for a hug. "You're back."

"Ugh." Nix groaned, pressing a hand to her head. "What the hell is going on?"

The familiar edge in Nix's grumpy voice was the best sound Lola had heard in days. She laughed, though it made her own skull throb. Her head felt like it might explode.

"What do you remember?" Lola asked, steadying Nix as she tried to sit up.

Nix squinted, her face scrunching in concentration. "Everything is so foggy, like a dream, you know? There are some memories but they're fading away. I remember some things—like the Harvest Ball. And..." Her gaze swept over the group, landing on Reiko. "Wait. Why is she here?"

"It's an extremely long story," Violet said dryly, though her pale face was drawn tight with strain. Her usual flippancy seemed more like a shield than ever.

Walt stepped forward, offering Nix his hand. "Let me help you."

Nix took it, groaning as she rose. Meanwhile, Marissa knelt by Lola and laid a hand on her head.

Lola winced. "Ow."

"Lola, do you have any idea what you just did?" Marissa's tone was half awe, half exasperation.

"An exorcism?" Lola guessed.

Marissa shook her head. "That was more than an exorcism. You forced open a portal to the Otherworld." Marissa sucked in a gasp of air. "It was so dangerous...you could have destroyed the whole island."

"I'm sorry," Lola said. "I didn't mean to—"

"But you didn't!" Marissa interrupted, her voice trembling with both relief and disbelief. "You opened a portal, held off the demons trying to come through, and even contacted a spirit from beyond. That's...unheard of."

"You heard her too?" Lola whispered. She wasn't sure if the voice had been real or just another thread of madness woven into the night.

"We all did," Gael said as he came to her other side, his strong hands coming around her and lifting her to her feet. Pain crashed in her head, and she swayed, but he kept her steady. His worried gaze met hers, and her shaking fingers brushed the furrowed lines on his face. She wanted to smooth them all away.

"What did the spirit say?" he asked softly. "I didn't understand."

"She called me daughter." A tear trickled down Lola's cheek. "She said she loved me."

"And?" Gael pressed gently. "Was there anything else?"

"She...she warned me. She said: *Beware the demon that wears the lover's face.*" Lola shivered, the weight of the words settling deep. What could they mean?

Her knees buckled, but Gael caught her, holding her until the wave of dizziness passed. "I've got you," he said.

"I'm okay," she whispered, though her body betrayed her.

"That's debatable," he muttered, but his tone was tender. He kept an arm around her as though to keep her from tumbling over. She welcomed the support; she welcomed his warmth.

"Seriously," Nix said, her tone sharpening. "Why is Reiko here?" She glared at the girl through narrowed eyes. Reiko silently retrieved her knife with her good hand, her injured arm hanging limp.

"She insisted," Lola said. "She's been...helpful. And she got shot saving us."

Nix's expression softened, though her suspicion lingered. "Fine then. But what's *Violet* doing here?"

"Something I keep asking myself," Violet said, her arms crossed.

Walt turned to her, his face heavy with guilt. "Violet, I—"

"Just shut up," she snapped, though her voice faltered. "This has all been very weird and I think you guys are even bigger freaks than you were before."

Walt slumped a fraction. "My dad trying to murder you and all?"

Her gaze softened. "I'll never forget you stopped him. That's what matters."

At her hesitant smile, Walt glanced up sharply. "Violet, I—"

A sound echoed up from the tunnels beneath them, a high-pitched chittering, like teeth clicking together in the dark. It bounced off the damp stone walls, rising in intensity as it approached. It wasn't just noise; it was rhythmic, deliberate. As if it was trying to communicate.

"What is that?" Marissa asked, her voice thin. Her glasses were gone, flung into the darkness during the fall, and her cheeks were streaked with dirt. Her breath hitched as the sound grew louder.

"Nothing good," Lola said. The noise wormed under her skin and burrowed deep. "It's whoever Mr. Seabourne was supposed to meet tonight."

"You mean whatever had the psycho drug dealer absolutely terrified? No thank you." Violet's lip curled in a sneer. "Can't you do something with your lights? Make the bad things go away?" She wiggled her fingers like a magician putting on a show, but her hands trembled.

Lola reached inward, desperate for the flicker of power she'd drawn from before. But the green energy was cold and flickering down to nothing. "I'm tapped out," she said, her voice barely a whisper. "There's nothing left inside of me."

"I got this." Reiko's voice broke the momentary silence. She hoisted her knife with a shaking hand and stepped in front of the group, her boots slipping on the slick stone. Blood soaked her sleeve, dripping from her elbow, but she gritted her teeth and raised her blade in an attack stance.

"Reiko, you're hurt." Lola moved towards her, but her knees gave way. She crumpled to the side, Gael catching her just in time. Even he looked pale, sweat sheening his face.

"I am a demon hunter," Reiko said, her voice level like she was reciting a mantra. Her body trembled but her eyes were steady. "I can do this."

The chittering grew louder and louder, scraping along the stone walls. And then, from the tunnel's throat, the creatures emerged from the shadows, bringing with them the reek of damp rot and old meat.

They scuttled forward on too many legs, emerging in a blur of motion that defied logic. Their bodies were vaguely human in silhouette, but *wrong*: tall and hunched, their flesh glistened with a slick blue-green sheen like beetle shells. Their eyes glittered, bulbous and glassy like dragonflies.

From their backs sprouted spider-like appendages, jagged and barbed, crawling along the walls and ceiling of the tunnel.

One of the creatures stopped when it came to the dim circle of light around them and tilted its head at an impossible angle. It opened its mouth far too wide and let out a shriek that made Lola's bones hum.

The group froze in collective horror as the insect-like demons clustered around the light.

A man—one that Lola recognized—pushed to the front of the demon crowd. He'd been at the Harvest Ball, the one that had terrified Mr. Seabourne.

The man's eyes gleamed with Otherworldly light, more obvious in the gloom of the tunnel. This time, he wasn't wearing a fedora, and the horns curving from his temples were fully visible, black and ridged like twisted obsidian.

The blue-eyed demon's gaze swept the group, glowing as it passed over each face before settling on Lola. He smiled, slow and deliberate. "Well," he rasped, voice like rust scraping along steel. "This is unexpected."

He took a step forward.

A sharp crack like shattering glass rang through the cavern.

—and the world exploded in light.

A burst of radiance flared, blindingly bright. Everyone dropped, shielding their eyes. The creatures shrieked, retreating in a frantic scuttle, limbs clicking as they vanished into the deeper shadows.

Silence fell then, broken only by their sobbing gasps.

At the centre of the group, Marissa stood with her arms outstretched, shards of broken glass glittering at her feet.

"It worked," she said, awestruck.

"You bottled sunshine," Lola said, remembering the conversation about Marissa's experimental magic project.

"One point to the librarian," Gael murmured, offering a shaky smile.

"What were those things?" Walt asked, still staring into the dark.

"Demons," Lola said. "Mr. Seabourne must have been working with them."

"No wonder he was so scared," Gael said. "I wouldn't want to get on their bad side."

"Those insect guys were bad enough, but the other one..." Lola trailed off, eyes narrowing. "He's smart, clearly running the show. But what did they want from Mr. Seabourne?"

She turned the question over in her head. Mr. Seabourne said he had been promised power. But demons never gave anything freely. What had he offered in return?

"Most importantly, are they gone?" Nix asked.

Lola tilted her head, straining to hear. The oppressive chittering was gone. "I think so," she said at last. "Marissa's flash job sent them running, *merci Dieu*."

"Can we please get out of here, then?"

"Hang on." Walt picked up the sputtering lantern and examined the mechanism of the passageway door, a splintered mess after taking a gunshot. "I don't think we can go back this way."

As a group, they turned to peer into the darkness.

"Do you know where these tunnels lead?" Lola asked.

"To the cliffs, eventually," Walt said. "Smugglers have used them for centuries."

"Then we follow the tunnels," Gael said. "We can't stay here."

"What about..." Violet nodded her head to Mr. Seabourne's still form.

"Leave him," Walt said shortly, not looking at the body. "He's not going anywhere. We can...we can figure out what to do about it once we're out of here."

Reluctantly, the group moved into the labyrinth of tunnels, their footsteps echoing along the damp limestone walls. The air thickened as they descended, heavy with moisture and something sour. Branches split off and circled back like veins through the cliffside, the stone honeycombed into a dizzying maze. No one mentioned how dangerously similar this felt to descending into the Well of Souls. Lola didn't dare say it aloud, but she prayed these passageways weren't boobytrapped. She didn't think they could survive another hit.

The trembling lantern cast only a feeble glow, barely cutting through the shadows. Pale moss coated the walls, soft and fuzzy like blooming mould. Pools of water collected in shallow depressions, and they splashed through the puddles with hisses of dismay.

Eventually, they ducked beneath a low arch and emerged into a wider cavern. The ceiling vanished above them, lost in the dark. Stalactites hung like jagged teeth, dripping in slow, echoing plops. Moisture shimmered on the walls, catching glints of light as they moved.

"What's that?" Marissa hissed, pointing to a natural alcove carved into the stone wall.

Inside were rows of jars filled with luminous liquids. Suspended within were grotesque shapes—twisted, shrivelled organs, floating like things half-alive.

"Oh my God," Nix said, pressing a hand to her mouth.

"Are these...body parts?" Marissa's voice cracked. She looked like she might be sick.

"*Merde*," Lola said. "I've heard about this. There's a black market for demon organs. They're incredibly potent, especially when used in dark magic. Powerful people would pay a fortune to get their hands on them."

"A market for demon guts." Gael grimaced. "Let me guess— Mr. Seabourne was trafficking the demon pieces through the island to the mainland?"

"And taking a cut, no doubt." Walt couldn't tear his eyes away from the glistening contents of the jars. "Another proud Seabourne legacy. My dad really was a winner."

"We need to leave," Lola said. "This stash alone could be worth more than anything in Seabourne Estate. Those demons could be back any minute."

As if on cue, the kerosene lantern sputtered. They took off down the tunnel, but hadn't made it far before the lamp let out one last flare and died, plunging them into darkness.

"That's just perfect," Violet said. "Trapped in a cave with insect-y guys. Surrounded by demon bits. This is exactly how I wanted to spend my afternoon."

Nobody mentioned that no one had invited her.

"What's that?" Nix said, her voice trembling.

They all fell silent.

Footsteps, heavy and fast, were pounding towards them through the tunnels.

THIRTY-NINE

A pale light flickered through one of the tunnels, growing brighter with every uneven footstep. Moments later, the sharp beam of a flashlight cut through the darkness, blinding them.

"Who's there?" Lola threw her arm up to shield her eyes, her voice tight.

The footsteps skidded to a halt, and the light shifted away from their faces. Slowly, the figure holding it came into focus.

"What the—" a familiar voice cursed, low and startled.

Lola blinked, her vision adjusting. "Matt?"

"Matt!" Marissa's voice cracked, and she stumbled forward, reaching for him like a lifeline.

"Marissa?" He caught her reflexively, his flashlight clattering against the wall as he steadied her. In her dishevelled skirts and fraying tweed jacket, she looked as out of place here as a china figurine in a war zone.

Matt glanced around at the rest of them—Lola, Gael, Reiko—his brow furrowed in confusion. "What the hell are you all doing here?"

"What are *you* doing here?" Reiko shot back, her tone cold and sharp. Her arms were crossed tightly over her chest, intimidating, though Lola noticed she was favouring the one coated with drying blood.

Matt looked as battered as they were, his black clothes streaked with dirt and a jagged slash of blood standing out against the skin of his cheek. His hair was matted with filth, his leather jacket torn at the shoulder.

"You're hurt!" Marissa's hand fluttered towards the wound on his face before hesitating mid-air.

Matt grinned, brushing her concern aside. "It's nothing; a little scuffle, that's all." He shrugged his shoulders as though to down-play what happened. "I was in the caves. There were these guys... weird guys. They came towards me, and I thought I saw..." A misty look came over his eyes, and he shook his head. "In the dark, my eyes were playing tricks on me. Next thing I knew, one of them clocked me. I fell to the side, and they passed me. Not my bravest moment, but I'm fine."

"And *why* were you sneaking around the caves?" Lola asked in disbelief. Matt had no idea how fortunate he was to be alive. "Seems like an uncomfortable place to hang out during a storm."

Matt hesitated, glancing between them before letting out a breath. "I saw a boat docking near the cliffs. It didn't belong there, and...well, I had a lead."

"A lead?" Lola arched an eyebrow, playing out a hunch. "You've been running your own investigation from Duchesne Island, haven't you?"

Matt's lips twitched. "Something like that. I've been tracking a smuggling operation. Months of work brought me to the island. Turns out I was right."

"About the Seabournes?" Walt's voice held endless bitterness.

Matt's eyes narrowed. "Yeah, the Seabournes. Well, Arthur Seabourne, specifically. I've been piecing things together and it all pointed back to Duchesne."

"That's the reason you came to Duchesne?" Marissa's hand

went to her neck, her skin mottled red. "You were undercover for a story?"

Matt seemed unable to form words for a second. "I...yes. I came here for the story. The editor opening at the *Daily* was the perfect chance to dig deeper. To single-handedly bring down an international trafficking scheme. It would be the scoop that would make my career..." He trailed off, his voice faltering.

"Of course, once you've finished with us small-town folk, you'll be back to the big city now, won't you?" Marissa stepped away from him, her hands clasping the frayed edges of her jacket.

Matt cleared his throat. "I haven't found much yet. Just the smugglers passing through these caves." His gaze swept over them, searching. He finally seemed to take in their different stages of dishevelment. "What are you guys doing in here, anyways?"

"We...went looking for Nix," Lola said and put her arm around her friend. "There are search parties all over the island; I'm surprised a keen-eyed reporter like you managed to miss that. But we found her."

Stunned, Nix waved. "Hi."

"I heard about it, of course. And you were...here. In these caves?"

"She got lost." Lola nudged Nix with her elbow. "Couldn't find her way out."

Nix glared at Lola, but Lola widened her eyes, imploring her silently to play along. "Yup, I was lost."

"You didn't happen to find anything else, did you?" Matt's voice was defeated, as though his big play hadn't worked out. "Nothing unusual?"

They all shook their heads. "Just a bunch of tunnels," Violet said. "Nothing other than that."

Matt seemed to fall back in disappointment, but he nodded and turned around. "Well, at least I found you. We should get you out of here. Lots of people are looking for you."

They followed the bright beam of his flashlight through the

tunnels. Matt walked confidently; Lola wondered how much he'd explored these tunnels and whether he would find the demon organs like they did.

Would the just-the-facts investigator be able to wrap his mind around the Otherworld, or would he do his best to convince himself nothing out of the ordinary was happening?

Lola would have to figure out something to do with the stash of invaluable Otherworld treasures before the demon traffickers returned. But right now, all she could focus on was getting one foot in front of the other.

Matt took a twist in the caves that led upwards, and after another fifteen minutes of trudging through the claustrophobic space, the stone walls opened to the cliffside.

The storm that had been brewing had evolved into a deadly tempest. The mass of clouds swirled charcoal and steel while howling winds drove sheets of rain horizontally into them.

Far below, waves battered the cliffs like the fists of a wrathful god, their thunderous roar shaking the earth beneath their feet. Salt spray mingled with the biting rain, stinging Lola's eyes as the storm ripped at her soaked clothes. The narrow path to the ridge seemed to shift and sway, a perilous thread stretched over the crashing water below them.

Far down below in the harbour, Lola thought she could make out the lights of a boat. But it would be suicide to head out to sea in these churning waves. She squinted but lost track and couldn't find the form again among the whitecaps.

Above them, bobbing lights congregated and flashed down on them.

"I see something!" a voice called, faint as the sound was whipped away in the wind. They made their way towards the light and soon were surrounded by a group of townspeople wearing rain slickers and holding flashlights.

Their shouts floated towards them. "We're looking for the Nix girl. Have you seen her?"

"She's with me!" Matt's voice held a tinge of bravado as though he was the one to have rescued her. Lola didn't mind; let the reporter take the glory. The less others investigated exactly what had happened tonight, the better.

"She's here! We've found Arabella Nix!" A cheer went up from the waterlogged searchers, and Nix was passed forward, hugged by countless arms, though she held herself stiff from her rescuers.

"Get them inside. She might need medical attention!"

Forty

After wandering through the tunnels, Lola had completely lost her bearings. But now, silhouetted against the darkened horizon, the Seabourne Estate loomed nearby along the ridge, all its lights burning bright against the storm. Heads bowed against the driving rain, they plowed forward.

By the time they arrived at the mansion, they were shivering, soaked to the bone.

The front porch lights glowed warmly, a beacon of welcome. Inside, the mansion was alive with light. Even though the sweeping staircase was still wrapped with rotting foliage, the estate seemed to have regained some of its majesty.

Standing at the centre of the grand entrance, rigid like a marble statue, was Mayor Seabourne. Water dripped from her soaked clothes, pooling at her feet. Her clasped hands trembled slightly, though her face remained stoic.

She went perfectly still as Walt stepped through the door, as though she didn't dare breathe. For a moment, Lola expected the usual cool nod. But then the mayor's mask cracked.

She took an unsteady step towards her son, then another.

"Oh, Walt," she whispered, her voice breaking.

In an instant, she was on him, pulling his tall frame down so she could envelop him in a hug. "It's all over," she said, her voice so low that only Lola caught the words. "Everything is taken care of."

For a moment, Walt stood stiff with shock. Then he sagged into her arms, burying his face in the damp wool of her scarf. A deep, weary sigh escaped him.

Lola's gaze fell on the mayor's sleeve, which had ridden up to reveal a dark smear of blood against pale skin. As Mayor Seabourne released Walt, she caught Lola's speculative look and tugged her sleeve down to cover the stain. Her composure snapped back into place.

"The power came back on about an hour ago," she announced, her voice firm and polished once more. "No explanation from the electric company, but I'm fortunate to offer everyone a warm place to shelter." She gave a practiced smile, a seasoned politician once again, ushering in the bedraggled group of teens and searchers towards the kitchen. "Come along. I'll see if I can figure out the coffee machine."

The gathering took on a brighter feel as the tension in the mansion eased. Laughter and chatter broke out among the searchers as they stripped off their drenched outerwear. The search for Nix took on the feel of a grand adventure now that she had been found safely and they were in from the cold.

Minutes later, the RCMP showed up, Sergeant Greyson leading a tearful Florence Nix and her tall, blond husband.

"Arabella!" Florence cried, rushing to her daughter. She enveloped her in a tight embrace, her sobs shaking them both. Nix, after everything, finally broke down, clinging to her mother as tears streamed freely.

Reiko stood apart from the reunion, her expression unreadable. Pale and silent, she watched Nix and her family with almost clinical detachment. Lola wondered how much blood the demon hunter had lost.

She approached, keeping her voice low. "You okay? Someone could take you to the ER for your arm."

Reiko's look would have withered flowers. "I'm fine."

"You were shot in the arm."

Reiko shrugged, though she winced at the movement. "I know how to take care of myself. Always have. I just have to get home."

Lola tilted her head. "Then why are you still here?"

Reiko stiffened, but before she could snap back at her, Lola raised a placating hand. "I'm not telling you to leave. You were unstoppable down there when it counted, and I want to thank you for that. But if you're staying on the island, we're probably going to have to figure some things out."

Reiko gave her a long, searching look. "I'll head out, then," she said, her tone uncharacteristically soft. "But maybe we'll have a conversation someday."

"Soon," Lola said meaningfully. She couldn't afford a rogue demon hunter on her island. But an ally who could handle herself against the Otherworld? That was something else entirely.

Reiko gave a stiff nod before striding out of the kitchen. Her steps were steady and graceful despite the blood loss. Lola watched her go, her mind racing with questions.

Sergeant Greyson approached then, notepad at the ready, his expression cautious. "So, Ms. Monteux," he began. "What exactly was your part in all this? Because I have no doubt you were somehow involved."

"We were searching for Nix," Lola said, smoothing out the frown that wanted to form. "We found her in the caves."

"Deceptively simple." He raised an eyebrow. "Anything else to add?"

Lola motioned for Walt and Gael to join her. Taking a deep breath, she spoke quickly, as if rushing would lessen the blow. "I do, actually. In our search, we found a body. In the walls of the lower level of the estate."

Greyson choked and nearly dropped his pen. "I'm sorry, you found a *body*?" He started to scribble madly on his pad.

"A very old one, if it helps."

"How old?" he growled.

"Quite old. I've been doing research into the history of the estate, and I believe a maid had been murdered there by the original Walter Seabourne in 1921. Her name was Alice McCullough."

"You've been busy."

She gave a one-shoulder shrug. "I was just trying to find a story for the school paper. Her body had been bricked over inside the walls; we found a way in and uncovered the remains."

Greyson stared at her, his lips pressing into a thin line. After a long pause, he let out a low chuckle. "Things are never simple with you, are they, kid?"

"I didn't plan for the night to turn out like this," she said, watching his reaction carefully.

Greyson shook his head, a rare smile tugging at his lips. "Just... try to stay out of trouble. If that's even possible for you."

"No promises," Lola replied with a faint smile of her own.

Greyson had turned away, already barking orders into his walkie-talkie about human remains. She watched him go and turned to Walt.

"I'm sorry. It looks like a world of trouble is heading your way."

Walt nodded solemnly. "It was coming."

"What about the study?" she asked. "It looks like we were performing satanic rituals." She gasped at the thought. "Don't let Matt anywhere near it—he'll never let it go."

Walt managed a thin smile. "I'll make sure he's not on the guest list."

The group began to disperse, but Lola lingered with Gael. Neither seemed eager to leave.

"So," Gael said at last, "did Greyson actually crack a smile?"

Lola laughed. "Maybe. Stranger things have happened."

"Listen, I wanted to say—" He stopped and cleared his throat. "Just...I'm sorry for these past few weeks. It was hard with you gone. And harder, somehow, now that you're back."

"I'm sorry too," Lola said. "For everything. I never imagined how things would play out." She swallowed, trying to find the right words. "There's no guidebook for this, is there? I feel like I'm drifting in the ocean, just trying to find a glimpse of land. And sometimes I think I'm close, and other times I'm in the middle of a hurricane."

"I get it," Gael said softly. "The thing is, I think I know where my continent is." His eyes burned into hers. "I'm just not sure I'll ever make it to shore."

"Maybe someday." Lola let out a tiny sigh, then held out her hand. "Until then, maybe we could be each other's lifeboat. No promises, just...someone to hold onto when the storm hits."

Gael took her offered hand. A spark of heat passed between their palms, lighting up her whole body. As though the last ember of shared magic had saved itself for them.

They both gasped and let each other go, staring in stunned silence.

"I should go," she said, her voice unsteady. Her body felt aflame, every nerve awake. When she turned back, though, she saw Gael still standing there, staring in wonder at his palm.

FORTY-ONE

"It's all there, Mrs. Nix." Lola slid the diary and the letters across the café table. "I've typed everything up so it's easier to read. These prove Alice was never a thief, and she didn't abandon her family without a word."

Florence Nix hesitated, her fingers brushing the edges of the worn paper as though touching them might summon ghosts. The Nix family sprawled across three tables in the Pain Perdu. Nix sat between her parents, her cheeks rosy and her eyes sparkling—almost herself again. Around them, her five younger brothers squabbled over mugs of hot cocoa, fighting over plates of flaky croissants, their chatter lively in the background.

Across from them sat Lola, Walt and Gael. Lola was wary about touching Gael. She wasn't sure how to navigate the crackling tension between them after the electrifying moment they'd shared. For his part, Gael seemed equally cautious, keeping a respectful distance but occasionally glancing her way.

Lola's last contribution to her research into Alice's life was the letter that was clutched in her corpse's withered fingers, which proved to be the last one written to her by Irene. In it, the heiress passionately wishes her maid a good life and bestows upon her the family sapphire jewels to be used to begin a new life on the mainland. Alice hadn't stolen anything; they'd been a gift.

Florence finally lifted the diary, her expression caught between reverence and unease. "I still can't believe it," she said. "Our family secrets, all laid bare."

The discovery of Alice McCullough's remains at Seabourne Estate had unleashed a media frenzy. Reporters had swarmed Duchesne Island, hungry for details about the century-old scandal and forbidden love between heiress and maid.

Lola had kept her lips sealed, but she suspected Matt had leaked parts of her unpublished story for the school paper. The result was an international whirlwind of attention.

"There've been offers from publishers," Florence said, sounding mystified. "They want to publish the diary and the letters, as well as an account of what happened all those years ago. The editor of the paper is trying to get the rights to the whole thing." She sighed and pushed the diary back towards Lola. "But this feels like your story. You did all the work."

Lola shook her head and firmly pushed it back. "I don't want any credit. This is your family's legacy. You should consider publishing it, though. The story is incredible, and it could bring some good out of everything that happened. I'm just happy Alice finally got the peace she deserved."

They had laid Alice to rest in the McCullough family plot with a proper headstone, a quiet ceremony that felt like a balm after all they had endured.

Florence blinked rapidly, fighting tears. "I can't stop thinking about her. The way she died...it's horrifying. I don't know how anyone could live in the house after that—" She caught herself and stammered. "I mean...I'm sorry, dear."

"That's okay, Mrs. Nix," Walt said gently. He looked lighter, unburdened. "Honestly, it's a relief. The house feels different now, like it can breathe again. My mom's already planning extensive renovations."

"And your father?"

Walt's smile faded. "No word. He was supposed to return to Port Despardoux the day Alice was found during the storm. But... nothing." He hesitated, glancing at Lola. The implication hung heavy between them.

"Perhaps he got lost." Florence's voice sounded uncertain.

"Perhaps," Walt echoed, his tone hollow, and Gael put his arm around his friend's shoulder. None of them knew what had happened to Mr. Seabourne's body after they left it in the tunnel behind the fireplace.

Walt had tried the passageway after the police had cleared out, finding it still worked when accessed from the fireplace.

His father's corpse wasn't where they had left him.

Walt wondered if perhaps he hadn't killed him after all—that his father had gotten up of his own volition. But Lola's mind flashed to Mayor Seabourne that day, drenched, blood-streaked and oddly triumphant. As though she'd taken care of her husband's last mess.

Lola didn't dare voice her suspicions, but she doubted Mr. Seabourne would ever resurface.

"I do wonder, though, what happened to the sapphires?" Florence asked, forcing brightness into her tone. "The tiara and the rest of them that Irene meant to give to Alice?"

Walt brightened. "That's the really good news. Forensic archeologists found the sapphire tiara and matching earrings in Alice's pocket when they removed her remains. My ancestor didn't know it, but they were buried with her."

"Imagine," Florence said in wonder. "After all that fuss, they had been at Seabourne Estate the whole time."

"The letter from Irene proves the jewelry was a gift," Walt said with a grin. "So, the Seabourne sapphires belong to you as her descendant."

"No!" Florence looked both overwhelmed and incredulous.

Walt chuckled. "The Seabourne Estate has no intention of contesting it. They're all yours."

Florence pressed her fingers to her temples as if warding off a headache. "I'm not sure I'd want to keep something so macabre."

"You might not have to," Lola said. "With all the interest in Alice's story right now, those sapphires could fetch a fortune at auction. I have some contacts on the mainland if you want to look into it."

Florence gave her a shrewd look. "You're an interesting character, Lola Monteux. But I'm thankful you kept on digging. It was worth it, in the end, to find out what happened to Alice." She patted her hand on the diary. "Between what the publishers are offering for the story and the sapphires, I might be able to pay off my debts at the store."

Lola repressed a smile. "You'll be able to do more than that, I think."

"Oh my, could I take a vacation?" Florence lay her head back in the chair. "To spend a week off my feet, it's all I ask." Her eyes popped open. "Oh, and Gael, I haven't forgotten your mother. I might sell the story, but the diary and the letters themselves are staying on the island. She might be interested in them as artifacts from Duchesne."

"That's awesome to hear, Mrs. N." Gael gave a bright smile. "She'll be happy to have them. She's working to put together a collection of Duchesne Island's history, using the treasure money to get it started. Alice's story will be a big draw once she gets it up and running." He glanced out the window and hesitated. "Looks like I gotta go. I have plans."

He stood and seemed as though he wanted to say something to Lola but swallowed it back at the last moment. He leaned down and gave Nix a big hug. "Glad to have you back," he said, causing the red-headed girl to glow.

"Catch you later," she said. "Don't become a total hyena."

Gael laughed as he left the café and approached the group

standing outside the doors, waiting for him. Among the group was Cassidy, bouncing on her toes as she greeted him.

Violet was there, too, searching through the windows of the café. Her gaze caught on Walt for a tense moment, but then Ethan steered her away.

Walt's body stiffened ever so slightly. Lola put her arm around him. "I guess those two made up."

Walt's jaw tightened. "I guess so."

"I'm sorry, Walt. I thought...well, I never actually know what to think about Violet, but it did seem like she feels something for you."

"Well, my father being a murderous drug dealer with ties to the Otherworld wasn't a great look. Neither was the fact that he tried to kill her." Walt tried to keep his voice light, but underneath it, she sensed the hurt.

"She's a fool if she lets that scare her off."

"She'd be a fool if it didn't." Walt shook his head as though to push any thoughts of the beautiful, fierce blonde girl from his head.

Nix came to sit on Walt's other side. She cuddled against him as though to make up for the distance Alice had put between them. Walt hugged her back.

"Can I just hate that Gael is friends with those hyenas?" Nix said. "And someone is really going to have to explain what Violet was doing at my exorcism in the first place."

Before Lola could respond, the café bell jingled and Reiko strode in, looking as out of place as a wolf in a henhouse. Her leather pants and ragged band tee, with the edge of a bandage peeking out around her bicep, drew stares from the Nixes.

"What are you doing here?" Lola asked.

Reiko leaned down, her grey eyes gleaming. "What are *you* doing here?" she countered.

"Enjoying a coffee?"

Reiko smirked. "But wouldn't you rather hunt down demon organs?"

Lola blinked. "I'm sorry, *what*?"

Reiko straightened, casting a quick glance at Walt and Nix. "If you're interested, I'm going back into the demon caves."

Lola exchanged a look with Walt, who shrugged. "I literally have nothing better to do," he said.

Expressionless, Nix stared at Reiko. "Yeah, okay, I'm in."

"I guess we're hunting for demon parts." Lola put down her coffee with a sigh. "And here I thought life was going to be boring now."

THE END

Acknowledgments

Books are built not only from ink and imagination, but from the quiet strength of the people who stand behind them. I am endlessly grateful to the following hearts and hands who helped bring this story to life.

To Marilyn Boake, my editor and one of the first true believers in Lola and her world. From the first page of the first draft, you have been there with your insight, your gentle honesty, and your unwavering dedication. Thank you for helping me find the truest version of this story.

To Nika Teran and the team at Brown Cat Press, thank you for your support, your patience, and your willingness to take a chance on this strange and magical little series. Your quiet confidence have helped carry this book farther than I could have imagined.

To Zach Magnan, who has never once asked me to explain why I needed to disappear into this story for weeks or months at a time. Your support has always been steady, offered without question or condition, like a harbour I could return to when the writing winds got wild. Thank you for letting me dream, and for believing—even on the days I didn't.

To Marilyn Smith, my most loyal reader and fiercest cheerleader, thank you for every kind word and enthusiastic message. Your encouragement has been a lantern on the darker days of this writing journey, and I'm lucky beyond words to have you in my corner.

And to every reader who has joined Lola on her strange and shadowy path—thank you. You are the reason these stories live.

About the Author

Cordelia Kelly is the author of the YA paranormal series *The Port of Lost Souls* and the standalone fantasy novel *The Sibyl and the Thief*. Her short fiction has been featured in numerous horror anthologies, including "Herbalista" in *Prairie Witch* and "Dare to Survive" in *Dark & Stormy*. She also released a chilling collection of horror shorts, *Then She Said Hush*, featuring her award-winning post-apocalyptic tale "Unfreeze."

When she's not crafting spine-tingling stories, Cordelia designs , creates vintage handdrawn maps of Canada at The Little Canadian Map Shop, and shares her love of nostalgia by writing recaps of R.L. Stine's *Fear Street* series on her blog, *Shadyside Snark*.

OTHER BOOKS BY CORDELIA KELLY

The Sibyl and the Thief

In the Port of Lost Souls series:

The Well of Souls
The Carnival of Fools
The Seabourne Legacy
The Salt Roses
The Book of Lead

Short story collections and anthologies:

Then She Said Hush
Goblincore
Prairie Witch
Dark&Stormy

THE SALT ROSES

A Port of Lost Souls Novel: 4

On storm-swept Duchesne Island, the supernatural isn't folklore —it's etched into the cliffs, stitched into the tides, and buried deep beneath the salt and stone.

Between witchcraft, demon studies and high school gossip, Lola is finally settling into island life. The vengeful spirit that once haunted Seabourne Estate has been banished, and the Otherworld has gone silent. As winter wraps the island in sea-ice, Lola dares to believe she might have a future here—with the people she loves most.

But her peace comes at a price.

To save her friends, Lola gave up her freedom—bound by a spell she's never confessed and a past she can't outrun. Now her visions have returned, sharper and more violent than ever, and something ancient is stirring beneath the island. Whispers echo from the sea cliffs, calling her toward the cavern lined with salt-stone rosettes. And beneath it all, a song—strange and sorrowful —is pulling her under.

As enemies circle and new threats gather strength, Lola must choose what she's willing to sacrifice to protect those she loves. Her heart. Her secrets. Even herself.

Because the magic that saved her once may not be enough to save her again.

Read more of the next book in the Port of Lost Souls series...

CHAPTER ONE

Chapter 1

The drop of ruby liquid trembled at the vial's tip, reluctant to fall. Finally, it splashed into the jar of clear solution, and thick grey vapour poured out. The smell hit them like an acrid punch: burnt matches and rotten eggs, with just a hint of underlying sage.

"What the eff is that?" Nix shoved her chair back until it slammed against the wall, scrambling away from the noxious fumes. "That's the worse one yet. Why did I agree to this?" She blinked rapidly behind thick goggles, gagging on the stench.

"Come on, it's fascinating," Walt said. He raised the jar, undeterred by the smell. The solution inside had turned a brilliant, poisonous green.

Lola peered over the open leather-bound book. "Marissa, you did it. This looks exactly how the book said it should."

Marissa gave a small, satisfied smile. Stray curls clung to her flushed cheeks and her blouse was clinging damp to her back from the exertion of the spell.

"My hunch was right," she said. "That blood comes from an Algith demon." She ran her finger down the page of a book of

Demonology. The etching shown on the aged paper looked like a walrus crossed with a sewer rat. "It's got healing properties. Not a bad ingredient to add to my witch's kit."

A snort broke the moment.

Reiko stood apart, arms crossed, inspecting the magical ingredients with a sneer. "Undocumented witch's kit," she muttered.

Marissa and Nix both glared at the demon hunter.

Lola bit back a sigh. She was the one who insisted Reiko be included when Marissa created potions, but the prickly girl made it hard to defend her. Sometimes Lola wished she'd lose interest so she wouldn't have to play the mediator.

The room was stifling with all five of them crammed into the back office of the Port Despardoux Library. No bigger than a janitor's closet, it was rapidly transforming into a proper witch's den.

Lamps with dim Edison bulbs cast golden pools of light over the cluttered worktable. Books bristling with Post-it notes, a mortar and pestle crusted with fine ash, and Marissa's sleek laptop crowded the surface.

Steel filing cabinets lined one wall, neatly labelled with everything from rare herbs to Bunsen burners. Incense curled from a chipped teacup, smelling of eucalyptus, though it did little to counteract the smell of burning hair that drifted from Marissa's newest concoction.

"Looks like you figured out the best use of that blood," Lola said, trying to keep the mood light before the tension boiled over. "You're really leaning into your witchy side."

"How could I not, when I have all these interesting jars of demon bits to work with?" Marissa jerked her chin towards the line of organic demon material they'd recovered months ago, deep in the caves of Duchesne Island.

Inside the murky liquid hung pieces of creatures that came from nightmares: acid green eyeballs, talons with razor sharp edges, guts that still squirmed slightly when tapped.

"Not everyone would be so cavalier about playing with demon

parts," Reiko said, her voice sourer than any seventeen-year-old girl's should be.

"Remind me again why she's here?" Nix narrowed her eyes at Reiko.

Reiko belonged to the Order of the Hanta Cythraul—the HC for short—a mysterious organization of demon hunters. The Order's motivations were murky, and Reiko's presence on Duchesne Island even murkier.

Reiko had helped them exorcise a ghost, though, which had earned her a seat at the table. Lola didn't trust her, but she also wanted to keep an eye on her.

Despite her obvious dislike of witchy magic, Reiko showed up to the library more often than not. And though she made dire comments about what they were doing, she was surprisingly helpful and less squeamish about some of the more disgusting tasks required. Lola didn't want to make an enemy of her.

Marissa opened the door, allowing the gasses to release into the hallway.

"Think anyone's out there?" Walt asked. "Smells like evil science."

Marissa frowned. "I hope not." She was the acting head librarian, but notoriously unhappy with sharing her collection with anyone, most notably the public.

"I don't think we need to worry about that," Lola said. The beautiful Port Despardoux Library was scandalously underused, in her opinion, but it served their purposes when they were playing with the Otherworld.

"I've finally worked through all the demon parts we salvaged," Marissa said, making some notes on her laptop. "That last one took me forever. I needed to wait for the proper celestial alignment."

Her cheeks glowed pink. The more the librarian tapped into her witchy powers, the healthier she looked. As though her essence had finally been awakened.

"Your potion stash would make any alchemist green with jealousy," Lola said. "If anyone knew about it, that is. And nobody ever should."

"You're right about that," Marissa said. "My collection would rival some of the most famous alchemists from back in the day."

"At the expense of the creatures they came from." Reiko's caustic voice sliced through their triumph.

"Seriously, why is she here?" Nix rolled her eyes so hard it looked painful.

Marissa squared off with the demon hunter. "What should I have done? Let all those parts rot in that cave? Leave them for the demon smugglers to come back and use them for profit?"

"Aren't *you* profiting off of them?" Reiko raised an eyebrow at Marissa. "You said yourself, your collection could rival any of the old masters."

"I didn't kill anything," Marissa said, affronted. "And some of these potions have real benefits." She held up the jar of green liquid. "I'm pretty sure this could be huge for cancer research."

"If only we had a steady supply of *Algith* demons," Walt muttered.

"Yes, thank you, Walt," Marissa said tightly.

Reiko eyed the jars. "If that's what lets you sleep at night."

Nix stood with a flourish and stormed out of the office. "I've had about enough of anything to do with demons. I need to get out of here."

The others filed behind Nix, leaving the ripe smell behind them. Lola was the last to leave, taking in the rows of jars in glowing hues. The rainbow colours lit the shelves like stained glass.

Entering the hushed expanse of the library, she inhaled deeply. The dusty space always held a suggestion of enchantment. It smelled of vanilla and pipe tobacco and now just a hint of sulphur: pure magic.

Reiko's eyebrows were slashed in a frown, and she looked like she wanted to argue more.

But Nix put her hand up. "No more evil science talk, I can't handle it. This winter storm has kept me inside for long enough and I'm going insane as it is. Let's talk about normal things."

"Normal things?" Lola asked, stifling a laugh. Since she had become human last spring, they had dealt with vampires, werewolves, desire spells and ghost possessions. Normal was a foreign concept.

"Yes, normal things. Like the new issue of the school paper. *Tea Time*'s been updated." Nix took out her battered phone, covered in rainbow stickers peeling at the corners.

"What's *Tea Time*?" Marissa asked, scrunching her nose. While the rest of them attended Port Despardoux High, Marissa had been homeschooled and was now halfway finished her master's degree in librarian sciences. So she wasn't up to date with the school paper, the *PD Tribune*.

It was Reiko's turn to roll her eyes as she checked her own phone in its functional black case. "It's this gossip blog. Everybody's obsessed with it."

Nix turned to her, eyes sparkling. "Oh, like you're not." Quick as an eel, she snatched Reiko's phone. The demon hunter's jaw dropped, and Lola suspected if it had been anyone other than Nix, that move would have earned them a broken cheekbone.

As it was, Reiko just started forward, trying to snatch it out of Nix's hands. "No, give it back!"

Nix danced out of reach, victorious. "See, she has the *PD Tribune* bookmarked on her phone. She's shallow like the rest of us!"

Reiko finally managed to get her phone back, her pale cheeks burning with high colour. "It's intel. Even gossip can give a heads up when things are starting to go funny." She shoved her phone into her back pocket and crossed her arms, as though daring Nix to go after it again.

Nix's grin was smug. "That's what I'm doing, too. Gathering information on my fellow classmates." She opened the website on her own phone. "This website is looking so slick, by the way. Violet's even got advertisers on here, now. I can't believe she pulled this together in a couple of months. I never thought she had the brains for it."

Walt glanced up sharply. "We don't know Violet's behind *Tea Time*. It was created anonymously."

"Violet being the creator of *Tea Time* is the school's worse-kept secret. I mean, she's the web editor, and then the gossip blog shows up randomly and nobody knows about it? It even sounds like her. Here we go:

'Okay, we know the science club is usually all about equations, robots, and that weird smell coming from Lab B… but word is, Quantum Cutie is tall, brainy, says 'photonic resonance' without blinking and is cute enough to make goggles look good. Is it suddenly cool to carry a calculator? Time will tell.'"

Everyone turned to stare at Walt, who's goggles were now casually dangling around his neck. "What?" he asked, flushing.

"Absolutely nothing," Nix said, exchanging a look with Lola at how clueless their friend could be. Lola bit back a grin. If she needed proof Violet was the voice behind *Tea Time*, this was it. The school's golden girl had been dancing around their tall nerdy friend for some time, though she'd yet to ditch her toxic actual boyfriend.

Nix cleared her throat. "To continue… *Is there more than school spirit happening between 'Pom Pom' and 'Ace'? The giggling cheerleader and the baseball nerd-turned-heartthrob have been spotted walking very close after indoor practice. Keeping each other warm through these frozen months, perhaps? The two of them should just get on with it'…*Oh." Nix turned beet red and slammed her phone down on the counter. The look she shot Lola was mortified, but Lola could only shrug.

"I know that Gael and Cassidy are a thing." She tried to sound casual but her throat was tight. "How could I not?"

They all looked to an empty chair at the table. Gael was noticeably missing from their witchy meetups at the library. Between training, helping his mother with research on the island and the after school crowd he hung out with now, he rarely had time for them.

Not that Lola had noticed, of course. He did show up sometimes, but it felt as though the amount of times he spent with their group at the library was far less than the amount of time he spent with Violet's crew at Lost Souls. With Cassidy.

"Actually, *Tea Time* seems to imply that Gael and Cassidy aren't a thing yet," Nix said. "If Violet wants them to get on with it, then that means they aren't there. Although…"

"Although what?" Lola slumped into her chair, acid rising up in her chest.

Nix shrugged and looked away. "Nothing. It just wouldn't surprise me. He looks so good with that crowd, doesn't he? With the beautiful people. Like he belongs with them."

Lola fought the urge to spit out that he belonged with her. She wasn't allowed to say things like that, though. She was the one who broke up with him, after all.

"Listen to yourselves," Reiko scoffed. "You're acting as though gossip and boys actually matter, when here we are with an arsenal of magical weapons and a potential demon problem on the island." Reiko held a jar of what looked like tiny kidneys; she shook it in her agitation, and Marissa gasped and grabbed the jar from the demon hunter's hands.

"We should be staking out the caves for demon activity," Reiko continued.

"They're not in there," Walt said, his voice flat with finality. "No demons have come back since that night."

Lola's glance was curious—how did he know?

Reiko's narrowed eyes seemed to be asking the same thing. "Well, we need to make sure they don't return; that they're never able to do this again."

"Never able to what?" Nix lasered in on Reiko with a vicious glare. "Kill other demons? I thought that's literally your job."

Reiko looked affronted. "What they're doing is horrible, keeping bits and pieces of other creatures. It goes to show how awful demons really are."

"But is it really any different from testing done in medical research labs?" Nix asked, squinting at the kidneys. "I mean, testing on animals to find cures for disease. Is that all bad?"

"I...that's not really...it's not for me to say."

"And I bet your Order would love to get their hands on Marissa's arsenal. Even though they were made from demon parts, *you* would use them. So how can you condemn the demons who smuggle the ingredients?"

"Wait, are we on the side of the demons now?" Walt asked.

"Let's just say I'm curious where the line is." Nix's gaze met Reiko's like a dare.

"Demons are bad," Reiko said, and winced, rubbing her forehead. "They're unnatural to the world and should be exterminated."

"Right. And there can be no nuance in there. Lola, want to weigh in?"

Lola knew the conversation might have ended with her, but the truth is she didn't want to weigh in. Because after eighty years of being a vampire, she sided more with Reiko: demons equal bad.

"Most demons *are* evil and do terrible things."

Nix turned her glare on Lola. "Seriously, I was looking for backup here."

Lola gave a weak smile. "Sorry, my experience with demons is pretty extensive. Maybe we shouldn't decide who lives or dies, but most demons wouldn't think twice about killing you, your friends and your family. And they shouldn't be given the benefit of the doubt. They should be stopped."

Nix raised her eyebrow. "And there's no room for atonement?"

Lola turned away from her friend's sharp gaze. "Some things can't be forgiven."

Staring at the table, Lola watched as Nix's freckled hand moved over to grab her own. "That can't be true," her red-headed friend said fiercely. "Everything can be forgiven."

Lola glanced up to see Nix's gaze burning out of her pale face, bluer than the sea. She wanted very much to believe her in that moment, but at the heart of it, Lola knew Reiko was probably right: the world would be a better place if all demons were exterminated.

www.ingramcontent.com/pod-product-compliance
Lightning Source LLC
Chambersburg PA
CBHW061015120726
47910CB00006B/1944